LUST . . .

His eyes flickered to the low scoop of my dress, then up again to my face. I sensed that what I had already suffered was nothing to what I must endure now. My heart began to beat wildly.

Before I had a chance to draw back, he had me locked in his arms. His hand cupped my breast and he kissed me savagely.

"Garfield, please, no . . ." But it was as though my protests aroused him to a greater frenzy, and his breathing became suddenly harsh as he ripped at the thin fabric about my shoulders . . .

A fugitive in a cruel and sensual land, Harriet Rogers would soon come to know many kinds of men. Garfield Hunt was only the first. . . .

THE WHITE KHAN

Big Bestsellers from SIGNET

If you wish to order these titles,
please see the coupon on the
last page of this book.

The White Khan

by
CATHERINE DILLON

A SIGNET BOOK
NEW AMERICAN LIBRARY
TIMES MIRROR

SIGNET, SIGNET CLASSICS, MENTOR, PLUME AND MERIDIAN BOOKS
are published by The New American Library, Inc.,
1301 Avenue of the Americas, New York, New York 10019

FIRST SIGNET PRINTING, MAY, 1978

1 2 3 4 5 6 7 8 9

PRINTED IN THE UNITED STATES OF AMERICA

Remembering Anne

THE
WHITE
KHAN

1

Only a handful of people came to the little cemetery at Mara Khel to see my father buried, and of those, I knew only two well. One was my brother Rupert, who, because he was only ten, stood pressed up close beside me at the graveside, dry-eyed and shivering a little, like a frightened dog. The other was Garfield Hunt of Banipore, the wealthiest merchant in northern India, who, I suspected, was present less out of respect for my father's cloth than for the fact that he had long wanted to be able to call me his wife.

The others were strangers, who had no real obligation to either my father or myself, save that they must have felt it fitting to bid farewell to yet another white man who had died, as many of them would eventually die, far from home and in a foreign land.

They were used to death, as was anyone who had served more than a few months in India, and I had little doubt that had I questioned any one of them, each would have had his own story of bereavement, of a wife or brother or child who had sickened from one of the many tropical fevers, died, and now lay buried in some parched half acre of ground, virtually identical to the one on which I now stood. In the background a small whitewashed church with a thatched roof, a cemetery with a mud wall against which neem trees grew, with tree rats quarreling in the branches. Big square tombs dating from the early John Company days, with urns on top of them, ranged alongside shabby little leftover graves of soldiers whose regiments had passed on, with stretches of yellow, sun-parched grass in between.

Man that is born of woman has but a short time to live and is full of misery. . . .

The chaplain's voice was crisp and military, because, like the four British soldiers who were easing the coffin into the ground, he had come for courtesy's sake from the Regiment of Foot that lay nearby. I watched the sweat making dark patches on the men's scarlet tunics, the veins standing out on necks constricted by tight-fitting collars, and wondered at the torments they must have been suffering encased in that heavy serge.

We therefore commit this body to the ground, earth to earth, ashes to ashes, dust to dust. . . .

The words rolled on and I did my best not to listen, because I knew that only if I managed totally to disassociate myself from all that was happening would I be able to get through the day at all. For myself it mattered little if I showed all the usual signs of grief, but Rupert had only me, which meant that I had to behave more like an elder brother than a sister, and elder brothers did not weep at gravesides. Any tears of mine would have to be shed in private. Not only was the loss of my dear father, and only close companion, unbearable, but a bleak future in this lonely and desolate land stretched ahead of me. Unless . . .

I forced myself to think of other things, such as the figure of Noor Jehan, the grave digger, hunched up against the church wall, the horses standing in a little group in the shade, with a *syce* squatting on his haunches beside them, the evening sun throwing shafts of light through the dust stirring above the turnpike. They were all things I was used to, and I suppose because of this I found them suddenly comforting.

. . . in sure and certain knowledge of the resurrection to eternal life, through our Lord Jesus Christ . . .

As I raised my head again and gazed beyond the gaping hole in the brick-red earth I suddenly became aware of one of the mourners who stood slightly apart, aloof almost, from the rest of the group. I was almost

2

certain that he had not been there a few minutes ago, and to the best of my knowledge I had not set eyes on him before.

Through the comforting privacy of my black veil I was able to study him and only then did I realize that, like me, he was paying little attention to the burial service. He was staring at me, quite openly, as if trying to probe what kind of person hid behind those stifling black folds.

He was tall and lightly built, with a complexion so burned by the sun that it was darker than that of many Indians, although his peculiarly piercing blue eyes could have belonged only to a European. He was wearing a suit of white linen, with a long jacket buttoned high at the throat, something in the manner of a Muhammadan's *archan*, with narrow breeches that gripped his ankles above well-polished boots, and was the only person at the graveside who was not in black.

He was, of course, bare-headed, and his dark tightly curled hair grew low on his neck in the manner affected by some of the more fashionable regiments. The lower part of his face was in shadow, but even so, I could see that he was a man of perhaps a little under thirty years of age, clean shaven, with the lean, high-cheekboned features that had much in them of the bird of prey.

I was looking at a man who would be hard to forget. I wondered who he was, why his interest in me was so strong that it was almost a tangible thing.

Earth fell with a hollow sound on the coffin and I felt Rupert's hand tighten on mine. We bowed our heads once more as the chaplain intoned a final prayer, and although the heat was such that the fabric of my black mourning dress was clinging to my back, I was suddenly aware that I felt desperately cold. There was a tightness in my chest that made it difficult for me to breathe, and for a terrible moment I thought I was about to faint. Then, as though from somewhere outside myself, I became conscious again of that small hand gripping my fingers and it was almost as though,

3

in that moment, it was Rupert who was giving courage to me.

Someone said, "It's time to go, ma'am."

I was still feeling a little dizzy, so, in spite of the possible impropriety of the gesture, I pushed the veil back over the flat, stiff lace hat I had been forced to borrow and took several deep breaths of the over-heated air. It was then that I caught the eye of the light-jacketed stranger. Before I could look away, he had stared me fully in the face, as though he were try-ing to memorize every single feature, then, with a small, brisk bow, he strode from the churchyard.

I felt a hand touch my arm lightly, reminding me to follow the few mourners back to the bungalow. Whether from the heat or the particular solemnity of the occasion, I felt as if I were in a dream. I found my-self looking around the drawing room as though I were seeing it for the first time and realizing that it was so exactly like half a dozen similar rooms that had passed as home over the years. The pale blue *dhurries* on the floor, made by the prisoners in the local jail, the long oak table that my mother had brought out from home. There was the desk in one corner made by the little carpenter in Lahore, with my father's papers still piled upon it, together with the Roorkee chair in which he used to sit in the evenings with his legs raised high and hooked around the wooden arms that were made extra long for just that purpose. With the exception of my mother's old dressing table in my bedroom, that was just about all there was of personal furniture. Every-thing else was hired from the contractor because it was easier and cheaper that way. Soon the trappings of a place that briefly had been my home would be no more than a memory—four whitewashed walls and a thatched roof that would belong to someone else.

For just a second I closed my eyes and railed against my position. There was little for a young, unmarried woman of no means in a great continent like this, par-ticularly one with the responsibility of a young brother. If ever I believed I had any choice, the final decision had been made for me by my father on his deathbed.

4

"Your health, ma'am, and our condolences."

I was jerked back into the present by the swirl of people around me. Hamidullah was going around with brandy and Madeira while the ceiling *punkah* swung slowly to and fro, stirring the heat-heavy air. It would have been a hundred times preferable to have gone out into the parched little garden, but I knew that custom decreed otherwise. I had been an onlooker at a good score of exactly similar gatherings, waiting with the women while the men made their ritual journey to the cemetery, then joining in the hushed conversation for the stipulated three quarters of an hour that was supposed to elapse before one could decently leave the bereaved to their grief.

Today there were only two women present, the plump and bustling widow who had been our nearest neighbor and Ursula Scott-Barnard, the married sister of Garfield Hunt. Together the Hunts came across to me and offered more condolences, but whereas Garfield's were softly spoken and genuinely sympathetic, I felt Mrs. Scott-Bernard spoke to me only out of duty. Though I had met her only twice, on both occasions she had shown me barely concealed dislike. Today was no different.

When they left me, I looked for Rupert and saw that he was standing, his face white and strained but strangely composed, speaking to the chaplain, and not for the first time I wondered if we were not wrong in the way we controlled our grief.

"My commiserations, Miss Rogers. It must be a heavy burden to have the grief of one so young added to your own."

I turned to find myself being regarded by a small, frog-faced man of middle years, dressed in a formal black coat of a curiously old-fashioned cut but clearly of the finest cloth. His silk-embroidered vest and stiflingly high stock gave him an air of elegance that must have cost him dearly in terms of sheer discomfort and yet failed to make him appear in any way ridiculous.

"Thank you, sir," I said simply. "I fear today has

5

been a taxing experience for him. He was devoted to his father."

The slightly protruding, moist eyes regarded me with a lively intelligence and yet real compassion. I wondered what chance it was that had brought him to Banipore in the first place, but without prompting, he enlightened me.

"Miss Rogers, my name is Joseph Whittle. Whittle of *Whittle's Gazette*, of which you have doubtless heard."

"Yes, indeed, Mr. Whittle," I replied. "I have even read it on occasion." It would have been strange had I not heard of the publication in question, which was by way of being the source of much of the gossip not only of distant Calcutta but much of up-country India as well.

Mr. Whittle said calmly, "I should be surprised were it to your taste. The scandal of Calcutta must make poor reading beyond the bounds of the city."

"Any news is welcome here in the North," I told him. "But I agree that I should not have imagined your readers would be overconcerned at the death of a missionary."

"The *murder* of a missionary, Miss Rogers." A couple of feet above my head the punkah stirred the heavy air without in any way cooling it.

"One of the workmen was addicted to *bhang*, Mr. Whittle. Under its influence he went out of his mind and attacked my father. You must be as aware as I that it is the kind of thing that happens all the time."

"I must confess I have not traveled in these parts for some years, but I was dining with Colonel Manson of the Eleventh Foot, and when I heard from the chaplain of your loss, I took it upon myself to pay my respects. I think I can guess what it is like to be a woman alone in this country."

"It was kind of you." I did not know whether to believe him or not, but it did not seem to matter one way or the other. At this moment I felt that nothing mattered greatly. But any further consideration was put

6

aside by Hamidullah's tall figure appearing suddenly before me.

"*M'emar argh gya, memsahib.*"

"I'm sorry," I said to Mr. Whittle, "but you must excuse me. The mason has come about the headstone."

"Allow me." The froglike little man took my arm and led me out to the blessed shade of the veranda, where a white-bearded figure in a saffron-colored turban rose from where he had been squatting to join work-worn hands in the ancient Hindi greeting.

"*Namiste, memsahib.*"

"*Namiste. Kitab hai?*"

Yes, he said, he had a book. He showed me the stained pages and their unexpectedly Western drawings of headstones, and I hesitated as an old school exercise book and a pencil were presented to me.

Mr. Whittle listened to our conversation with a little frown. "What does he want?"

"The inscription," I said, a little surprised.

I wrote, "Charles Barret Rogers, 1810–1872" in bold capitals, and paused uncertainly.

What did one inscribe to the memory of someone like my father? I asked myself. A man who had come to this wild land from the gentle countryside of New Hampshire when little more than a boy in search of adventure. A man who had earned his living in a score of ways until, in his own time, he had found his vocation and devoted his life to India as a missionary. It had, I thought, been a strange quirk of fate that should have decreed that a man so universally loved and respected should have died in a place like Mara Khel, where he had been planning a school for the children of the local tribesmen. Almost anywhere else, so many would have been sorrowing at his graveside, but here . . .

"Would your father have wanted anything else?" Mr. Whittle seemed in some strange way able to read my thoughts.

I shook my head. "No," I said firmly, the decision made. There was a lifetime of work for India to remember my father by and that was enough.

I gave the book back to the mason and watched him

7

go down from the veranda and across the compound. Once out of the shadow, the saffron of his turban glowed the same deep yellow as the setting sun.

"You speak the vernacular well," Mr. Whittle complimented me. "I must confess that after fourteen years in the country it remains for me a closed book. I fear you, an American, put us English to shame. But then you were born here, were you not?"

"No." I shook my head. "I was born in Tamworth, New Hampshire, when my father had taken my mother on a visit home. Then, when we came back, I learned Hindi from my *ayah*."

"Yet you went back to your own country for your schooling?"

"Oh, yes. I was sure then that I had forgotten every word of it. Indeed, it was not intended that I should come back here." I paused, remembering a way of life that seemed so very long ago.

"And?"

"My mother died of cholera six years ago."

"Yes," Mr. Whittle said unexpectedly. "I know."

How had he known? I wondered. Reluctant to ask, I went on. "I was sixteen then and my brother was only four. My father had his work to do and so . . . well, I came back to look after them."

"It must have been a very lonely life for you. This is a very small community."

"Solitary, yes, but not lonely. We were very happy together." It was true, I thought, and I remembered riding with my father before breakfast on a brisk winter morning, the smell of woodsmoke that drifted over the land at the end of the day. With him there had always been a closeness to the country that had made the lack of other companionship unimportant. Now those days were gone as though they had never been.

Oddly, I found this strange little man easy to talk to and I believed he genuinely had my interests at heart. As we turned to go into the house I stopped and said to him suddenly, "Mr. Whittle, you must know many people in these parts. There was a stranger at the graveside. . . ."

8

"A tall, striking man in a light jacket?"

"Yes. Do you know who he is? He walked away as soon as the ceremony was over."

Mr. Whittle said rather shortly, "I believe he told someone his name was Adam McKenzie." He allowed himself a small, grave smile. "I could not help observing his keen interest in you, Miss Rogers."

I knew that color stained my cheeks. "I, too, Mr. Whittle, but I know not why." Adam McKenzie, I thought. I should remember that name. I turned toward the door. "Shall we go in?"

But Mr. Whittle still stood there. And then he said quietly, "I have no wish to intrude on your affairs, ma'am, but it would have been out of character if your father had accumulated riches on earth. Your brother will soon be of an age when he should go home to school. Would it be presumptuous on my part to ask what plans you have made for the future?

I said bitterly, "India is a country that offers singularly few alternatives for a single woman forced to earn her own living, Mr. Whittle, and I have no doubt that you know them as well as I. With luck, I suppose I might find work as a lady's companion, though I cannot imagine I should earn enough to pay for Rupert's schooling. It is he whom I must think of now."

"True. So what shall you do?"

I looked out toward where the shadows were beginning to stretch out from the walls of the compound and listened to the creaking wheels of the bullock carts on their way back from the mill. Very soon, I knew, the first stars would show in the deepening blue of the sky and Hamidullah would come and light the old brass lamps that hung beneath the ceiling cloths and then even this day would be over. The promise I had made to my father as he lay dying came back to me with renewed force. For a little while I believed I had freedom of choice, but now I knew I had none.

"You may rest assured as to my welfare, Mr. Whittle," I told him quietly. I hesitated. "I gather that you are familiar with Mr. Garfield Hunt."

"An editor's responsibilities require that he be famil-

9

iar with all classes of society. However much he may deplore them."

I took a step back. "Then I can only hope," I said without any change of expression, "that your opinions are ill judged. Because very shortly I am to become his wife."

He stared at me for a long, silent moment, then gave me a formal bow. "My felicitations, ma'am."

"Thank you," I replied. This time I knew his words were spoken only out of courtesy.

"If I can be of service to you at any time, I am yours to command. Remember that, Miss Rogers." His eyes rested on me with a strange intensity of feeling. "One day it could be important. Now, if you will excuse me, I should return to my hosts. Alas, the time of a guest is seldom his own."

As I came back into the drawing room his words were still with me. I thought it unlikely that we should meet again. I was wrong. It was to be under very different circumstances, and I should have been married for two months of living hell.

"Marry me," Garfield had said to me, not once but several times, and I had put his offer aside with as good grace as I could, for although I had no desire to be his wife, I liked him well enough. As for his character, he was a highly respected man and well known for his charitable works.

I had not refused him without much thought, for I was strongly aware that there were a score of girls who would have jumped at the chance. Rich, distinguished-looking, and in what I judged to be no more than his early forties, Garfield Hunt would have been a feather in the cap of any ordinary girl without a fortune and with no family name of influence behind her. I understood he had been married once, when quite young, and his wife had died within a year. Had it not been for my dreams of Edward, I might well have considered what I could regard only as an inexplicable but flattering offer.

But in those few short weeks before his regiment's

transfer, Edward—so young and dashing and ardent—had roused in me that wild, sharp longing that cannot be denied—or forgotten. Indeed, it had taken me as long to forgive Edward himself as the cruel fate that had separated us. Of course I knew that a young officer would have been rash to think of marriage so early in his career, yet the fact that he had gone without putting the avowal of his eyes, his arms, into words had left a bittersweet restlessness in me that still lingered, even after two years.

After he had gone, the letters that I longed for never came, and later I had had time to blame myself for what had at first seemed so like a betrayal. Perhaps if I had responded more frankly to his advances instead of gently holding him at a distance . . . obeyed the dictates of my own desires instead of those strict rules of behavior that society had laid down for a young woman faced with her first experience of courtship . . . perhaps Edward would have spoken that last night after the regimental ball when he had led me again out into the scented gardens, had taken me in his arms under the waxen flowers of the frangipani. And how often had I dreamed that scene again and given it in my dreams a different ending! How often, in the loneliness of those long hot nights, had I, instead of shrinking in fear and modesty from those fierce kisses, reciprocated with shameless fire! Thus had Edward long since changed from lover to dream lover, so that only in the reality of my father's illness had those foolish dreams finally faded. When my father died, I was no longer the young girl dreaming of the might-have-been but a young woman with the responsibility of the future thrust harshly upon me and me alone. With Rupert to worry about and with, perhaps, the first frost of cynicism upon me, I had forgotten Edward long before the promise made at my father's deathbed.

Now his words, so weakly spoken that I had to bend close to hear them, were imprinted on my mind. "I am sure he is a good man, Harriet, and he will take care of you and Rupert. Promise me, Harriet, that you will marry him. Before I . . . go . . . I must know you will be safe."

I had taken the pale hand, outstretched toward mine, and pressed it gently. "You are not going, Father, please . . . you can't leave us."

"Promise me, Harriet."

"I promise." My voice was barely above a whisper, but my father heard and smiled. An hour later he was dead.

Now, after so short a time, Harriet Rogers had ceased to exist, and in her place was what *The Pioneer* called "the young and beautiful Mrs. Garfield Hunt of Banipore."

I had not thought of myself as beautiful, although I had never been short of partners at the few regimental balls I had attended, and Edward had paid me the most wonderful, poetic compliments. But now, with Lelune, my ayah, to tend my red-gold hair, and with the magnificent crinolines in lustrous Indian silk I was able to wear in the evenings, perhaps the people who saw the outer trappings of wealth might be forgiven for seeing beauty. But they had not stood in front of the mirror seeing the cheeks grow thinner and paler day by day, the leaf-green eyes that now had a dead look, or the once-soft mouth that now found it more and more difficult to smile.

They did not see the Mrs. Garfield Hunt who found herself walking alone on the well-tended grass leading down to the river's edge—alone—because if she stayed in the house one more minute she would probably break down and scream.

It was the night of Diwali, the commencement of the Hindu New Year, and as I walked I felt some of the wretchedness slip away from me. Diwali is also the Festival of Light, and even as a child I had been fascinated by the sight of thousands of tiny lamps flickering along the walls and roofs of Hindu dwellings as far as the eye could see. Seen at close quarters, each one was no more than a tiny earthen pot holding a wick that floated in clarified butter, but watched from a distance, it was as if great hosts of fireflies had settled on

12

the world, outlining homes and temples and shops with pinpoints of flame, creating some vast tropical fairyland.

But I knew well enough that to the teeming hordes who lived out their lives beyond the compound walls of the European homes, Diwali was more than a spectacle. This was the night for casting accounts, when every merchant and shopkeeper was bound by holy writ to strike his balance for the past year. Somehow it seemed only appropriate that I should do the same.

I looked back at the house behind me—a great square of whitewashed brick, built for some merchant prince back in the days of Clive. In the light thrown by the Diwali lamps flickering from the roofs of the servants' quarters, the wooden shutters over the windows seemed to have taken on the appearance of bars.

The lawns that ran down to the river were lush and green. At this season of the year most people's gardens were parched and dead, but here a dozen *malis* sprayed them with river water gathered in goatskins. Poinsettia and flame-of-the-forest trees grew in orderly profusion around an exquisite Mogul summerhouse that Garfield must have found perhaps a thousand miles away and had reerected, neither knowing nor caring that its fragile northern beauty was wildly out of place among the rococo extravagances of Bengal. Forty servants devoted their lives to this monument to the power and wealth of one man, yet it was probably fair to say that I, for all the diamonds at my neck and the fashionable gown of palest green satin that had newly arrived from the famous Monsieur Worth of Paris, was as much a servant as any of them. Oh, to go back in time, to break that promise too easily given, to be the poor companion to some lady in Calcutta . . .

"Harriet . . ."

I caught the flash of a white nightshirt against the dark green of the bushes, then Rupert was beside me, and I touched his damp hair reproachfully.

"What are you doing here? You know it's time you were in bed." Soon, now, I thought, he would be going to school in England, to a normal life with other boys

13

like him. I must not forget that my marriage had at least made that possible.

"Oh, Harriet, it's so hot in my room."

"Isn't there a boy wetting your tatting?"

My father would have none of it, but here one of the sweeper's innumerable family sat outside the window and tossed water over the grass-packed screen every half hour in order that a breath of cool air might filter through to the room beyond.

"Oh, yes, but it's so much stickier here than at home." He sighed. "Oh, how I wish we were home again, Harriet. Here, it is—"

"Hush," I said quickly, not wanting to hear. "This is our home now, remember. You may stay out for five minutes, but no more, mind."

"Oh, thank you, Harriet, I shan't be long, I promise." His pale face lit up with a smile that reminded me of my mother's, and then he scampered away across the grass. I had turned back to my thoughts and solitary contemplation of the river when a shadow darkened the wide portico of the house, and I caught my breath as my husband came slowly toward me.

"What are you doing out here alone, my dear? It is getting late."

"I'm sorry," I said. "I hadn't noticed."

He was holding a cut-glass goblet in his hand and he held it out to me. "The *abdar* tells me that Spencer's delivered some samples of their latest consignment of wines today. Try this. I think you will like it."

The glass he handed me was frosted with cold and as I showed my surprise a look of satisfaction crossed his face. He did not smile, and indeed it had but lately occurred to me that such an expression was totally alien to him. Yet he felt pleasure in his possessions and satisfaction in his ability to command ice-cold wine in spite of stifling heat.

"There are few households, even in Calcutta, tonight where a glass could be served as chilled as that. They tell me the last shipload of ice from New York was sold a good month ago."

"Indeed?" I sipped the wine and then, because it

14

was clearly expected of me, I asked from where this particular ice had come.

"I have my own icehouse, out beyond the stables. It is twenty feet deep and well lined with sawdust. I've had ice down there that's outlasted a year." He studied my face. "Is the wine to your liking?"

I was immediately filled with suspicion. Garfield never asked for my opinion. Nevertheless, I had to answer. "It is very agreeable," I said.

Watching him over the rim of the glass, I wondered how a few short weeks could bring about so much change in a man. Except, of course, he had not changed; it was simply that he no longer felt it necessary to conceal from me the long-hidden darker side of his nature. As he stood there, tall and masterful, in his dark tailcoat of fine London cloth, a white cravat at his throat, I could not help thinking that few women would have done other than envy me in such a partner. He was a figure admired widely in the society of Banipore and I doubted not that there had been many a whispered conversation over the teacups on the question of how a little unknown mouse had managed to secure such a prize. Only Mr. Joseph Whittle had had some insight into my husband's character, into his tyranny, his lust for power. In his own subtle way he had tried to warn me.

"Agreeable?" Garfield's full lips twisted into something that was more a sneer than a smile. "Are you sure, my dear, that your wide experience of fine wines has made you a sound judge?"

Here was the bite in his tone, the steel behind the mockery, that during the past weeks I had come to realize was to be my lot. Each time he spoke to me with some civility I prayed the change had come, but it was as though now that he possessed me, some devil within him drove him to humiliate one he had sworn to love.

For myself, I had never pretended that I returned his avowed affection and had promised no more than loyalty and a proper devotion to his well-being. That, he had assured me, would be sufficient for the present.

15

Within the bonds of marriage, affection—love, even— might well come later.

God knows I had lived long enough in the East to be prepared for the physical aspects of marriage, yet I had in no way imagined how gross were to be the realities of our life together. In some curious way it was as though the very strength of his appetites were his undoing, as though he hated himself for gratifying his passions and then hated me for possessing the body that enslaved him. I had learned to recognize the pattern, the look in his eyes that I had come to dread. I could foresee it all with unfailing accuracy—the brief yet not ill-humored courtship as desire grew strong within him, followed swiftly by a savage consummation. It was then, his passion momentarily spent, that Garfield would turn on me with words of refined cruelty, as though punishing me for the power I exercised. It was a power that I was more than willing to forgo. Hurt and not a little sickened, I might have been an apter pupil had my efforts been rewarded with any expression of affection. As it was, each day brought only more misery, more revulsion, and the small, shrill beginnings of what I recognized as fear.

"I asked you, my dear," Garfield said with terrifying softness, "if your experience of wines makes you a sound judge."

Perhaps I was far enough from the bedroom to have some small amount of spirit left, because instead of saying no, of course I knew nothing of wine, I forced myself to smile and said, "Sufficient experience to know that a wine should be chilled and not frozen, Garfield. This is so cold that none could say if it be good or not."

"I stand corrected." His lips moved in the travesty of a smile, but deep within his eyes I saw something change. I had gone too far and shown him that I was not yet beaten into submission. He reached out and took the glass from me and, with a flick of his wrist, tossed it into the river.

Trying to keep my voice steady, I said, "I do not think there was any need to do that."

"No? Perhaps you are right. As your most devoted servant I must stand corrected." His eyes flickered to the low scoop of my dress, then up again to my face. I sensed that what I had already suffered was nothing to what I must endure now. He said thickly, "Your *very* devoted servant."

Feeling my heart beginning to beat uncomfortably, I backed away. "It doesn't matter, Garfield. Call for another glass."

"To hell with the wine." Garfield could move surprisingly quickly for a man of his size, and even though I knew well enough what to expect, he had me gripped in his arms before I had a chance to draw back. He kissed me once, hard and savagely, and then, as he drew back, his hand cupped my breast.

"Garfield, please, no . . ." All at once my own fears were forgotten as I remembered Rupert, who must return from his ramble at any minute. But it was as though my protest had awakened some kind of frenzy in the man before me, and I heard his breathing become suddenly harsh as he ripped at the thin fabric about my shoulders. His fingers caught one of my earrings, and as the flesh tore I gave an involuntary cry of pain.

I think my cry surprised Garfield, for he drew back, and even as he did so a small, furious figure in white burst from behind the bushes and threw himself at Garfield.

"No! No! No!"

There was more than a small boy's instinctive defense of a well-loved sister in Rupert's desperate attack. At any other time Garfield would have plucked him up and cast him aside much as he would have freed himself of an overexcited terrier, but the sheer unexpectedness of Rupert's arrival, coupled possibly with his dislike of being caught fondling me outside the privacy of our room, took him totally by surprise. He gave a muffled exclamation, knocked Rupert away with a swift, cuffing blow, and stepped backward—into the swirling waters of the river sweeping silently past, three feet below.

17

"Garfield!"

I stared after my husband in horror, not so much for his predicament as for fear of his anger when he regained dry land. But there was no answer.

"Garfield!" I screamed. I ran to the edge and stared down into the dark depths. For a moment I thought I could see him, but it was only a log drifting down with the tide. Then all at once I saw an arm come out of the water, farther out in the current than I had expected. There was no answering cry. The arm disappeared. Smoothly, like yellow oil, the river ran on silently into the darkness of the night.

2

How long I stared at the river as though expecting it to return Garfield to me, alive and well, I do not know. Probably it was for no more than a few fleeting moments, during which my mind tried to grasp the enormity of what had happened. Then I shouted desperately for help, and was answered by the patter of bare feet as three of the servants ran toward me.

"Hunt sahib has fallen in the river," I said hoarsely. "Find a boat."

They stared at me as though I were mad.

"A boat! And hurry . . . he may have been carried away by the current."

The youngest of the three seemed to grasp the situation, for he nodded suddenly and ran off toward the end of the garden, and after a moment his companions followed. I heard a confused babble of voices, which seemed the inevitable accompaniment to any action, followed, surprisingly swiftly, by the appearance of a flat-bottomed boat with the three men aboard, being poled out into the stream.

"It is unlikely that they will find him. The river runs swiftly here."

I turned to find a pair of limpid dark eyes regarding me with an expression that I had neither the time nor the will just then to attempt to fathom. Yet instinctively I recoiled from the man who had come upon me unawares.

Victor de Souza was Garfield's chief clerk. There

should have been nothing frightening about the immaculately dressed, sallow-faced young Eurasian who had never treated me with anything but dutiful courtesy. Yet, illogical though it may have been, I had always sensed an unspoken antagonism between us, and at this moment I felt it stronger than ever before.

My fear of what might have happened to Garfield drove me to speak sharply. "Then we must act quickly. Do not stand about doing nothing. Call some more . . . no, call all the servants to look for him. He may have caught hold of a log or reached one of the banks. Please hurry, Mr. de Souza."

"The servants have already been summoned, Mrs. Hunt. It is better to come indoors and bring the boy with you."

I might have argued with him had it not been that I looked down at my brother, standing staring at the river, his whole body trembling. When I held out my hand to lead him away, he came without a word. Had he wept or attempted, as is the way of children, to blame me for what had happened, I should have infinitely preferred it to the white-faced, total silence he maintained until his bedroom door was shut behind us and we were alone. I sat down beside him on the bed and put my arm about his shoulders, wishing desperately I could summon up some words of comfort.

"Harriet." He turned to me and seized my hands with sudden earnestness. "Harriet, it was an accident, wasn't it?"

"Yes," I assured him, "it was indeed an accident. Had Mr. Hunt not struck his head as he fell, you may be sure he would have suffered no more than a ducking." And that, I knew, was the truth. All I wished, most fervently, was that it had been my hands and not those of my brother that had set the fatal train of events in motion, but it was too late for wishes. I had to live in the world as fate had decreed it should be and so, I feared, had Rupert.

With the odd, jerky mannerisms inherited from his father, he broke in on my thoughts.

20

"Were you so very unhappy with Mr. Hunt, Harriet?"

I turned and looked at this child who seemed to have insight far beyond his years. He met my eyes steadily and with the compassion of one who fully understood the full meaning of the question he asked. And yet, I thought, it was a fair question and one that deserved an equally fair answer.

"Yes," I said slowly, "I was very unhappy with him, although I would bring him back to life this minute if it were possible."

"But it isn't possible, is it, Harriet?"

I gripped his hand hard. "No, my love, I don't think it is, and the best thing we can both do is to try to put it behind us." I somehow managed to smile reassuringly into the small, pale face. "It was very gallant of you to come to my defense. The fall was an accident. And now it's time you went back to bed and tried to get some sleep."

He gave a small sigh and, almost as though he were speaking to himself, said, "And then perhaps we can both go home." Home. But where was home for me now, if not in Banipore?

In the big oval drawing room I found Victor de Souza waiting for me. I remember thinking that he must have called at least some of the servants back because the punkah was swinging steadily from the ceiling, the greased rope creaking faintly where it disappeared through a hole in the wall.

"Drink this, Mrs. Hunt. It will be doing you good."

I took the heavy cut-glass goblet and sipped, discovering with surprise that it was half full of cognac. Not that it mattered. Victor, after all, could have had little opportunity for discovering which glasses were supposed to hold brandy and how much. Nevertheless it was a mild shock to find him standing in the middle of Garfield's drawing room holding a glass in his own hand. Garfield would never, never have offered him a drink in the drawing room or, for that matter, anywhere else.

"This is a great tragedy, Mrs. Hunt. May I offer you

my deepest sympathy." The Eurasian's dark, spaniel-like eyes, oddly expressionless, stared into mine.

"That is kind of you, Mr. de Souza, but I, for one, have not given up all hope yet. Are the servants still searching?"

"Of course." Victor sipped at the amber liquid in his glass, then turned to stare at the rather muddy painting of one of Garfield's ancestors that hung above the fireplace. It showed a Jacobean soldier whose haughty glance had in it something that was guarded and almost furtive, so much so that Garfield, in a moment of rare humor, had suggested to me that he wondered if the painter ever succeeded in getting paid for his work. Now the strange expression seemed to captivate Victor. At least, that is what I thought. But then Victor swung back to me and, in a voice as smooth as silk, said to me, "That is a most interesting picture. One could almost swear that he has seen something that he wishes to keep to himself. Something that he will reveal when it suits him best. Do you not agree?"

I took a sip of the fiery liquid and found it comforting. But I was holding the globe of the glass so tightly that I feared I might crush it.

"Yes," I said, praying that my voice, at least, was steady.

Perhaps I was wrong in seeing some hidden meaning in his words, yet it was a strange fragment of drawing-room conversation to offer at such a time. I tried to tell myself that it was because the little Eurasian felt ill at ease in his surroundings. But his general attitude was very far from that.

He glanced again toward the picture and now there was no trace of his earlier carefully phrased formalities.

"A man in such a position would have great power, would he not, Mrs. Hunt? He would indeed be a fortunate fellow." And then, before I had an opportunity to be even fully aware of the rising tide of fear within me, his manner had changed again, and there was only respect and consideration in his voice as he went on. "But you must be excusing me, Mrs. Hunt. It is late. If

22

I may say so, a good night's sleep will be most beneficial. Tomorrow things will not seem so dark."

"I expect you are right, Mr. de Souza. Good night."

Only when he had gone and the door had closed behind him did I allow myself to drop my guard. I sank down into a chair, trembling all over, my head swimming, but whether from the shock of Garfield s death or the brandy or de Souza's sly innuendos I did not know.

Had he really been hinting that he had seen Garfield's death, or had I, with my heightened sense of guilt and my frantic desire to protect Rupert, read more into his words than had been intended?

Suddenly, from the depth of utter weariness, I knew that nothing could be resolved until the morning. Perhaps then I would see the awful happenings of tonight in a different light. I turned and stumbled toward my room. Lelune, the sixteen-year-old Kashmirian ayah whom Garfield had engaged for me on my arrival, was waiting for me at the door. Her eyes slid to the torn shoulder of my gown, and only then did I think, De Souza must have seen it, too. I would gladly have dismissed her had it not been for the fact that with fingers clumsy from exhaustion I should make a poor showing at unfastening the dozen or more tiny pearl buttons that ran from neck to waist.

I stood like a statue while the girl deftly undressed me, clucking maternally as she fingered the ruined satin. From outside the lattice of the window there no longer came the distant shouts of the men who were searching for Garfield's body, and instead the song of the bulbul, the little Indian nightingale, flowed on, liquid and clear. It was a sound that had entranced me so often before on happier occasions and now, as I listened to those magical notes rising and falling, something seemed to snap inside me and I found tears running down my cheeks.

I did not know why I wept. Certainly it was not for Garfield, although Lelune could not guess that. Her tears joined mine as she drew back the covers of the

23

bed, for she was a Hindu and her mind could conjure up no worse fate than widowhood.

In the weeks that followed, I almost found myself sharing the girl's view. It was true that I had been wretched in my brief marriage to Garfield, yet there were times when it seemed as though its miseries had been preferable to the new and oddly unwholesome atmosphere that now seemed to be my portion. Callers, official and otherwise, reflected an attitude that I hoped owed little to England and much to our country of adoption. Short days ago I had been a bride and the toast of the station, welcomed everywhere with pleasure and attention. Now I was plainly that most dreaded pariah, a widow—and a young one. Women who had but lately welcomed me into their homes with open arms plainly regarded me as inevitable competition for the favors of their menfolk, and the men themselves, while still too civilized to disregard the requisite period of mourning, showed with their eyes that they were invigorated at the prospect of competing for the favors of one who was no longer troubled by the presence of a virginity she feared.

I remembered a friend of my father's who had, in days long past, once watched a Hindu woman burn herself alive on her husband's funeral pyre and reported that she had gone singing to her death. Perhaps, I thought grimly, I should find more favor were I to go *suttee*. At least I would cease to exist as a kind of predator.

Almost worse than these men, however, were those who regarded me with uncertainty. Suspicion would perhaps be too strong a word. But I believed I knew what was in the minds of these friends of my late husband. Nearly every night of his life he had walked down by the river. Yet, only two months after he had married a young—and possibly unsuitable—bride, he had slipped and drowned. Their sympathy for my loss lay perilously near the surface and I realized day by day that there was no one in this community to whom I could turn for help and advice.

Yet, mercifully, there were other preoccupations.

24

Chief among these were visits from Inspector Crendal of the Indian police, visits that, had it not been for the purpose they served, I might well have viewed with apprehension. As it was, I was glad enough to welcome the stocky, red-faced Irishman, whom I had met once or twice at station gatherings and disliked heartily and unreasoningly on sight.

"You must be allowing me to keep my records straight, Mrs. Hunt. Just a statement of the tragedy and the way you remember it happening now, an' then we'll be forgetting all about it."

I told myself that there was every reason why he should question me and none at all why I should resent him, yet resent him I did. There was something about his affability that could not be dismissed as being no more than a personal characteristic, something that struck me as being essentially false. But I had heard Garfield observe, on more than one occasion, that he was a good policeman, as far as policemen went, which in the social scale of Banipore was not very far, and doubtless he was tired of being patronized. Nevertheless he listened quietly as I told my story and I think he believed me.

"Just so, Mrs. Hunt. I'll not be saying it's a thing that could have happened to anybody, but it certainly seems to have happened to your husband. Doubtless you'll be hearing no more about it."

Why "doubtless"? Or was it merely a trick of speech? Then I decided there was no point imagining threats when none were intended. After all, I had imagined Victor was threatening me, but he had spoken no more to alarm me, even on the day he brought me the news that Garfield's body had been recovered some five miles downstream.

"I'm glad to hear that," I said to Inspector Crendal.

"You'll not be planning to leave the station, I imagine?"

"No."

"I'll bid you good day, then, Mrs. Hunt."

I wondered what the answer would have been had I said yes, but had not the courage to ask. Instead I watched him ride away down the dusty mall, an ordinary enough but vaguely disquieting figure. The British were not expected to break the rules, and the Indian police, with their white officers and native constabulary mounted and trained after the fashion of the military, were there to put down the everyday crimes of theft and horse stealing about the bazaars and caravansaries. Yet everybody knew that there was always a handful of white prisoners in the bigger jails. It was something few talked about—the law was the law for both black and white—and even in the little, closed community of the cantonments it was accepted that, if you broke it, the affable man with the silver badge who sat beside you at dinner would exact its penalty with regret but total impartiality.

In some fatalistic way I was not surprised that, during the days that followed, Inspector Crendal did in fact call on me twice more, on both occasions with some trivial point that may or may not have been his real reason for coming. There was no change in his manner, and he left me with no more definite conclusions as to his real feelings than I had formed before. But I did remember another comment that Garfield had made about him over the convicting of a particularly despotic planter. "That man has the tenacity of a terrier who worries at a bone. He will never let go until forced to."

It was just after one of the inspector's visits that Mr. Whittle came to call briefly and ask after my welfare. I was in a particularly low state that day and when he spoke kindly to me, I was sorely tempted to confess to him what had really happened. But I stopped myself. Sharing the burden would not make it any easier and, I suspected, might make my problems even more acute. Nevertheless, before he left, he once again reminded me that his help was available should I so require it. As before, I thanked him, certain that this kindly but eccentric little man saw a great deal further into the human mind than an ordinary newspaperman.

The most welcome of my visitors was Mr. McKay, the bank manager, on whom I called initially to seek

26

advice as to how I stood with regard to money for the day-to-day running of the house. It was said that he had occupied the same old-fashioned office at the back of the bank building since before the Mutiny, and faced with his gray, shrunken figure crouched behind the enormous teak table that served him as a desk, I could well believe this to be true. Yet the eyes behind the gold pince-nez were at first sight encouragingly kind, and as he came forward to take my hand I had a feeling that here, at least, was a man on whom I could rely.

To my relief, he cut short his commiserations and turned quickly to business.

"You'll be wanting some funds to see to the running of that great place of yours, I'm thinking. Forty servants or more to be paid for, for a start. I told your husband he was a fool to buy such a place, but he wouldn't listen." I started to speak but he went on. "Mrs. Hunt, it was my privilege to look after your husband's affairs for well nigh twenty-five years, as well as being interested in his business on my own account, though you won't have been knowing that, I'm thinking."

I shook my head. "No, Mr. McKay. But, then, I know very little of business. Garfield never discussed it with me."

"Well, commerce is not a woman's business anyway. Ye'll not have seen the will?" He peered at me over the top of his glasses. "No? Then it had best wait for Mason and Hawkes in Delhi to deal with, but I know enough of Mr. Hunt's intentions to say that ye'll be a wealthy woman—an uncommonly wealthy woman, come to that."

I felt no elation at the news. All I had ever wanted from my marriage was security for Rupert, and as Garfield's widow I was reasonably assured of that. I said, "I presume, Mr. McKay, there will be some delay before the formalities are completed?"

He nodded. "Aye. But I'm not a partner for nothing. I can take it on myself to advance you any reasonable

27

sum against your expectations. Had you a figure in mind?"

"My brother, Rupert, must go to school soon." I hesitated, not wanting to make too much of the issue, yet knowing the sooner I got Rupert away, the sooner he would forget all that had happened—and the more easily I would sleep at night. I went on doggedly. "His education has already been sadly neglected through no fault of my father's, but further delay would not bode well for his future."

"Ye'll not wish to be going with him yourself? It might well complicate legal matters were you to leave India so soon."

"I can join him later. For the moment I'd be happy if I could make some arrangement for him to travel to England in the care of some family going there on leave."

"And when he gets there?"

"I have an aunt who married an Englishman; I am sure that between them they would make a suitable choice of a school." I had never met my Aunt Laura's husband, a country doctor in Gloucestershire, but from what I had heard they had a large and happy family and I had little doubt that they would gladly do all that was necessary.

The bank manager scribbled on a piece of paper, then leaned back in his chair. "I can see it would be desirable to establish your ability to pay for the education your relative is to be asked to arrange. Would you consider fifty thousand rupees adequate for that purpose and also to meet the demands on your purse during the next few months?"

The sum startled me. "Mr. McKay," I protested, "that is a great deal of money. . . ."

"In sterling it approaches four thousand pounds. In view of your expectations the figure is not inappropriate."

The following day the mail arrived from the South, bringing with it a letter from Garfield's solicitors. Only then did I realize fully what it was the bank manager had been unable to tell me. Garfield, with a lack of

28

foresight amazing in a man of his character, had failed to make a new will upon his marriage, which meant that the whole estate belonged automatically to me. Like all other legal firms, Mason and Hawkes was reluctant to commit itself but gave the opinion that, when probate was granted, it was unlikely that I should receive much less than the rupee equivalent of one hundred and fifty thousand pounds.

I think it was the cold reality of the figures that shocked me. There seemed to be an enormous difference between knowing that I was to inherit a considerable sum of money and being aware of the actual amount, even though I already knew in my heart that I could never take it. Enough for Rupert's schooling, yes. I had decided that Garfield owed me that. Perhaps enough to allow me a modest independence, for there was nothing worse than to be a burden to others. But when the legalities were settled, I would find some plausible way of distributing the money in accordance with the last will. Which meant, I told myself, that the bulk of the estate would probably go to Ursula. True, she had been no friend to me, but as Garfield's sister she had as much or more right to the money as I.

It was probably these reflections that prompted me to call on Ursula the following day. Formal courtesy decreed, as I was well aware, an invitation before a visit. Banipore, with its two hundred British residents, had really very little in common with those isolated little communities that had been my home as often as not through the years. Most of them had no more than an irreducible minimum of civilians, usually consisting of the deputy collector and his wife, the magistrate, the local police officer, and perhaps a doctor. But now I lived in a station that boasted its own general and two infantry battalions as well as a regiment of artillery. It had its own polo ground and a real bandstand in the center of the mall and an accompanying formal pattern of social life that one disregarded at one's peril.

Nevertheless I told myself that whether she liked me or not, Ursula and I were sisters-in-law, and so I changed into the simple black taffeta dress with its matching hat that was to be my uniform over the next year anytime I appeared in public. The hat, which I had attempted to dress up with a piece of black chiffon, did not suit me, making my complexion even paler than it was. But at least, I thought wryly, the very dullness of my appearance would probably give Ursula a certain satisfaction. True, as Garfield's sister she was condemned to the same mourning hue, but only for six months, and then with the knowledge that it was not greatly different from the somber grays and mauves that she habitually favored.

It was no more than half a mile to the Scott-Barnards' bungalow, close to the old cavalry lines, and I might well have walked the distance with enjoyment. But at the last minute I reflected that my arrival on foot would only have confirmed my lack of breeding in Ursula's eyes, so I set out in the fashion that Banipore doubtless judged as appropriate to my station, in the Calcutta-made phaeton, drawn by two grays, Karim Das on the box, with my faithful Hamidullah beside him and the dog boy running alongside with the two dalmatians.

The sun was almost down and the *bhistis* were sprinkling the dusty mall with water from goatskins, so that the air was filled with a sharp, fresh smell so different from the heat of the day. We swung into the semicircular drive that led up to the broad steps of Ursula's bungalow and I went up to the front door, beyond the thatch-covered veranda, to be greeted by a white-coated *khitmagar* wearing a broad belt of his master's regimental colors.

"*Meri salaam memsahib ko dena.*" Lionel Scott-Barnard was fifty miles away in camp with his regiment, so there was no point in announcing myself to him. Yet, as I was ushered into the overfurnished drawing room, I did not regret his absence, for on the few occasions we had met he had shown little inclination to be friendly. Rumor had it that he lost more at the card tables than he could afford, and I suspected that Garfield had not been inclined to make good his brother-in-law's losses, for the bungalow had the slightly shabby look of a home that had neither money nor care expended on it.

Ursula greeted me distantly, making no attempt to hide either surprise at my unannounced arrival or indifference at the prospect of my company. There was a glass on the table beside her and her normally florid face was more highly colored even than usual.

"I hope this is not inconvenient," I said. "It seems a long time since we met at the funeral and—"

"And so you assumed that within the family you could forgo the customary formalities." Without an accompanying smile the words were a reproach and I found myself regretting the impulse that had brought me to her home without due warning.

"Yes, I suppose I did." I did my best to keep my voice level. Then, on impulse, I appealed to her. "Ursula, I know that I am not the person you had hoped Garfield might marry, but surely that is behind us now? Couldn't we be friends?"

"Friends!" I was shocked by the venom that Garfield's sister put into the word. She took a step nearer and I smelled the scent of brandy on her breath. "Friends! Do you expect me to be friends with a chit of a girl who has taken every penny that should have been mine? You talk about not being the kind of person I had hoped my brother would marry. Garfield had no intention of marrying *anyone* until you flaunted yourself at him. Even then he didn't want you. It was just your body he wanted and he was prepared to pay for it. . . ." She caught her breath suddenly, and for a moment I thought she was going to fall, but she recovered herself with an effort, groped for her glass, and drained it clumsily. "All these years . . ." The words were slurred, almost as though she were speaking to herself. "All these years I've waited. And now . . . nothing."

With a feeling of revulsion I turned away. I realized that at the back of my mind there had been a hope that it might be possible to suggest tactfully that I didn't want Garfield's money, that she could have it,

31

for all I cared. Whereas now . . . I said quietly, "You're quite right. I should not have come. Nor shall I ever come again."

"Then go, damn you, and leave me alone."

I left her, sick and shaking. There was something obscene about the sight of someone baring her very soul in such a way, and I cursed myself for being such a fool as to have invited such a display of hatred. All the way back through the lengthening shadows of the mall, I sat with my hands pressed together in a vain endeavor to keep them from trembling. Hamidullah looked at me compassionately as he handed me out of the carriage, and as soon as I was alone in my own sitting room he reappeared bearing a glass on a small silver tray.

I looked at it with surprise. "What is this, Hamidullah? I did not ask for anything."

"Brandy-pani, memsahib." His lined face was expressionless. "Drink. I think it will make you feel better."

"Thank you." I sipped the amber liquid and felt its warmth steadying me. I should have known that very little escaped Hamidullah's eagle eye, and I was thankful that he had accompanied me to Banipore. Always he had had my father's interests at heart and now, I supposed, had mine.

He was still standing there. "The chief clerk is outside. He wishes to speak with you. Shall I tell him the memsahib is too tired?"

"Mr. de Souza?" I tried to remember if there was any matter outstanding with the Eurasian but could recall nothing. "No, Hamidullah, ask him to come in."

He bowed slightly, but in the doorway he paused as if to say something more. Gently I chided him. "I am perfectly all right now, Hamidullah. I will see him."

Victor de Souza seemed to have lost some of the assurance he had shown on the night of Garfield's death, but as he came toward me across the polished *chanum* floor there was something in his manner that caused me even greater disquiet. Just what it was I could not tell, yet as I looked into his moist, dark eyes I felt an unreasoning pang of apprehension.

"You wished to see me, Mr. de Souza?"

"Yes, madam, there is a small matter I am most eager to discuss with you."

"Well?" I waited and, rather childishly, pointedly refrained from offering the chair that Indian courtesy demanded. I detected a spot of color darken his olive cheek.

He said smoothly, "It is by way of being a problem in my family, madam. My brother is at present working with the railway in a poor sort of job. Really, it has no future. I am always telling him that."

"Indeed?"

"Indeed, yes, madam. But now he has fine opportunity for going into business on his own account. Only there is big difficulty in finding money for his share in project, so I am thinking that perhaps out of kindness you might be helping."

To hide my feelings I stood up and walked to the fireplace. Then I asked quietly, "How much money is your brother needing, Mr. de Souza?"

Neat, well-kept hands spread out in a deprecating gesture. "Not a great sum, madam. Twenty thousand rupees."

It was impossible for him to have seen the lawyer's letter, I told myself, yet it was a wild coincidence that he should have chosen today to make the demand. He could, of course, have been aware that it had arrived, and as Garfield's chief clerk it would have taken no great flight of imagination to put two and two together. He, more than anyone else, could have guessed what Garfield's estate was worth.

I said, "But I do not even know your brother, Mr. de Souza. What makes you think I might be willing to advance such a large sum to someone I have never met?"

"Because, madam," Victor said in a voice as smooth as silk, "I can be helping you."

I felt my hands grip the edge of the desk so hard that its finely polished mahogany bit into my fingers. I

33

longed to reach out for the brandy glass but guessed that de Souza would take that move as a sign of weakness. Instead I did my best to look politely puzzled. "In what way is that?"

For a moment the man paused, as though at the very last moment his courage had failed him. But the pause lasted only the briefest instant. "I wish only to help madam forget what happened on the night of Mr. Garfield's death. The . . . accident." He raised his eyes and looked me full in the face. Now there was no doubt at all what he was saying to me.

The trembling in my legs was so great I knew they would soon no longer hold me up. So I sat down in a high-backed chair and let my hands rest upon my lap. I knew not what to say.

Victor de Souza took a step nearer and there was no mistaking the underlying threat in his voice.

"So, madam, is my brother getting the money?"

There was, of course, no brother. Suddenly my dislike of this greedy, obsequious man became almost a physical sickness. It was all I could do to stop myself striking out at him. Then I remembered Rupert. I could do nothing, nothing at all, until my brother was out of this house.

I fingered the silver pen and inkstand on the table as though I were considering his words. Then I took a deep breath.

"Mr. de Souza, as you know, these things take time to arrange. I have yet no money of my husband's in my possession. When I do, I will give the matter serious consideration. Until then you . . . your brother must be content to wait."

For a moment I thought he might try to press me, but he seemed to think better of it. He nodded. "So be it, madam. We will talk again later. I will tell my brother that his future looks promising."

The door closed behind him. I took a deep draft of the brandy, and though it burned my throat, I felt that my head was clearing. I had done the right thing and played for time.

"Hamidullah!"

He must have been very near, for the door opened almost immediately and the tall, white-coated figure moved with his effortless hillman's lope across the carpet.

"Memsahib?" His eyes were suddenly watchful as he noticed the pallor of my cheeks. "Memsahib, it is better that you do not allow the chief clerk to intrude upon you again."

"Yes, perhaps." I brushed aside his concern for me. "I want you to pack my brother's belongings at once. But do not let this be known to any of the other servants."

"He goes on a journey?"

"Yes. In your care."

"So be it. And to where do we make a journey?"

"Pack the clothes first. I will tell you later."

What was it Joseph Whittle had said to me both at my father's funeral and when he had visited me after Garfield's death? *Should you have need of me at any time, I am at your service.* The words, I knew, were not uttered lightly. If anyone could have guessed what I had endured as Garfield's wife, it would have been Mr. Whittle. And by good fortune I had only recently heard that he was visiting a military station a bare fifty miles away.

I sat down at the Venetian escritoire for which Garfield had repeatedly told me he had paid five hundred English pounds. For a moment I sat looking at a blank sheet of crested paper, seeking the words I needed. Then I took up my pen and wrote briefly to Mr. Whittle, consigning Rupert to his care and asking if he would make what arrangements were necessary to have the boy sent to his aunt and uncle in England.

When I laid down the pen, I sat staring, unseeing, at the wall for a long time. For it had suddenly come to me that after tomorrow I might never see Rupert again.

3

The next ten days found me in a condition bordering on despair.

I had always felt alone in Garfield's home, but with the departure of both Rupert and Hamidullah, the place seemed like a stifling, ornate prison. Had there been friends nearby, at least I could have sought in their companionship a warmth and sense of personal contact that might well have sustained me. As it was, I filled the long days as best I could by riding in the cool of the early morning and concerning myself for the rest of the time with the trivialities of housekeeping, only too well aware that night, when it came, would bring with it little sleep.

Worst of all was the waiting. Waiting for Victor de Souza to make his next move. If he had any feelings about my action in sending Rupert away, he did not show them. Since I had spoken often enough of the matter of my brother's education, I prayed the move would have seemed natural to him in spite of the departure without warning.

Although I saw little enough of him during those days, I knew that he studied every movement I made. Among the servants he was a powerful man. There would be a dozen eyes watching me on his behalf.

It was a great relief when Hamidullah returned, bearing a letter from Joseph Whittle confirming that he willingly accepted the responsibility I had put on him and that he would shortly write to me again, as soon as he was in a position to report on the arrangements he had made. Hamidullah assured me that no one had seen Rupert and himself leave the great house. He had made certain that their departure took place when all the servants save the night watchman were asleep. I thanked him warmly. At least Rupert was safe. Perhaps now I would be able to sleep in peace.

But the relief I felt was not to last for long. When I returned from an errand one evening, de Souza was waiting for me and I knew by the look in those dark, greedy eyes there would be no more postponing the moment I had been dreading.

"I think, Mrs. Hunt, that the time has come for us to be making a more realistic financial arrangement. My brother . . ."

The words were so very like the ones I had already heard a hundred times in my own mind that they had lost their capacity to dismay. As I stood facing Garfield's chief clerk once more in the big, oval room that I had come to hate, I realized that I had prepared myself for the demand better than I had supposed.

My voice was commendably steady as I said, "Come, Mr. de Souza, both you and I know that your brother's business exists only in your imagination. How much do *you* want this time?"

He spread his thin hands in a gesture that I found suddenly more irritating than threatening. "Madam, what are you offering?"

"I am offering you nothing," I told him sharply. "It is you who are demanding."

"I am not a covetous man, Mrs. Hunt. But I should have been a poor kind of businessman had I not some idea of what Mr. Hunt's estate will be. Shall we say at least a crore?"

I drew in my breath harshly. I had expected nothing like this. A crore was ten million rupees, more than seven hundred thousand pounds. The sum was ridiculous, far in excess of the true figure.

"I am afraid," I said coldly, "that you are under a misconception."

"Misconception?" De Souza raised his eyebrows.

"Then it is possible that I might not be able to continue a service I am at present doing for madam."

"Which is?" I asked with a sinking heart.

"Mrs. Hunt, my service is this: I am forgetting what I am seeing through window on the night of your husband's unfortunate death."

"You have already told me that, Mr. de Souza. But you have not told me what it was you saw." I was gradually regaining my courage. Now that Rupert was safe, I almost welcomed his bringing his threat out into the open.

The answer came immediately. "I saw you thrust him into the river. Also, when he tried to swim, you struck him upon the head with a heavy stick."

"But that is nonsense! You must have taken leave of your senses!"

I had been prepared for the truth but not for this. "You could not possibly have seen that." It was, I suppose, a naive outcry, but the words sprang to my lips instinctively.

Had Victor de Souza been an Italian, he would almost certainly have shrugged his shoulders, but as it was, he made a curious little jerking movement of his head that in India means the same thing. "I have many witnesses, madam. All will agree with what I say."

I knew there was little doubt of that. My mind went back to the time, a couple of years before, when I had asked my father about a row of men squatting in the sunshine outside a courthouse, and he had laughed and told me that they were witnesses waiting to be hired. At the time, I had thought he was joking. Now I had been in India long enough to know that he had told me a plain fact. If de Souza said that half a dozen of the other servants had seen me kill my husband, I was quite certain that he could produce those men to swear to just that.

De Souza's smooth voice went on. "Particularly my conscience troubled me. It is with regard to the departed's sister, madam. Daily I feel that Mrs. Scott-Barnard should be informed of the true facts of the case."

38

Ursula! This man was a devil, I thought. I could imagine only too well the readiness with which my sister-in-law would listen to his lies.

I must have shown my dismay. Certainly he believed he had me in a corner at last. His oily voice broke into my thoughts. "So, madam, we are coming to an agreeable arrangement?"

Suddenly the combined tensions of the last few days worked on me to produce not fear but white, blazing anger. I had suffered abuse from Ursula because I knew her to be a lonely, bitter woman who had found herself balked of the one thing that might have made an unhappy marriage bearable. But to be persecuted by a man like Victor de Souza, for no better reason than that I was a woman alone and apparently at his mercy, was unendurable. I suppose that had I been more in control of myself, I should have been sensible and told him not to be a fool, trusting in long years of service to have its effect. But anger knows little discretion, and instinctively I struck back in the way that would wound and humiliate him most.

I said in Hindi, "There will be no financial arrangement—I repeat, *no* financial arrangement. You have my leave to go. Now."

His immaculate European dress, his open contempt for all things Indian, showed how deeply Victor resented his own mixed blood. Now he found himself not only addressed in a language he would have preferred not to acknowledge but in the person appropriate to inferiors.

I do not think I have ever seen such naked hatred in any man's face as I did in Victor de Souza's as the words sank in. He stood staring at me for a moment, his eyes wide and luminous, then he said in a soft, deadly voice, "So be it, Mrs. Hunt. Murder is an ugly charge to face." Silently he turned and strode out of the room, slamming the door behind him.

At the finality of that shut door, I slumped back in my chair, suddenly sick at heart. Had I made a terrible mistake? I had openly challenged the man who had threatened me, of that I was not ashamed. But it was

39

one thing to be defiant in the first hot flash of anger and quite another to consider its consequences in the cold light of reason. I stood by myself in that hated room of Garfield's, calling myself a fool and yet at the same time wondering what other course had been open to me. On no account could I have given in to blackmail on such a terrifying scale. But if de Souza's threats were real, I was indeed in danger. Where, I wondered desperately, could I go?

A door creaked in front of me and I jumped like some animal of the wild, only to relax again as I saw that it was only Hamidullah, regarding me with stern compassion. Not for the first time, I was thankful I had insisted he stay with me in my new home. There was something wonderfully comforting and familiar about the aquiline brown face beneath his customary white turban. He was a Pathan, one of a Mercurial people, traditionally hostile to the British, yet capable of fierce loyalty to those for whom they felt respect. At this moment there was a stillness about him that smacked strongly of his northern forebears, the dignity of a proud though sometimes cruel race.

Abruptly Hamidullah said, "Memsahib, you must leave this place. Even now that half-breed bastard is on his way to the police."

"So, you know. . . ." I was not surprised, for he'd always known everything.

"There are things in a great house like this, memsahib, that cannot be kept secret. I have watched and I have listened. Do you wish that the chief clerk should die?"

The suggestion was made so casually that for a moment I did not take it seriously. Then it came to me suddenly that Hamidullah's stubborn loyalty could well make him capable of violence on my behalf, should he deem it necessary.

"No," I said, "the sahib is not to die."

"Sahib?" he said scornfully. "What talk is this of sahibs? He is a . . ." And he used a word that made me jump. "I tell you, he will either let you hang or wrench from you every anna until you be starving in the

40

streets. Out of memory for your father, who is dead, I say this. Now, let me cut the man's throat and be done."

"I have said that there shall be no more dying." But though my words sounded brave, I knew they had a hollow ring.

"Then, get from here, memsahib, for the love of God. You have friends who would shelter you?"

I shook my head. "I have no friends to whom I could ask that. If the police want me, then they must come. I have done no harm to anyone, whatever the witnesses may say, and I'm not afraid to stand trial."

"And the boy?" Hamidullah demanded. "What of him? He is not yet clear of the country. He may be safe from the chief clerk, but the police will find him if they choose to. But if you protect him, as you must, then I fear a trial would go badly with you. Mr. Hunt was a well-known man. Already there is talk about his death. The police inspector has visited you too often. For a little while longer . . . a month . . . two months at the most, you must be clear of the law, so run while there is yet time."

"Run?" I turned to the tall window and stared out over the lengthening shadows of the garden as the quick Indian dusk wrapped darkness across the land. The scent of woodsmoke drifted in on the cooler air and from somewhere out of sight a jackal howled at the new moon. More to myself than to the big Pathan I said, "Where should I run to? There are not many Englishwomen up here in the North. Wherever I ran I should soon be brought back."

"From any land under the rule of the raj, yes," Hamidullah agreed. "But in India there are many lands, and in some of them the old ways still hold good. In the South there are many princes who would offer you hospitality and then doubtless sell you to the highest bidder. But in the North the old laws are never broken. In the hills there are khans who would receive you as an honored guest. Is it not written in the thirtieth *sura*, 'The just man careth for the wayfarer and shall surely prosper'?"

It was true, as I well knew, that the Muhammadan laws of hospitality were rigidly laid down in the Koran, but at the same time there was no knowing how strict about his religion any particular khan might be. In theory he might be obliged to give me sanctuary within his own borders, yet I had little doubt that the British government had means of applying effective pressure if it so desired. In times gone by, the whole of India had consisted of independent kingdoms, large and small, and the most important had long ago fallen under British control. Those that retained their independence were either so powerful and so cooperative with the white raj that it was politically inexpedient to disturb them or so tiny that they were of little value. I would do Rupert and myself little good where I simply to step from the frying pan into some unknown fire.

As if reading my thoughts, Hamidullah said, "I will take you to my own country. Your safety shall be on my head."

I smiled in spite of myself. "Hamidullah, you are a Pathan. Would you have me offer myself to the Marsuds or the Atta Khel, who kidnap white women for their ransom?"

" 'Trust a dog before a harlot and a harlot before a Pathan.' " Hamidullah bowed slightly as he quoted the old saying of the frontier. "It is true my mother was a Pathan, but my father was from Khudistan. The khan is of your people—have you not heard?"

The white khan of Khudistan. The phrase came back to me from half-remembered stories. Years ago, in the old days of the East India Company, one of the wild band of European mercenaries who had earned a precarious living selling his sword to the highest bidder had settled in a lush, uncharted valley high in the northern hills, where it was said his son ruled to this day. I had half dismissed it as a traveler's tale or at best as the story of some poor, half-crazed refugee from his own kind, native in all but color, yet counting himself a prince because he ruled a village or two in some forgotten valley.

"Yes," I admitted, "I have heard of him. But is it true?"

"Oh, yes, memsahib. And despite his blood, he has no time for the British. His borders are closed to travelers and were you to gain his hospitality, no man should bring you back."

Even if the police eventually forced my return, I told myself, it was not something that could be done in a day. It would give me the breathing space I so desperately needed. By the time anyone traced me, Rupert would be on his way to England, and then it would matter little what happened to me.

"Very well," I said, "let us go to Khudistan."

Hamidullah inclined his head. "So be it. Pack only what is needed. But with your own hands, memsahib. Do not speak of this to your maid. I go to saddle the horses."

I thought of all the servants in the house and I knew how they watched me. With a sudden feeling of defeat I said, "Someone will ask why you want them. And in any case, we shall be seen as we leave."

"Much may be done with money, and so perhaps the head syce will be elsewhere. As for our going, that, too, can be arranged. The memsahib should be ready in half an hour."

"Very well," I agreed, "in half an hour." I found I was content to leave the manner of my escape in the hands of the one person whose loyalty was not in question. And though I would not have confessed to anyone at that moment—least of all to myself—the prospect of escape from the stifling atmosphere of Banipore to an unknown future in Khudistan filled me with a sudden tingle of excitement.

I packed what bare necessities I needed in a leather saddlebag before changing into a dun-colored riding habit of a shade similar to that which, since the Mutiny, was beginning to replace the old familiar red-jacketed army uniforms, and a matching stiff-brimmed hat. Then I folded a white shawl of Kashmirian wool, light enough to carry across my saddle but warm against the evening cold of the hills.

I gave a final glance around the room, at the rows of elaborate gowns, the silver toiletries that Garfield had given me, the multitudes of shoes. I had had them all for so short a time and yet, now that I was to abandon them, it came to me that I did so without regret.

Suddenly my thoughts were interrupted by a panic-stricken cry from the servants' quarters, followed by a rush of footsteps in the compound below.

"Ag ligya! Chalao! Chalao!"

There was indeed a fire. As I ran to the window and pulled back the shutter I could see its rosy glow against the night sky. A great tongue of flame was licking up the side of the kitchen, set back some twenty yards from the house, and I could hear it crackling viciously as it reached the thatch. In the flickering light I could see scantily clothed figures rushing confusedly here and there, presently to be joined by Victor de Souza, issuing orders. If there was a moment in which to make our escape, this was clearly it, and as if in response to my thoughts, there was a tap on the door.

"Quickly, memsahib," Hamidullah hissed, "we can go unseen while they busy themselves with the fire." And as I joined him on the stairs he added, "The building will burn for some time, never fear. With my own hands I soaked it well in oil."

There was little I could say to that, although I found my eyes suddenly stinging with tears. There was no reason why this man should risk his life for me. It could only be that he had loved my father, and now that his old master had gone, all his fierce hill loyalty had been transferred to me.

"Do not delay," he said as I paused at the open doorway. "The half-caste bastard has returned and this time will stop at nothing."

I nodded without speaking and followed his tall figure across the veranda and into the shadows of the garden beyond.

Flames from the burning building were turning the night sky orange, but the bulk of the great house hid us from the direct glare, thickening the shadows to an inky black. With all the servants trying to quell the flames, there was no one to bar our way. Within minutes we were outside the compound, where two horses stood tethered beneath a tree. One was my own gray, the other I recognized as the great black stallion that had been Garfield's mount. Hamidullah would have enjoyed taking him, I thought, remembering the reputation Pathans enjoyed as incorrigible horse thieves.

I must have hesitated, because he came back to me and saw me into the saddle. Behind us, the flames were mounting steadily higher, and a crowd was gathering rapidly.

"Ride, memsahib!" Hamidullah urged. "The vultures gather already. See those three riders beyond the flames—if I am not mistaken, de Souza's hirelings are already here. Make for the pike. It is better that I play the syce tonight."

I nodded without speaking and urged my mount forward. Hamidullah was right, no one would remark on a memsahib out riding with her groom following close behind, whereas we would have been distinctly noticeable the other way round. Tonight we wanted to pass unseen.

I cantered down the mall with Hamidullah at my heels, skirted the empty darkness of the polo ground, and then wound my way through the bazaar until the buildings thinned and ahead was only the lonely turnpike, heading north.

Many times since, I have remembered parts of that journey, and although I have never again covered quite the same ground, my memories of much of it are as clear as though they belonged to only yesterday. We traveled steadily rather than as fast as was formidable, both to save our horses and to avoid drawing attention to ourselves, winding up through the foothills, the endless, blue-hazed plain behind us and ahead the great, towering ranges of the high mountains, beckoning us on.

At first the road was busy enough with the regular traffic of those parts, camels packed high with carpets from Afghanistan and beyond, light-footed ponies with almond-eyed drivers bringing down trade goods from

Gilgit and even Tibet. Mixed in with these long-distance travelers were the bullock carts belonging to local villagers, their wheels creaking their way to the nearest market or family wedding, with the farmer perched precariously on the axle tree and his wives, formless shapes in all-enshrouding *boorkahs,* tramping the dusty road behind him. Soldiers on leave, wandering holy men, the occasional armed retinue and elaborately painted carriage of some local chieftain all helped to make a composite picture of Indian life. I saw no one I recognized, nevertheless I kept my hat pulled low over my brow and a chiffon scarf wound loosely around my face.

Watching the various figures emerge from the gently stirring clouds of white dust and seeing, as though for the first time, the rays of the rising moon strike slantingly through it, I realized how much a part of this vast country I had become. I could look out across the fields toward the little villages blurred in the moonlight, with the low-lying smoke from their fires, and picture in my mind the kind of life that was lived there, because I had witnessed it with my father a hundred times. India, seen from the foreign, isolated world of a cantonment, could mean little enough to one who made no attempt to understand it. But here on the road it was vibrant with life and color, and it seemed to me that each step carried me not so much away from one world as into another.

I had asked at the outset how long the journey would take, and Hamidullah had said only about a week, but with the inflection that I had long ago realized meant that he either did not know or at least had no intention of telling me.

For three days we made our way north along the busy road, stopping each night at the old travelers' post bungalows that were scattered along every Indian highway; here the inevitable ancient custodian would produce a simple meal cooked either by himself or by one of his many relations who inhabited the sprawling quarters at the rear.

On such occasions Hamidullah would treat me with

46

the usual formality appropriate between a servant and his mistress, busying himself with the horses as soon as we arrived, appearing again in the morning, silent and quietly efficient, with the horses perfectly groomed. Only when we had ridden on for a while and he had made quite certain that we were not being followed would he draw his mount alongside mine, so that we might talk as we traveled.

I do not know how many years Hamidullah had been with my father, but it must have been a great many and it came as something of a shock to me to realize that we had never spoken of anything more than everyday domestic affairs before. Now, as the British ways dropped from him, he spoke as a man of fifty to a woman less than half his age. Of exactly what we spoke I can no longer fully remember, save that he was able at a glance to identify not only the religion and race of anyone I might pick at random from among those thronging the road but usually their *zat* and occupation as well. He spoke of the crops in the fields as we passed and of the life the villagers led, the age-old battle of poor men against the weather and the soil. And as I answered him, sometimes in his own language, it became somehow easier to think in that tongue, too, so that in a very little while much that had been, as I thought, indelibly Western began to wear noticeably thin.

I realized that in spite of my urgent need to escape from what inevitably I would have had to face back at the great house, I was more content in my spirit than I had been since my father died, and, yes, since Edward had gone out of my life. I knew not what awaited me in those great dark mountains, but for the moment it was enough that I had found a kind of peace.

After the third day I drew a sigh of relief when we left the turnpike to strike off along a small track that climbed steeply up into the hills. Now we no longer saw people, save at rare intervals, and even then it was seldom that we passed within speaking distance of each other. Indeed, it was noticeable that as soon as we saw someone approaching in the distance, the tiny figure would, more often than not, turn aside from the track as though to avoid meeting us face to face.

But my sense of security was to be short-lived. "Men travel no more than they have to in these parts," Hamidullah informed me grimly. "On the public highway only a fool seeks to do his enemy a mischief, but here . . ."

"Here?" I said uncertainly.

"Here matters are arranged differently. Should any man feel that he has scores to settle, then he can attend to it in his own way. True, such things are against the law, but the police officers cannot be everywhere."

Hamidullah's words made me glance uneasily over my shoulder toward the ground we had already covered. The countryside had changed. Below us stretched the vast plain we had left, a patchwork of fields laid out as though for our inspection. I could see the road we had traveled, winding its way into the distance, flanked by the little huddles of buildings that made up the villages through which we had passed, until the whole merged into a shimmering blue haze of heat. But now on either side of us the hillsides were brown, relieved only by outcrops of stone and the occasional bush of thorn. At rare intervals we saw small herds of fat-tailed sheep, grazing quietly on what appeared to be no more than barren earth and guarded by a single boy who squatted watching his charges, hugging a long staff held upright like a pole. Overhead, in the cloudless blue sky, kites wheeled tirelessly, their wings outstretched to catch the shifting current of air.

The next night there was no dark bungalow to be found and we sought shelter at a tiny hamlet that nestled in its brief oasis of green, where grass grew around a spring of cold, clear water. The villagers provided an empty hut for me willingly enough, and although they eyed me curiously, they appeared satisfied with whatever story Hamidullah had thought fit to tell them in some thick and to me unintelligible dialect of the hills. Then, as though by magic, trees appeared again and our horses climbed through great groves of

48

deodars, and their hooves crunched over a carpet of sweet-scented pine needles.

Yet despite the beauty of the place, I felt some of my contentment slip away. Hamidullah was uneasy. He no longer talked to me of the country through which we passed but was for the most part silent, quickening the pace almost imperceptibly. I began to see in him the same buccaneering look that I had noted often enough in the hills, where the young men had swaggered through the bazaars with roses behind their ears and little gilded cages for their fighting quails held carelessly in their hands. It was because of this that Hamidullah's wariness seemed out of character, and I asked him if he sensed that someone had picked up our tracks after all.

"If the memsahib's enemies follow us at all, they are at least a day behind us," he told me briefly. "Yet three men have been behind us all the morning."

"Three men?" Fear tingled down my spine as I turned and looked for myself, but nothing moved among the great trees. Puzzled, I said, "Are you sure?"

"Yes, memsahib, I am sure. Three mounted on hill ponies and carrying rifles."

"Don't all men carry arms in these parts?" I tried to reassure myself. "It doesn't mean they intend us harm."

Hamidullah jerked his chin in what I recognized as disagreement. "Honest men do not carry army pattern muskets. Either they are deserters or have killed honest men for the sake of their arms."

Killed honest men. Criminals. Had de Souza hired *dacoits,* I wondered, to track me down and carry me back? Surely he would not dare? And yet, I thought, there might be very little such a man would shrink from to recapture a goose that might lay for him such golden eggs.

As Hamidullah spoke, the trail we were following came out from among the trees and I caught my breath at the sight that lay spread out before us. Almost at our feet the land fell away in a sheer precipice that formed the side of a narrow valley, at the bottom of which a silver thread of water ran between trees and what seemed toy-sized fields. A hundred feet below us a single eagle soared and planed majestically, and in the crystal-clear light the further hillside seemed so near that it could almost be touched. Beyond, the peaks of still higher hills climbed one above the other until they were no longer just hills but mountains thrusting jagged peaks toward the sky.

Hamidullah grunted with what I took to be satisfaction, then pointed toward the head of the valley. "So, I have not lost my way at least. Thither must we go, memsahib, toward the high hills." He glanced reflectively along the way we had come. "Fool that I was not to have brought one of Hunt sahib's rifles. Wait here awhile, and I will ride back a little and see how close our friends be."

He turned the big stallion in its own length, careless of the drop that lay within a yard of the animal's hooves, then suddenly sat up very straight in his saddle. For a long, timeless moment he seemed to remain there, like a statue, and then, again like a statue, toppled over as the report of a rifle crashed out in the silence.

"Hamidullah!"

Frozen with horror, I watched him hit the ground as red splashed suddenly on the white muslin of his shirt. I saw him roll like a rag doll over the edge of the cliff and plummet down to the valley below, silently, turning infinitely slowly, growing smaller and smaller, until the man who had been my friend was no more than a tiny white smudge, finally swallowed up in the greenness below. From the other side of the valley the echoes of the shot that had killed him slapped back at me three, four times, then dwindled away into more silence.

I must have been paralyzed with shock until my eyes saw, a quarter of a mile below me, three ragged-looking horsemen moving out from the shelter of the trees.

I remember only the pure terror of that moment. Never had I felt so alone. I have no memory of urging my mount forward and upward, and indeed little enough of my flight. Yet it must have been swift enough, for in my mind there is still the sound of the gray mare's hoofbeats on pine needles, the animal's labored breathing, my own sobbing shock and fear, and the flickering transition between shadow and sunlight as we raced from clearing to trees. Nor have I any clear recollection as to how long that wild ride lasted. I must have reached some kind of summit, or perhaps it was simply a goat track that led down toward the valley, for all at once I was leaning back in the saddle, trying desperately to keep my seat as we plunged downward, sliding and slipping down what must have been a well-nigh-impossible incline.

Probably it was on the very edge of that slope that I lost my pursuers, for their shouts dwindled and died behind me. For a time that could have been measured in either seconds or hours for all the meaning it had for me, I existed in a strange world of my own, detached utterly from knowledge of my surroundings and fear of any consequences. Then the sweating arch of the mare's neck was no longer in front of me. I heard, as if from a great distance, the crash of her fall; I was flying through the air and the hillside rose up swiftly and darkness engulfed me.

4

The bed on which I became aware of the world again seemed a familiar thing. I lay with my eyes closed, conscious at first only of my wildly throbbing head and then of the curious sensation of reclining on something that held my body comfortably yet inflexibly. Despite the pain, I could remember waking in such a way so often that for a moment I believed that in some extraordinary way I was in my own room at home. Then I moved cautiously and was rewarded with a squeak of cords. I had slept on enough *charpoys* in my time to recognize well enough the sound of an Indian string bed, which was as distinctive as the hammocklike feel of the thing. I moved again, and a woman's voice said in Hindi, "Tell the father of my sons that she wakes."

I had no desire yet to open my eyes. It seemed less painful to lie where I was and imagine my surroundings. But nothing could shut out the events that had brought me here. Hamidullah, soaring like a small white bird to a death that should never have happened. For me he had sacrificed so much. Grief engulfed my mind in a despair from which all fear seemed to have gone. Whom, now, was I to turn to?

My own fall I remembered clearly enough and I prayed that nothing terrible had happened to the gray mare. Considering the steepness of the hillside, she might well have broken her neck. I moved restlessly in the confining cords and heard the moan of pain from my lips.

"Tell the father of my sons," the voice had said,

52

which suggested that I was among some kind of community rather than an isolated family. And Hindu rather than Muslim, judging by the reluctance of the woman to speak her husband's name.

The scent of woodsmoke was in my nostrils, as was the clean, bitter smell of the cow-dung paste with which Indian villagers renew the surfaces of their walls and floor. There was another scent besides, and it took some little time for me to identify it as coriander, so I guessed that the unseen woman beside me had been crushing the seeds in preparation for a meal. But what meal? How long had I been here? The effort must have exhausted what little strength I had, for instead of forcing my eyes open, I slept.

When next I woke, the pain in my head had receded to a dull throbbing. This time my eyes flickered open immediately, and through an open doorway I could see the pale green dusk of the hills and the narrow outline of an almost new moon. With not too much effort I managed to turn my head and found a woman squatting on her haunches by the side of my bed, a hunched figure with a cheap pink sari drawn over gray hair. She wore a *bindi* in the center of her forehead, a single smudge of yellow ocher, and as she saw me move, her almond-shaped eyes became even narrower as she smiled.

"So, daughter, it seems you have come to no harm after all." She stood up, not ungracefully, considering her bulk. There was a briskness and an authority about her that led me to suppose that she was the village headman's wife. Practical, too, for when I did not immediately answer, she said more slowly, "Do you understand me?"

I managed to smile. "Yes, Mother, well enough." On the plains there would have been elaborate ritual of greetings and even more elaborate respect. Wherever I was, I guessed it to be sufficiently remote for the usual tedious differences between East and West to have no meaning. Probably she felt more curiosity than anything else.

"Good." The woman strode out into the open and I

53

heard her giving news of my recovery to unseen people while I took the opportunity to glance about me.

It was a very simple home of one room, with mud walls and a roof of thatch. What furniture there was consisted of two other charpoys, a solid wooden box, and the usual cooking utensils of polished brass. The only decoration was a cheap mirror. In a little alcove fashioned out of clay stood a crudely painted image of the elephant-headed god, Ganesha, remover of obstacles. It was difficult to imagine living with fewer possessions, and yet I sensed that as far as the owners were concerned, it was enough.

The woman came back, still alone, and asked me if I could bring myself to eat.

"I don't know," I told her. "I do not think I can stand up."

I learned then that it had been Gopal, the headman, who had found me while searching for an adventurous sheep. He and his brother had made a litter from tree branches and somehow managed to carry me down to the village. Yes, my mare had been standing grazing nearby, quite unharmed, and they had led her in without difficulty. They had seen no sign of my attackers, but it was true that there were many such people about. They themselves formed armed parties when they moved from village to village. Someday the police would come up from the plains and carry the bandits off to a British jail—her dark eyes snapped fiercely—but not yet. They were poor men and probably nobody had ever heard of them in the land beyond the hills.

I listened to the earnest, rambling account, only half taking it in. At least it seemed as though I had only fallen foul of a band of local robbers and not hirelings of de Souza. Somehow it still seemed terribly wrong that I should have the good fortune to be alive and cared for while Hamidullah lay dead somewhere among the undergrowth.

I said, "I had with me a servant . . . a friend. . . ."

"He, too, was found, but he is dead . . . both he and his horse. We have sent a message to a village nearby where there is a Muhammadan shoemaker, who will no

54

doubt see to it that the man is buried in accordance with his faith. The saddle and harness of the horse have been brought here, for they are of fine workmanship and worth many rupees.

"Thank you," I managed to say. I had listened and I had learned. I had even taken a few mouthfuls of the dish of spiced vegetables the woman had handed me, but now I wanted nothing more than to rest again as the pain in my head grew to intolerable intensity. As I turned to her I wanted to at least satisfy her natural curiosity as to where I had come from, but instead I said, "Please don't send me back. Don't send me back to the plains. Do you understand?"

"Yes, we understand, you are safe here. You shall not be sent back."

Was it compassion or cupidity I saw in their dark eyes? I had no means of knowing, but in the days that followed I knew that my new friends had kept their word. At first, in a feverish half world between waking and sleeping, I knew terror, for it seemed that I was imprisoned within a box that moved. Then, as my senses took in a plaited-wicker roof a little above my head and curtains to either side, it came to me that I was in a palanquin, the ancient coffinlike mode of conveyance boasting four poles, each supported by the shoulders of a bearer. Even now I have not discovered how the people of Gopal's little village should have come by such a thing.

As a mode of travel the palanquin could not have been overly comfortable for a person in the best of health, even when carried over a level road. For someone such as myself, half blind with the pain in my head and every inch of my body seemingly a bruise, it was a kind of nightmare. Mercifully, I must have spent my time in a fainting condition, for I remember little of that journey. Sometimes at night I was aware of blissful relief that we had stopped and that the good-natured face of Gopal's wife was close to mine as she wiped my face with cool, damp cloths and urged me to eat a little before she settled me, like a sick child, for the night. And on at least one occasion I woke crying out that they should not blame Rupert for what had happened, but my words were in English, so it is unlikely they were understood.

It must have been a strange treatment for whatever injuries I had sustained, yet a morning came when I drew back the curtains of the palanquin and stared out at the world with the knowledge that, if not fully recovered, at least I was a good deal better. I realized that no longer were we traveling uphill but were making good time over a high, grassy plain where poppies grew amid the lush grass. In the distance the snow-capped peaks of mountains rose toward a steel-blue sky, but I knew that in the crystal-clear air they could well have been fifty miles away for all that they seemed near enough to touch.

"Where are we going?" It was a measure of my weariness, I thought, that I had not asked before.

It was Gopal who answered my question. The headman, a stocky fellow with legs corded like trees, stepped back and greeted me courteously before saying, "We go to the palace of the khan, at Ranipur."

"The palace of what khan?" I demanded.

"The khan of Khudistan. Who else?"

Khudistan! It seemed in that moment a kind of miracle that I should have been brought by chance to the place that was to have been my original destination.

"This khan . . ." I began.

"He is of your race. Beyond doubt he will have womenfolk to care for you."

"But is it necessary to go so fast?" I could not see the men who were carrying me upon their shoulders, but I could hear their labored breathing and felt an instinctive revulsion from treating fellow human beings like beasts of burden. "Surely there is no hurry. Cannot the bearers rest awhile?"

Gopal's weathered face was troubled. "For two days we have been followed. Three men on horseback, likely enough the same who slew your friend. We brought two men of our own village with muskets, but when we came to this land they turned back, for it is

56

an act of war to bear arms on a stranger's soil. But the horsemen followed on. The gods alone know if we shall have the strength to escape them until we reach the palace." Gopal glanced behind him and his copper-hued skin paled visibly. "May they burn in hell! They are already upon us!"

The ground came up to meet the bottom of the palanquin as the unseen bearers hastily put down the poles, and I made my way out, in somewhat undignified fashion, on my hands and knees. I looked around me and saw that the flower-covered plain, which had seemed limitless from one side of the palanquin, was broken by a great spur of deodars that extended from some apparently limitless forest that vanished in the blue haze hanging about the base of the distant hills. Directly behind us, no more than half a mile away, three horsemen rode toward us at full gallop.

Gopal looked at me. "They are the same men?"

I did not have to look twice; the one in the white shirt riding in front was unmistakable. So I had come this far only for it all to end like this. I knew in my heart that these were no common dacoits. The face of de Souza rose up before my eyes and I wondered if he himself was one of my pursuers or if they were no more than paid ruffians who were simply employed to catch and return their prey. I suddenly felt sick, not for myself but for what I was about to bring on the heads of a handful of simple people who had done no more than try to help me.

I glanced at the group around me. Gopal, his wife, and eight other villagers, who had obviously been taking turns as bearers. Only Gopal carried so much as a stick that might serve as a weapon. It was not fair that they should hazard their lives to save mine.

"Listen," I said urgently, "tell those men that I will go with them but that they must not harm you or any of your people. Do you understand?"

I do not know whether he would have agreed or not, for at that moment a troop of perhaps fifty horsemen appeared from behind the spur of trees. At first sight of them my heart sank, to lift again almost immediately as I realized that this was no further pack of human wolves but a disciplined body of cavalry, for the sun caught the tips of lances and the polished brass of saddlery. They approached at full gallop, and as I stared at the sight, wide-eyed, the tight phalanx split, one half wheeling to form a wide circle to enclose the three men who had sent Hamidullah to his death.

Those dacoits were on us now, yet hardly aware of us, for they stared, wild-eyed, at the newcomers, as indeed did I. They were Indian troopers, dressed not in regulation cavalry uniform but in light-yellow quilted jackets such as the Sikhs wore against the redcoats at Sabroan, in the days when Victoria was newly queen. Boots and breeches they had none, but they rode their sure-footed little ponies in the baggy white Muhammadan *shilwars* which matched the snowy turbans wound about their heads. I could see they were irregular troops by British standards, probably raised locally for some special purpose, but the discipline and precision of their attack could hardly have been bettered.

Within feet of me, the white-shirted dacoit pulled his sweating horse round in a tight circle, loosed a shot from his carbine at the nearest yellow-jacketed man, then with his two companions urged his mount back the way it had come.

From the throng of riders someone rapped out an order and the cavalry squadron came snorting to a halt. Then a fusilade of shots rang out and three crumpled heaps were left on the ground beside their riderless horses. The cavalry laughed and joked until a further order brought silence. Only then did a single figure detach himself from the main body and trot his mount toward the point where I stood.

He rode, whoever he was, with the sun behind him, so that he was almost upon me before I discerned much more than that he was mounted not on a hill pony but on a magnificent black thoroughbred. Then Gopal gave a little gasp and with joined hands and bowed forehead made hasty submission, his fellow villagers following suit.

"The gods help us—it is the khan himself!"

The villagers had backed away, so I stood alone, my head held high, staring at the oncoming horseman whose arrival had been so timely, until his body blocked out the sun and I was able to see him properly for the first time.

I suppose it was because I was standing on the ground and he was above me on that great black horse that my first impressions were of the lower part of his body rather than the top. In what seemed a long minute but was probably no more than fleeting seconds, I took in an immensely long leg, with white doeskin breeches above highly polished black boots, the feet thrust into chased-silver stirrups, the spur chains with the warm gleam of gold. His yellow silk jacket was immensely long and embroidered with flowers worked in seed pearls. The sword that hung at his side was no cavalry saber but a long Sikh *kirpan*, its scabbard a gleam of gold, gems glinting at the hilt and in the fringed sash hanging from the turban that framed a somber, dark, hawklike face.

"Good day, Miss Rogers." He studied me impersonally, then his gaze flickered over my companions. With a single smooth movement he swung a long leg over the back of his charger and dismounted with a jingle of spurs. "Apparently we were in time, for you appear to have come to no harm."

"But how . . ." I was still staring at him, now in complete amazement at his calm recognition of me, when he turned to face me fully again and I saw the piercing blue eyes that I had seen once before, over the grave of my father."

"Why," I exclaimed, "I remember you at my father's funeral!"

Suddenly I took in the incredible fact. Adam McKenzie was the white khan of Khudistan!

"Your memory flatters me, ma'am."

I felt a strange little shiver as I came under the deep scrutiny of that gaze. I think I must always have known that I would see this man again, although never

59

in the wildest moments of my imagination under such a circumstance as this.

Conscious of my dirty, ragged appearance, I said, with some attempt at formality, "We are very grateful to you . . . sir. Had you not chanced to be here . . ."

"I should not say it was by chance that we are here." Adam McKenzie's voice was flat and impersonal, but there was a hint of amusement in those extraordinary eyes. "Your arrival on my lands was reported to me, so I thought it appropriate to provide a fitting escort for a visitor. And certainly one who was in need of protection."

I gestured toward the three bodies. High in the sapphire sky the vultures were already wheeling. "Was it necessary to kill them out of hand? Without any kind of trial?" I felt my voice shake and the knowledge made me angry with both him and myself as I said, "It was barbaric."

"Barbaric?"

"For God's sake, Mr. McKenzie, you didn't even know who they were."

"I am not Mr. McKenzie here, Miss Rogers, but the khan sahib. And you may as well learn from the start that my people are accustomed to swift justice. The lives of these men were forfeit on three counts. They entered my country without permission and bearing arms. They fired on my men. And, if my information is correct, they murdered your servant some days ago."

I did not question how he knew that. Somehow I accepted it. But my anger at his summary justice had not yet abated. "And so," I taunted him, "like the emperor Akbar, you decided that you would carry out sentence on the spot."

For a fleeting moment anger crossed his face and I knew that this man was not accustomed to having his motives challenged. Then, just as quickly, amusement returned and he said very quietly, "Come, Miss Rogers, you have been in this country long enough to know better than that. Akbar was a patron of the arts and no mean philosopher, but he would have had those men flayed alive and hung up as a warning to others to

60

mind their manners. At least give me credit for awarding them deaths that were swift and a good deal more honorable than they deserved." Abruptly he dismissed the subject. "Now I shall offer you some refreshment before completing your journey. We have only about twenty miles to go, but the sun is hot. Are you well enough to ride?"

"I think so." I looked at Gopal and his friends, who were standing back in respectful silence. "You will see that these people get home safely? They cared for me when I was injured, then brought me all this way simply because they thought they should find someone better able to look after me. . . ."

"It would be more accurate to say that they didn't relish the prospect of having a white woman dying on their hands. Still, they served you well enough. That was reported to me, too." My host smiled suddenly. "I'll see to it that they are adequately rewarded. Now, shall we go?"

I ignored the brusqueness of his order and pointedly took my time in bidding Gopal and his wife farewell. Only when I had expressed my thanks to the very best of my ability did I allow myself to be drawn away to where a tent had been erected and a Bukhara rug laid out to cover the ground. The fact that there were no cushions or furniture of any kind did nothing to detract from a sense of *Arabian Nights* fantasy as I sat with my host and sipped the silver goblet of *sherbert* a white-coated servant had produced apparently from nowhere.

"This is delicious," I said. "Do you always travel with such ceremony? With tent and carpets . . ."

"Ceremony is important to these people. They like to look up to their ruler, which means a certain amount of magnificence. That is something about India the British government has yet to learn. It imagines the ordinary people like money to be spent on sensible things like schools and hospitals, whereas in reality they would be much more impressed with a better show of ceremonial elephants."

He looked at me over the rim of his goblet and his

lips curved upward in a slight smile so that it was hard to tell whether he had been speaking seriously or not. Then he went on abruptly. "Miss Rogers, there is a question you have been waiting to ask me for the past hour. I can see it in your eyes. I assure you that you have my permission to ask it."

For just a moment I hesitated, then I, too, smiled. "And you, sir, have my permission to explain why it was that you came to my father's funeral."

"Your father once did my family a service. I was in the area and it seemed fitting that I should pay him a tribute."

I looked at him in surprise. "He never mentioned your name. When I first saw you at the graveside, I had never set eyes on you before."

The man opposite me said slowly, "There were . . . special circumstances regarding the association. I doubt that your father spoke of it to many. Not even to you."

"Then why did you leave without introducing yourself to me?"

He shrugged his broad shoulders and in the soft light the pearls woven into his silk tunic shimmered with the movement.

"Again, because had I done so, I should have had to explain one or another of my reasons for being there. One I have acquainted you with. The other is that I had intended asking you something I had already discussed with your father—the possibility of your taking up employment with me."

"Employment?" I thought I could not have heard him correctly.

"Yes. Of a very special kind."

"Then why did you not broach the matter to my father?"

"Because I understood that you were contemplating marriage, which, in the circumstances, was likely to be much more to your advantage. There was little point in putting forward a proposition that could be of no practical use."

"I see." I said quietly, "It is my turn to explain something to you. My husband is . . . dead."

"So I understand. In . . . unfortunate circumstances, shall we say." He met my eyes and it was all that I could do not to look away.

I had been a fool to imagine he would not know. It seemed that the remoteness of the khan's kingdom in no way prevented his knowing everything. Everything? I asked myself, and again I felt that strange little shiver. But the khan went on. "Since you have chosen to confide this much to me—Mrs. Hunt, is it not?— perhaps it would be best if you told me still more. I assure you that I shall respect your confidence, but it is necessary that I understand the situation fully."

"Very well." I do not know why, but I felt little hesitation in doing as he suggested, and I was surprised at the ease with which the words came. I told him of the misery of my marriage, of Garfield's accidental death, of my persecution by de Souza. "And so," I ended, "I find myself a widow and with no home to which I can return. So perhaps it is right that I should consider . . . employment."

For a long moment he made no reply, staring past me at the distant shimmering hills, as though his thoughts, too, were far away. Then he said quietly, "Yes, I can see that we might possibly make an arrangement that would be convenient for both of us." He looked at me with narrowed eyes. "You are American, of course. I was forgetting."

"Yes." I nodded. "Does it make any difference?"

"None whatever. Sometimes I think that were I not khan of Khudistan, I might well choose to make my life in that strange new country of yours. It was just that it struck me that you must feel very much at a loss just now, alone in a strange land."

"It is hardly strange to me," I pointed out. "I have lived here almost all my life."

"True." The khan gave a short laugh. "Well, I can offer you sanctuary if that is what you want. And as for the employment I have to offer, it is as part companion, part governess, part friend."

"To whom?"

The ruler of Khudistan put his goblet down carefully, and I noticed that such was his presence that there seemed nothing unusual about our having such a conversation in the open air with a group of wild horsemen grouped nearby. He said slowly, "To my sister, Sabina. She is eighteen years old and an intelligent young woman. Unfortunately, although life in this part of the world has many advantages, it can be restricting to one whose experience of anywhere else is . . . limited. Sabina also lacks the companionship of someone nearer her own age. She is lonely and, I think, bored. I had hoped that in addition to repairing certain flaws in her education you might enjoy her company for its own sake."

I said quietly, "I'm sure I shall. But as you say yourself—for a girl of eighteen . . ." I glanced about me. "Is there really nowhere for her to go apart from here? Surely you have friends in Calcutta or Delhi?"

When those strange blue eyes met mine, they were without expression. "The situation is—unusual. But you will come to understand the difficulties later on. For the moment I'm mainly interested in whether or not you would undertake the work involved."

I felt I had no choice if I were to seek sanctuary in his kingdom. Nevertheless I had to show some independence in the matter. "I should like to meet your sister," I said.

"Naturally, that is understood."

"And . . ." I hesitated. "You must understand that I have had no experience. If your sister needs a governess . . ." I left the sentence unfinished.

Adam McKenzie shrugged his shoulders. "That is probably all to the good. What Sabina needs is companionship of the right sort and guidance rather than any great quantity of book learning." He looked at me reflectively. "I have already ascertained that your own education would fit you perfectly adequately for the position. And, after all, you were for a short time a schoolteacher, were you not?"

I said uneasily, more and more aware of the depths of his inquiries about me, "Yes. But more by force of circumstance than anything else." It had been two years earlier, during a terrible summer on the plains when malaria and cholera had combined to decimate the members of the local mission, so that in consequence I had undertaken to help in their little school for a while. I added, "There is a difference between teaching seven-year-olds and a young woman more than twice that age."

"It is of little consequence," he said, dismissing my scruples. "I have already made up my mind. I suggest you accompany me to my palace at Ranipur as soon as you are rested. There you can meet my sister and see for yourself that the work is less difficult than you seem to imagine."

"If you will be so good as to have my horse brought to me, I am ready now."

He regarded me narrowly. "You are sure you can ride? It will be easy enough to pay the men who brought you this far to finish the journey."

"I am perfectly sure." In fact, I was far from sure, but some foolish quirk of pride would not allow me to waver. Already I knew that if I was not to be totally dominated by this man, I must assert my right to a pride of my own. Fortunately for me, it proved to be easier to sit in the saddle than to stand, although by the time the five-hour ride that followed was over, I was nearing the end of my endurance. Nevertheless I stayed the course somehow, and so it was that, at the head of a jingling, many-hued band of horsemen who might well have come from the pages of some romantic picture book, Adam McKenzie and I rode through the blue-tiled Mogul archway that flanked the city gates of Ranipur, where lay the palace of the khans of Khudistan.

5

As we rode through the winding streets and up toward the palace I looked about me with wonder and admiration. The town was set on the side of a hill, so that the streets descended in a series of terraces, the buildings the simple, flat-roofed, mud-and-whitewash structures of the Indian far north. Yet beyond the individual dwellings I caught glimpses of astonishing magnificence—the azure dome of a mosque whose beauty caught at one's heart, great fluted columns that towered to the sky, the mighty Mogul arched elephant gate let into the remains of what had once been a curtain wall.

Adam McKenzie—or the khan, as I was to learn to think of him—kneed his horse closer to mine and gestured upward toward the palace. "In the old days it was just a fort—probably built by some warrior princeling back in Mogul times. It's still strong enough, but my father rebuilt it as a palace for his own use."

I followed the direction of his pointing finger and took in the building that dominated the town. The rays of the setting sun had caught the walls and turned them rose pink, giving a softness to what I guessed must still be a formidable structure. There were no windows in the great expanse of sandstone, only a single massive gateway tall enough to admit not only a riding elephant but the *howdah* upon its back as well. Along the battlements were spaced four delicate stone cupolas, the appearance of which so lightened the ef-

66

fect of the whole building that it seemed to float weightlessly, like a rosy cloud in the evening light.

"It's beautiful," I said. My heart was beating uncomfortably, and even the effort of speaking two words seemed to have made my head swim. I told myself firmly that it was the height that was taking its toll on me as much as anything else, but even so I swayed in the saddle through sheer weariness until Adam McKenzie's hand gripped me by the shoulder, ramming me into the saddle.

"You should have rested earlier," his voice said curtly. "I'll have an ayah take you to your quarters as soon as we get in. You can wait until tomorrow to see Sabina."

"It might be best." My voice sounded thick and woolly, and I was no longer making any attempt to guide my horse, just allowing her to pick her own way up the steep streets as she chose. Only half conscious, I took in the sudden dark shadow of the gateway as we passed through it and felt the cool of the shaded courtyard within. Someone helped me to dismount and I remember thinking with a kind of bewilderment that this strange, detached sensation must be what people meant by being asleep on one's feet. Somehow I walked but without any real awareness of where I was being led. Then there were women's voices and gentle hands unfastening the buttons of my now torn and shabby riding habit. Then, blissfully, there was a bed beneath me and this time no creaking strings from a native charpoy. I tried to speak, but before the words could come out, sleep had enfolded me.

When I woke, sunlight was slanting through the arched windows and I followed the shafts lazily till they splashed in great puddles of gold on a marble floor. With a feeling of comfortable curiosity I studied the rest of my bedroom, taking in walls of blue Persian tiles, divided into panels by columns of gilded wood. On the wall facing me a vast ormolu mirror reflected not only myself but the bed in which I lay, gilded like the walls, with its head carved to resemble the partially extended wings of a swan. From the ceiling a punkah

67

curtain of embroidered silk swung silently back and forth, stirring the still air.

I sat up, remembering everything that had brought me to my present surroundings, anxious to see more of them. I swung my legs over the side of the bed and slipped to the floor, only to find a young, fine-featured ayah awaiting me.

I smiled at the girl. "What time is it?"

"It is almost noon. The lady Sabina awaits the memsahib in the garden."

"And the khan sahib?"

"I do not know. Usually in the mornings he rides to inspect his lands or attends to his business affairs."

I looked about me for my riding habit, but the girl shook her head and smiled. "Memsahib, we tried to wash your dress, but it was too badly torn. The lady Sabina asks that you will wear this until she can find something suitable for you."

I saw that she was holding out a sari, its delicate creamy-yellow silk perfect for my own coloring. I let her help me into it, winding its folds skillfully about me. When she had brushed my hair she allowed me to look in the ormolu mirror.

For a moment I did not recognize myself. The sari emphasized the slenderness of my body, and the way the girl had allowed my hair to fall loosely about my face seemed to give me a softer look. With all the traveling of the past days my skin had lost its pale, lusterless look that two months of marriage with Garfield had given it. Instead it glowed with a warmth that I knew the ladies of the plains would have disapproved of but that I felt suited me and the new life I was now facing.

Ready at last, I made my way from what appeared to be a separate wing of the palace to a great flight of white stone stairs, which led in turn to the circular hall below. I could only imagine where the stairs and the furnishings of my bedroom had come from—possibly some house that had been sacked and looted during the Mutiny. I glanced upward at an enormous chandelier suspended from the ceiling above me, the profusion of tables and glass-fronted cabinets glimpsed through the open doorways of adjoining rooms, Bukhara and Aubusson carpets or magnificent tiger skins covering marble floors. There was a bizarre opulence about the furnishings of the palace that dazzled the eye in a bewildering display of treasures from East and West.

As I paused for a moment to look about me I realized that the reckless splendor of the palace sprang as much from the building itself as from its contents. Behind the draped tapestries and gilt-framed landscapes could be glimpsed the crude strength of whitewashed walls, and I was reminded at once that this had once been a fortress, built to withstand the most fierce battles.

Before me now, a white-coated servant was opening a great door of polished mahogany, and so I passed through it and out into the garden beyond.

It was, in fact, more courtyard than garden, a walled haven of rose bushes set in the intricate convolutions of a maze. Somewhere a fountain splashed gently, a sound accompanied by the chattering of birds. I turned to look for it and found myself facing a great jasmine, in the shade of which a girl sat watching me, a silky Afghan hound stretched out, sphynxlike, at her feet.

"Good morning, Mrs. Hunt. I am Sabina McKenzie. Won't you come and sit where it's cooler? I'm sorry there was only the sari for you to wear, but we can see about some proper clothes for you later." The words tumbled out with a kind of breathless intensity, as though the speaker lived in fear of being stopped before she could get them out.

"Thank you—and I think the sari is beautiful. I had not realized it would be so cool to wear." I walked toward the jasmine and the dog followed me with his eyes. Not until I was in the shade myself was I able to study the girl who had spoken, and as she rose to greet me I caught my breath, for seldom had I seen such flawless beauty.

Sabina McKenzie's hair was raven black, falling straight and glistening to the nape of her neck. Her face was a perfect oval with enormous dark eyes that regarded me with an almost childlike excitement, and as she smiled I glimpsed pearl-like teeth that seemed almost unnaturally white against her lips. Her skin was olive, soft, and without blemish, and at that first meeting the thought that struck me was that here was a face that might have come directly from the brush of one of the court artists to Akbar the Great. My second thought, hard on the heels of the first, was that the beauty of Adam McKenzie's sister was more of East than of West. No woman could look like that without some Indian blood in her veins.

I said to her now, "I feel I am imposing too much on you and your brother. Not only do I arrive as an uninvited guest, but almost without a single possession except my horse and what little remains in the saddlebags."

"Then it will be my pleasure to help you choose a new wardrobe. Like that I will learn of the latest fashions from the city! Adam tells me all too often that my dress is not always seemly for the sister of the khan."

As she stood up I saw that she was wearing a loose white muslin shirt of the kind that could be bought in any bazaar and beneath it the wide-hipped, calf-hugging breeches commonly worn by the men of Jodhpur. With her slim figure and astonishing attire it might well have been a boy who stood before me, one long-fingered hand toying with a drawing board.

We sat together and I gestured toward what I saw to be the half-finished charcoal head of the dog. "You are an artist, I see?"

"An artist? Oh, I wish indeed that I might be!" Whatever her parentage, her English was as cultured as that of the khan, beyond question the tongue she had been born to. Impulsively she thrust the drawing board at me. "What do you really think of it? Oh, Mrs. Hunt, shall I ever be even reasonably competent, do you think? I have been told I have talent, but then people are always trying to be kind, aren't they? Nobody ever believes that you really want to know. Can you draw? You must show me. Promise?"

I listened to the breathless flow of her eager chatter

70

as I studied the sketch in my hand. My own knowledge of such matters was limited indeed, yet there was a sureness of line that surprised me. Untutored the work might be, yet it breathed life and held a strange individuality that made me reluctant to hand it back.

"I think it's good," I said. "I do not believe your teacher is being kind. He tells the truth." The words were inadequate enough, yet I need not have worried, for Sabina's quicksilver mind had already abandoned one subject and was hot on the chase of another.

"Adam says that you know everything about what's happening in the world outside. You must tell me all about it. Have you been to England?"

I laughed. "I'm afraid not. I was born and went to school in America." Barely were the words out of my mouth than I felt a pang of remorse. It was so easy to talk of life anywhere overseas, and yet here was a beautiful young woman condemned to live a life of almost complete isolation and who probably dreamed romantically of places she had only read about in books. I remembered, too, the sad little pretense of the Eurasian officials of the railways and post and telegraph department who spoke of "going home" to an England they had never seen and in all probability never would see. Was it possible Sabina felt the same?

"Perhaps," I said with some caution, "one day you will also be able to see the world. We must try to talk to your brother—"

"Oh, no," she interrupted, "You do not understand." She leaned forward and lowered her voice, as if she feared someone might be listening. "You see, it is Adam who wants me to go when I am older, who thinks that I must long to go to what is after all his ancestors' country. But Khudistan is *my* country and I love it here. I am happy. Everything I have known all my life is here, but I do not think Adam will ever understand that. Oh, I am eager to learn all about the world, and I hope you will tell me what I cannot read in books, but with that I shall be content. Adam says I will go only when I learn to 'behave like a lady,' by which I think he means dressing like one." She gave a little chuckle. "Do you think I look very terrible like this?"

In truth she looked surprisingly attractive in her unconventional attire, and I found myself somewhat at a loss how to say otherwise. "I think," I said carefully, "that people would think you perhaps a little too unconventional if you appeared like that in London or New York."

Sabina's chuckle turned to a peal of laughter. "Oh, but I should do no such thing. Here I'm always riding, you see, and Indian ladies don't use a sidesaddle. But there is nowhere here to buy fashionable clothes."

"You could order them from Hamilton's or the Army and Navy stores in Calcutta," I suggested. "Better still we will send for a catalogue and choose that way. I expect there are *durzis* who could copy dresses from a picture if we told them what to do. I shall certainly have to do that."

"I suppose so. But until you came, there has been no one to advise me. You *will* do that for me, won't you?"

"Of course, I shall enjoy it. If you can draw so well, we may have no need to wait for catalogues. There was one I had . . ." My voice faded. For the first time in many days I was reminded of my life with Garfield. I turned quickly away from those thoughts and said briskly, "Surely, Sabina, you cannot wear riding clothes all the time?"

The girl smiled fleetingly. "No, of course not. In the evening I usually wear a sari because I am half Indian, after all. That is one of my favorites you wear now. But it's the *other* half of me that needs helping, so that I may please my brother without being banished from Khudistan. Mrs. Hunt—"

I interrupted her. "If I am to call you Sabina, then I am Harriet."

"Harriet . . . I like that. It sounds like the name of a very highly educated person."

It was my turn to laugh. "Does it? Well, I fear that I am really a very ordinary person and still somewhat at a loss as to what I am to teach you."

72

"Oh, that is easy," Sabina told me promptly. "We have talked about clothes. I should like to know how to dance in the English way and what books to order from Spink's and how to play the piano and speak French. . . ."

"Why on earth," I asked, "should you want to speak French?"

"I don't know," she admitted frankly, "except that I read somewhere that all well-educated ladies play the piano and speak French, and when people of importance come to visit my brother, I should not like them to laugh at me."

I looked at the exquisite creature regarding me so solemnly now with those huge dark eyes and I said gently, "I don't think anyone will laugh at you, Sabina. But if you really want to learn French and to play the piano, I'll do my best to teach you what little I know. But do you *have* a piano?"

"Oh, yes, my father had one brought from Calcutta. I think it was carried over the hills by elephants when I was a little girl."

"It will probably need tuning by this time."

"Will it? I didn't know. Can you tune it for me?"

I shook my head. "I'm afraid not."

"It doesn't matter. Adam will send for whoever is necessary. . . ." She broke off as the dog at her feet raised its head. "I think there is someone coming."

Perhaps I should have guessed, for fate can be a quixotic thing, but of course I could not have. I watched the figure in dusty boots and cord riding jacket walk toward us; the sun touched on the wheat-blond hair and I caught my breath. Had Sabina not at that moment been trying to settle the great dog, she must have noticed how I first stiffened and then stared, scarcely believing what I saw.

Edward Ashworth stopped, had time to meet my astonished eyes—returning my stare with a searching half smile in which the lack of any surprise told me that he must already have known I was here and thus had the advantage—before turning to make a formal bow in the direction of Sabina as she straightened up to greet him.

As if from a long way off I heard Sabina introducing us. "Captain Ashworth, Mrs. Hunt." Why, in that moment, did neither of us say we had met before? For my part, I was still speechless, though I trust that by now I had regained my composure. I saw that after two years he had changed but little—a trifle heavier, perhaps, which gave him an air of greater maturity than I remembered, and his skin tanned a deeper brown in contrast to those sun-bleached streaks in his hair, the gray eyes perhaps creased a little more at the corners from two more years of squinting into that same blazing sun. But the eyes had not changed—nor, it seemed, the expression in them, though that vanished again as Sabina finally straightened up from chiding the Afghan for its growling suspicion of the visitor. As he looked at me, passing the secret, unspoken message with his eyes, I felt the same crushing grip about my heart, the same breathlessness that had overtaken me when he first took me in his arms at that far-off regimental ball. No, I thought in dismay, nothing much had changed.

"Your servant, ma'am," Edward was saying, and I realized that he thought it best to pretend that we were meeting for the first time. "A new arrival is always welcome in Ranipur. May I wish you an enjoyable visit."

"Mrs. Hunt is here for more than a visit," Sabina pointed out. "She is to be my companion—and friend, I hope."

"Indeed." This time Edward's eyes did betray a fleeting something—surprise? anticipation?—before he quickly smiled. "Then I'm sure we are even more fortunate than I supposed." He turned to Sabina. "It was, in fact, Mrs. Hunt I came to see on an official matter."

"Then you knew I was here?" I said.

"As British agent I was automatically informed."

For just a moment an expression of pique crossed Sabina's face, to vanish as quickly as she got to her feet. "Then I had best leave you," she said. "Perhaps,

Captain Ashworth, you will take some refreshment? Please ask the servants for anything you may require."

"Sabina, please stay," I said quickly. "I am sure there is no reason for you to go."

She laid a slim, cool hand on my arm. "It's all right, Harriet, I'm sure Captain Ashworth does not need me to help him with his official business, and besides, the grooms have been waiting for me at the stables for the past half hour. Come, Sikundar."

I watched her go with the great dog loping easily at her heels. Only when she had vanished from sight did I turn to look at Edward; there was a kind of panic in me that made me look away again.

He stood gazing down at me for a long moment, then dropped to the marble bench beside me. "Don't turn away, Harriet. Let me look at you." He did so, searching my eyes for what he had once seen in them.

In my care to let him see nothing, to resist at all costs the spell that had once enslaved me, perhaps a faint skepticism entered my regard, for he said softly "You have changed. You were so shy . . . you have grown up."

"Not surprisingly," I told him. "Two years is a long time."

"Too long."

I raised my eyebrows slightly. Why could I not be natural? "A great deal has happened in that time," I heard myself remind him.

Edward frowned, looking at me carefully, wondering, perhaps, how to break through my crisp formality or whether to accept and follow it.

"Forgive me," he said quietly. "I should have offered my condolences. You are recently widowed, I believe."

I said shortly, "Yes, my husband was drowned."

"My poor Harriet. Then you have known sorrow. Is this what has changed you?"

It would have been easy to make no answer, but some instinct deep within me rebelled against taking compassion that was not rightly mine. I said steadily, "My sorrow was when my father died. I agreed to

75

marry Mr. Hunt because it was . . . expedient to do so, or so I thought at the time. But I cannot pretend that it was a success."

"Harriet—" He put a hand out to cover mine on my lap. It was only the lightest touch, yet it recalled vivid memories. I was angry that he must have felt the trembling in my fingers before, on the pretext of rearranging the sari on my shoulders, I withdrew it.

"And you," I asked in the same too-brittle voice, "you are married?"

"No."

"So you still prefer your freedom." Nothing could keep the dryness from my tone, try as I may. "I expect it is the artist in you—"

"I thought I preferred my freedom, Harriet, but—"

As if I had not heard him, I went on brightly. "How is your painting? I imagine it is you who are giving Sabina lessons in art. She seems to think much of you."

Edward went on searching my face for several seconds before, with a little shrug as if of resignation, he stood up and began slowly to pace the terrace.

I prompted. "She has talent, has she not?"

He had little option, then, but to abandon his attempt to break the formalities—although I was perfectly aware that he would return to the attack at the first opportunity. He shot me one quick look of appeal before replying to my question.

"Yes, I do my best to help her. Sabina is full of enthusiasms. Though if truth he told, she has a considerable natural gift. It may be that one day she will need a far better teacher than I can ever hope to be."

"Edward," I said, "Mr. McKenzie—the khan—however you may call him, wishes me to act as a kind of companion and tutor to his sister."

"It sounds an excellent idea."

"Perhaps, but I find it all very confusing. He is clearly English, she of mixed blood. Can you tell me something of the family?"

Edward looked at me with surprise. "You mean," he said, "that you have never heard about the white khans of Khudistan?"

76

"Something, but a long time ago. Only the name it-self is familiar. I have no idea who they are or how they came to this place."

"It's a curious tale. I thought everyone knew about it by now." He took out a slim black Trichanopoly cheroot and raised his eyebrows in query.

"Of course."

He lit the cigar with care, crushing the vesper care-fully beneath his heel. I had to look away from that face—the profile with its straight nose, the shadow of the long lashes pointing down the high-shelved cheekbones—to concentrate on what he was telling me.

"The first khan—Adam's father—was a free lance of the old school in the days when India was full of little private armies belonging to one raja or another. Most of them were commanded by French or English merce-naries who lived by their swords and usually came to unpleasant ends. A few of them—men like George Thomas or the Frenchman, Peron—amassed huge for-tunes and were probably more powerful than the men who employed them."

"I have heard of them," I said, my interest fully aroused, "and I've often wondered what sort of men they were."

"All sorts," he went on, his eyes on my ankles as I felt increasingly his awareness of me. "Officers who had been dismissed from the regular army after some scandal. Country gentlemen who had lost their estates at the gambling tables, quick-tempered fellows who happened to kill the wrong man in a duel. George Thomas was supposed to have been a sailor who deserted his ship by jumping overboard at Madras. The only thing they had in common was a knack for lead-ing men. The best of them had real generalship they would never have had the chance to exercise in any other way."

"And you say Adam McKenzie's father," I put in, "was one of those . . . free lances?"

Edward nodded. "And one of the best. Of course, his early life is something of a mystery, but I've heard it said that he was a Scottish laird who was tricked out of his lands by an English nobleman who arrived with a regiment of British troops to help him take possession of the ancestral home. McKenzie gathered his tenants together and fought a running battle with the redcoats for about three days, during which he killed milord with a claymore before finally blowing the castle up with gunpowder rather than let it fall into British hands. After that he fled the country with a price on his head and ended up in India, where he took service with one of the Maratha chieftains and apparently worked his way up to the point where he was a sort of general. He was enormously powerful and—judging by the way his family still lives—enormously rich as well."

He puffed away at his cheroot and for a moment I thought he had come to the end of his tale. "Go on, please," I said eagerly.

"Well, sometime during the thirties he married the daughter of the collector of one of the Punjab provinces—a Scot, like himself. The girl's father did everything he could to stop the marriage, but she was of age and apparently had a mind of her own. And from all accounts old Duncan had a way with him. Not that it did him much good, because a couple of years later she died giving birth to Adam.

"After that, Duncan McKenzie rarely contacted his own countrymen. All that was known of him was news of an occasional campaign in one of the wars that were always being waged between the princely states. People who met him said that in dress and manner he had become almost wholly Indian and that he had taken an Indian wife."

I nodded. "And she was Sabina's mother?"

Edward nodded. "Yes, a Rajput girl of good family. It says a lot for old Duncan's standing that such a marriage was allowed by the girl's parents. But by then, of course, he was a legendary figure and a good deal more powerful than many of the rajas." Edward glanced at me again, with this new, searching look so curiously appealing it was all I could do to maintain my calm, and then stared abstractedly over the garden, his eyes following a little group of doves that strutted busily among the flowers. "I think that all this time Adam's father was still at heart intensely loyal to his own country. Certainly there was never a suggestion that in any of the private wars he fought he ever did anything that was opposed to British interests in India. I imagine his attitude was that it was a big country and there was room for them both. So when the Mutiny came and the British were fighting for their lives, Duncan McKenzie offered not only his services but those of three well-equipped cavalry regiments as well."

I could guess what officialdom's answer to that offer had been. "And I suppose he was told that his services were not wanted."

"Yes." Edward shrugged his shoulders. "Perhaps it was understandable. Overnight scores of native regiments of the Old East India Company's army had risen against their officers and killed every European in sight. What the authorities wanted in 1857 was more British troops. You can't altogether blame them for not wanting McKenzie's private army of wild horsemen, even if he did swear that they were loyal. Commanding officers always believed their men to be trustworthy, even if it cost them their lives, and Duncan's men were just as doubtful as any other Indian troops. Only, unfortunately, the old chap didn't see it like that. He considered the whole thing to be a slur upon himself. From then on he seems to have severed all connections with his own people and with many of his Indian friends as well. With a small band of his most trusted followers he headed north, settled in this valley, and decided to make it his own private kingdom. The British hadn't even heard of the place and nobody else seemed to object, so that was that."

"He died here?"

"Lord, yes. About five years ago. Which was when Adam became khan."

It was an extraordinary story, yet perfectly possible. There was something about India that had always drawn the strange, sometimes gifted misfits of other nations and eventually claimed them as her own, especially in the days when the land had not been part of the British Crown but just a trading monopoly of London's all-powerful East India Company. The Company's power had ended with the Mutiny, yet its influence still lingered. "Is Sabina's mother still alive?" I asked.

"The begum? Yes, she's a formidable woman and getting on now. Sabina was born unusually late in the marriage for an Indian woman. If it weren't for the begum's wanting to keep her near her, Adam would have packed Sabina off to England long ago. I've never met the begum, of course. She lives in the old ways and rarely comes out from behind the curtain."

"It's strange," I said thoughtfully, "that a woman who lives in *purdah* should allow her daughter to dress in such an extraordinary fashion."

Edward laughed. "You sound shocked," he said.

"Not shocked. A little surprised."

"By all accounts the begum is no fool. She knows— better than Adam, I sometimes think—that the old ways are passing. She's prepared for the girl to learn about the way people live in the rest of the world because she thinks it's necessary. But, breeches or not, you'll notice that Sabina is never left unchaperoned— ever. Everyone is delighted that I should help her to paint, but if I were ever to overstep—the slightest familiarity—I doubt if I would leave this place alive."

"You mean that seriously?"

Edward gave me a strange look. "Oh, yes, I mean it seriously all right. The khan may seem like an English gentleman to you, but I assure you that in some ways living in Khudistan is like living in India two hundred years ago. You take liberties at your peril."

"What a strange man he must be," I reflected. "So handsome and cultured in some ways, yet apparently so barbaric in others. He is courteous and kind, yet so fierce, too. I am rather afraid of him. I cannot quite make him out."

"I shouldn't try," Edward said shortly. "No one ever gets close to the khan. He is very remote."

"Remote—or lonely?"

80

My companion stood up abruptly. "Well, I shouldn't advise you to try to find out. He has never looked at a white woman since his wife died. I expect he will avoid you as long as you are here—" He stopped, impatient to drop the subject of the khan. "Harriet, I must go now, but . . ."

"What about Sabina? Didn't you come to give her a lesson?"

"Not today." Edward's gray eyes rested on mine. "I had heard you had taken up residence in the palace. Perhaps I should have waited—but I had to see you."

I laughed. I did not mean to taunt him, yet I said, "You are so starved of the company of your country-women? It certainly is not your style, is it?" Perhaps I was thinking of the odd bits of news that had filtered back to me since his departure from Lahore—his name linked first with a notoriously generous widow and then with a girl named Beatrice somebody, a colonel's daughter, with whom an engagement had for some time been rumored, although it had never come to anything. If gossip was to be trusted, it seemed that the liaison had been broken when the colonel married a second wife, to whom Beatrice had taken such a violent dislike that she had been packed off home to England. Of course such rumors were rife among the army towns and as likely as not were groundless. Yet I could not imagine that Edward had exactly lived a monklike exis-tence since I last saw him, and here he must certainly be excessively lonely. Perhaps, I thought, that ex-plained his posting here. Had he proved too attractive to some senior officer's wife? But that was surely carry-ing my cynicism too far. Was I, no longer a virgin and myself alone and clearly vulnerable, expected to fall like a ripe plum at the first shake of the tree? The sharpness in my voice surprised even myself as I re-peated, "Not your style at all, surely?"

For a moment his face closed; his jaw clenched on what might have been anger. Immediately I was sorry and bit my lip—while he stood considering me for a moment and then smiled a rather grim, crooked smile.

"Have you really changed so much? Can you be so cold? The Harriet I knew was so gay and warm—"

And trusting, I thought. But my heart lurched, knowing I had succeeded in hurting him, and foolish tears pricked at my eyes. Why was I treating him like this? To punish him? To punish Edward—who had probably never had the slightest conception of the suffering he had once caused me?

"Oh, Harriet . . ." He had seen my moment of weakness and suddenly he was sitting beside me; his hand caught up mine in a hard grip that I did not even try to resist this time. "Do you know how beautiful you are? Do you know how many times I have remembered—"

"No . . ." I shook my head. "Please, Edward . . . let us not try to turn back the clock." I had succeeded in composing myself, and I withdrew my hand. Perhaps I was more exhausted from my ordeals of the last months than I knew or more in need of love than I wanted to admit—but I knew in that moment that if I did not stop him now, the last of my resistance would be swept away. The very proximity of him, the scent of his tobacco, the hard grip of his hand, threatened to send all my defenses toppling. A momentary weakness, I told myself, a momentary nostalgia that, once given in to, would put me back into that particular power Edward once had over me—albeit perhaps unknowingly.

I stood up. He said something gently behind me, but I did not hear it. A servant had come out to water the flowers on the far side of the terrace and that helped to bring me back to myself. I turned to him.

"Did you say that you had come to see me on an official matter?"

He did not answer for a moment, refusing to accept even temporary defeat. His gaze went from my eyes slowly to my mouth and back to my eyes. Then, suddenly, he smiled and—typical of him, of that impetuous, mercurial quality in him that could be so disarming—he stood to attention and gave a little salute, making a comically official face.

"Her Majesty's government agent at your service, ma'am! Whose humble duty it is to make the usual inquiries—report the arrival of any interesting newcomers."

"Report?" I frowned, suddenly anxious. If he reported my whereabouts to the authorities, all my efforts to find a secure hiding place would have been in vain. "What sort of report?"

"Usual routine," he said, serious now. "I always have to send in details—"

"Edward." I tried to make my voice sound natural and unstrained. "Is it really so necessary to report on every single person?"

"Well—yes." Now he eyed me curiously. "Why do you ask?"

I drew a deep breath. The last thing I wanted to do was put myself under any sort of obligation to Edward; nor did I wish to tell him of the circumstances of my flight from Banipore. Yet I had somehow to try to protect my privacy here.

"Because," I said firmly, "I'd be grateful if you would not report my presence here. At least not for the moment."

There was a moment's silence. Before the question in his eyes could be put into words, I said quickly, "Please do not ask me to explain. Perhaps sometime—but now now."

"You realize what you are asking me?"

"Yes, I know. I am asking you to disregard your orders. It can't matter all that much, can it? You might very well not have heard that I am here. Couldn't you pretend that you hadn't . . . just for a little while?"

There was curiosity in his eyes but sympathy, too. Nor could he quite conceal his satisfaction in having regained the upper hand. "Very well. For you—I will close my eyes. You'll probably get me court-martialed, but for the time being I'll tell myself that my orders don't apply to Americans. But you must promise to tell me what this is all about as soon as you can. In fact there is a lot I don't understand. There seems to be

83

some mystery surrounding your arrival. I gather that you were being pursued."

"By bandits, yes," I said quickly. "But that is not unusual in these parts, is it?"

"Or by a pestering admirer, perhaps?" His eyes sparkled again, but I did not smile. "Don't worry," he said. "I will do as you wish. And now, in return, you shall do something for me. Come riding with me tomorrow morning and let me show you something of your new territory."

"Well, I am not sure what—"

"And, by the way, a sari becomes you well."

I felt the color mounting to my face in spite of myself.

"I will come at first light tomorrow morning if that will suit you?"

Then, before I could answer, he made me a deep, mock bow. "Your servant, ma'am." A quick smile straight into my eyes—in which I did not miss the flash of triumph—and he was gone.

I sank down onto the seat and covered my eyes. Edward—the same Edward . . . the same magic. I did not know whether to laugh or to cry. How was I to avoid falling under that spell again? But I must, surely I must avoid it. In the first place I was, after all, supposed to be in mourning. . . .

But that was not what really troubled me. I knew now that I did not really know Edward—there were whole areas of his character that I had never explored. All I was sure of was that the physical attraction between us was still there and that, given half a chance, my heart could break again. I could not trust myself— or him. It would be far better if I saw as little of him as possible and, when meetings were inevitable, that I should continue to remain as aloof as was consistent with common courtesy. It was with this resolve firmly made that I set off in search of Sabina.

6

It was a little after seven on the following morning when Edward and I allowed our horses to find their own way down the track that led from the town to the luxuriant floor of the valley.

The previous day, when I had asked Sabina what I might wear for riding, she had responded carelessly, "Do not worry about details, Harriet, it has been taken care of."

She was right. When I awoke in the cool morning, I saw, hanging up outside my wardrobe, an exact replica of the dun-colored habit in which I had arrived; only this one was in a soft green and the material was lighter, more pliable. Beside it was also a simple morning dress in fine blue lawn, with pearl-gray buttons running down from the neckline to the sharply nipped-in waist. Indian tailors were always quick and efficient, but it seemed that in Ranipur even higher praise was called for.

Edward and I were not alone. Sabina, escorted by a henna-bearded syce, rode with us, the girl smiling and chattering in high spirits. I had not asked her to accompany us. Indeed, it had been with surprise that I had found her already at the stables, supervising the harnessing of her mount when I arrived. I was relieved that I was not to be alone with Edward.

"They tell me you are riding with Captain Ashworth this morning," she had said. "May I come, too?"

"Of course. He was kind enough to suggest showing me some of your beautiful country." For a moment I wondered if she resented the fact that Edward should have made such an offer in the first place. It would have been natural enough in her restricted life, and, indeed, she would by no means be the first pupil to fall in love with her teacher. But there was no antagonism in her liquid eyes and no edge to her voice as she made her request, and I dismissed my momentary doubts as unfair.

Now, as I followed Edward, who must have thought that I had invited Sabina to join us and was at pains to conceal his annoyance, I eyed the great glowing ball of the sun which was already rising high above the dawn haze, and was suddenly glad I had come to this extraordinary kingdom of Khudistan. For the first time since Garfield's death I felt a sense of freedom, even a sense of well-being. I leaned forward and stroked the gleaming neck of the horse that had carried me so faithfully to my new life.

Ahead of us Sabina rode astride her beautiful Arab, which gave me a twinge of envy—comfortable though I was in my new habit. I had ridden like that often enough as a child. Perhaps I, too, might do so again.

"The river is high at this time of year." Edward flung out an arm toward a winding gleam of silver ahead. "It's the snow water from the high hills."

I looked back at the town, perched like some fairy-tale stronghold against the side of the hill, and then up the valley to where the trees grew black and tall in great forest banks climbing to the sky. I watched an eagle circling infinitely high above me, wings stationary as it rode on the rising currents of air, and suddenly I wondered how the first white khan must have felt when he set eyes on the hidden valley. There was a peace and beauty about the place that made it seem curiously unreal and the air was so crystal clear that the distant trees seemed close enough to touch, just as I could hear the rusty squeak of a bullock cart's wheels as it made its way through a village that I guessed to be all of two miles away. A hare, startled by the slow-moving hooves approaching its hiding place, leaped up and ran, all ears and legs, for some safer hiding place.

"It is a good place, is it not?" I looked up to find Edward watching me with a smile on his lips, and I realized he must have read the pleasure in my face. "Perhaps it is fanciful, but there are times when I have imagined that the garden of Eden was not unlike this. Today it seems even more so."

I answered without looking at him. "I think it must be one of the loveliest valleys in all India. I only hope that we do nothing to spoil it."

"It *is* beautiful," Sabina agreed, "but I'm afraid I'm not able to appreciate it this morning. Suddenly I have a terrible headache. If you will excuse me, I think I shall go back."

"And I will come with you, of course," I said quickly.

Sabina shook her head. "It isn't necessary, and I shall be able to ride back myself very quickly." Then in Hindi, as her syce prepared to accompany her, "Nor is there need for you, Imam Bux. Accompany the captain sahib."

The man said doubtfully, "Lady, it is an order from the khan. . . ."

"And it is also an order that you go with the Englishman," she snapped. While we still watched her uncertainly, she had wheeled her Arab and without a backward glance galloped back along the way we had come. The syce reluctantly fell in behind us.

"Are you sure it's all right for her to go back alone?" I asked Edward doubtfully.

He shrugged his shoulders. "Whether it is or not, there's nothing to be done about it. Sabina has a will of her own and if she has decided on something, nothing is likely to dissuade her. Let her go."

It was not for me to question someone who knew Adam McKenzie's sister far better than I, but I felt uneasy as we rode on. Was it intuition or mere imagination that told me that the headache was a mere excuse to return? And alone. But why? I wondered. Why should Sabina have come all this way just to turn back on some mission of her own? Again I wondered whether she resented Edward's attentions to me. I decided to clear up the matter at once.

"Perhaps she feels possessive about you," I said lightly. "Is she in love with you, do you think?"

Edward's astonished stare and then his burst of spontaneous laughter reassured me. "Good heavens, Harriet, what an idea!"

"Well—but she is very attractive, isn't she? Surely any man must find her attractive, and at her age she must surely need some admirer—"

"Ah," Edward said, "who knows? She is a wily minx despite her childish ways . . . but as to any attachment to myself! How much you have to learn, Harriet! Her brother would have my skin were she even to look at me in that way!"

"Why?" I persisted obstinately. "I should have thought an English officer would be perfectly acceptable as a suitor—to her brother as well as to herself."

"A penniless soldier for the khan's sister! A captain's pay! My dear girl—you may have only just arrived, but you have certainly seen the manner in which Sabina lives in the palace! Can't you see that anyone bidding for the hand of Sabina would have to bid very high indeed?"

"But—under the circumstances," I said after a moment's hesitation. "As she is of . . . mixed blood—"

"*Especially* under the circumstances. Good heavens—surely you can see that?"

"Yes." I was not sure that I did, but I said no more upon the subject. But more than ever I wondered whether I should have allowed Sabina to ride back alone.

The feeling of faint disquiet was only gradually dispersed by the continuing wonder of the countryside that, little by little, revealed itself to me. In truth I could have asked for no better guide than Edward, who seemed to find a deep satisfaction in sharing his own appreciation of his surroundings with me. As we rode through the scattered hamlets, with their patchwork of fields, bright green with the ripening millet, it seemed to me that there was a prosperity and security here that could not just be attributed to the climate and the rich alluvial soil of the valley. Khudistan might be backward in its development as a state—indeed, Edward had hinted that progress was virtually nonexistent—yet it seemed that the ordinary people drew some very real satisfaction from this strange survival from the past. The high-cheekboned, slightly Mongolian faces that regarded us as we passed held none of the servility of downtrodden peasants, and their sturdy children ran to greet us across the fields. A prayer wheel before the door of a thatched dwelling caught my eye and I remarked that its owner must have found his way down from some Buddhist community even farther to the north.

"Possibly," Edward agreed. "It's hard to say what there is to find in the Far North of this country. There's a place up there that's absolutely forbidden to foreigners because the land is supposed to be especially holy. I've often thought it would be interesting to see exactly what kind of ceremony goes on there, but I imagine it would be more than one's life was worth to try to find out."

"Have you asked Sabina?"

"Once. She said she hadn't even been there herself, and I believed her. I doubt if anyone but the khan himself could give an answer."

"Then perhaps I will ask him sometime when the opportunity arises."

"With all due respect," Edward said dryly, "what makes you assume the khan would be prepared to satisfy the curiosity of a total stranger?"

"I am not a total stranger to Adam McKenzie," I said coolly. "My father knew him. In fact," I added, taking some satisfaction from Edward's look of amazement, "he once did him a service of some kind. What the nature of it was I do not know, but it was enough to bring your white khan to his funeral."

"Good Lord." After a moment Edward said, rather sharply, "Then perhaps this explains your seeming fascination for him."

"Fascination? I hardly think that is the word. You

89

assume too much, Edward. I am only saying that as his guest I suppose I have the right to show an intelligent interest in his kingdom and its customs—"

"Good luck to you, then," he said. "But bear in mind that the khan is not much accustomed to discussing his affairs with anyone—let alone a woman and an intelligent one as that!" His laugh held a note of derision and I felt faintly irritated until he added, "What a different person you have become, Harriet, in these two years. Forgive me if it takes me a little while to reconcile Mrs. Hunt with Miss Rogers! It is only that I should not like you to be hurt by the khan."

It was my turn to laugh, but gently. "Thank you for your concern, Edward. But I think I can defend myself." My words expressed far more confidence than I felt, however; perhaps I was pretending a little more bravado than was honest simply in order to discourage the inclination Edward evinced to seek to protect me. For I was even more aware this morning than I had been last night that, should I lower my guard even slightly, he would take advantage of it.

Edward turned his mount in the shallows of a stream. "We'll go back this way, then I can show you where I live."

I realized as he spoke that I had somehow taken it for granted that Edward's home was in the city, but when we came upon the simple, thatched bungalow set in a clearing within sight of the river, it seemed exactly the kind of place that he would have chosen. Yet it was with a certain wry acceptance of the simplicity of it all that he invited me inside and called for glasses of lime juice.

"It's a poor sort of place, I'm afraid. Some homes have the benefit of a woman's touch or the beneficial influence of money. I'm afraid I'm able to give mine neither."

An elderly bearer brought the glasses on a tray and said something in a low tone about a message while I took the opportunity to look about me. I saw that it was indeed a dwelling that was sadly lacking in comfort, bleaker even than the many similar homes I had

90

occupied with my father when times were hard. The single square living room had no more than a couple of cheap mats to cover the hard mud floor, and the ceiling cloths were old and stained. There were the usual few sticks of furniture brought in from the local bazaar, a jumble of books and sheets of drawing paper on an old deal table, a couple of leather and canvas camping chairs. A great feeling of sadness came over me as I thought that Edward, the talented young officer I had known and briefly loved, should be living like this.

If there were any relieving features in the room, they were an exquisite bronze head of a boy that looked almost as though it could have been the work of Cellini, and a pair of superb double-barreled Purdy shotguns that lay on the table ready for cleaning—objects oddly at variance with their surroundings. Somehow I had never given much thought to whether Edward had money or not, and I wondered why I was surprised that not only was he poor but, judging from the tone of his voice, he resented the fact. Could it be, after all, that in my ignorance and infatuation of two years ago I had failed to see that pride—or, at least, a lack of confidence—could account to some degree for the fact that Edward showed no inclination to marry? Somehow the thought touched me deeply. For whereas he, with his artistic resources, might be content enough to live in such modest circumstances as these, it was possible that he had not the confidence to expect a woman to share them. I was so ignorant of financial matters I did not even know what a captain's pay would amount to. Comfortable enough, I should have thought, yet without any capital behind him . . . Suddenly and for no logical reason I was glad he knew nothing of my present financial situation as Garfield's widow. And then, as quickly, I diverted my thoughts; for days and weeks I had almost forgotten Garfield and the very name in my mind now seemed both abhorrent and unreal to me.

I looked up as Edward turned away from his bearer and said, with a look of annoyance, "Word has just come that the khan will be sitting in judgment this afternoon. It is the new moon tonight. I should have remembered."

I said in puzzlement, "Sitting in judgment on what?"

"Whatever cases are brought before him." He led the way back to the veranda and offered me a rattan chair. "The khan rules his kingdom in the old-fashioned way—although there are some who would probably say that it was none the worse for that. Once a month he sits on the *gaddi*—the throne of judgment—in the Hall of Audience at the palace, and he's there to dispense justice to anyone who asks it of him. It doesn't matter who you are; prince or pauper, you're entitled to stand up and state your case. If you think that your neighbor is encroaching on your land, it's up to you to bring evidence to prove it. If, for example, a peasant woman reckons one of the shopkeepers in the bazaar is using a doubtful pair of scales, she asks the khan to look into the matter. He listens, then makes up his mind. There are no lawyers, no jury. The khan's judgment is final and possibly, by our standards, a little . . . draconian."

I found myself remembering stories of similar lawgiving by the emperors of old and decided that perhaps the simple expedient of a personally administered justice accounted for the less than servile appearance of the villagers. There was, I had to admit, something very engaging about the idea of a humble man claiming his rights in person.

Edward was pacing up and down the room restlessly, looking distinctly put out, his expression that of a small boy who had been told to do something he disliked.

"Do you have to go this afternoon?" I asked him. "Is that what your message was about?"

"Yes, I'm afraid so. It's a damned nuisance. And quite unnecessary. Why must the khan choose today of all days to demand my presence? One might almost imagine . . ." He broke off.

"Imagine what?"

"Does he know you are riding with me this morning? Did you ask permission or leave a message?"

92

"No." I frowned, surprised. "Should I have done, do you think? It did not occur to me."

"It is possible that as your employer he might have expected it," Edward said irritably. "That would be just like him. And this summons could be his way of reminding us of his authority."

"Oh, but that is nonsense," I protested. "But, of course, it is possible that Sabina may have mentioned that we were going riding. . . . I am still a little worried about her," I said, making to get up. "Perhaps it was remiss of me not to have ridden back with her."

"Remiss be hanged, Harriet! You are not an ayah, for God's sake! Nor am I to be treated like a servant."

I stood up. "I may not be an ayah," I agreed, "but I am still a kind of servant, and there is no point in ignoring the fact."

Frangipani flowers hung their heavy, waxen heads over the corner of his small veranda, and to bring an end to the conversation I walked out to look at them.

"Do you remember the frangipani in the temple gardens?" Edward spoke beside me. I turned and found the gray eyes on mine with an expression that brought a slow flush to my cheeks. "I broke off a flower to pin on your dress and it stained your gown—remember?"

I knew that it was not the flower stain that he was reminding me of but the moments that had followed it—first his apologies, his efforts to rub away the milky stain with his handkerchief, and then the hands that had left my gown to cup my face—the memory of that burning kiss burned in my memory now, and I knew that Edward saw it before I dropped my eyes.

"It would be best if I returned to the palace," I said. "You will need time to get ready if you are to attend the audience, and I must go to see how Sabina is."

"As you will. I will see you back to the gates."

For a brief instant we stood together and I felt my heart beating uncomfortably hard within my breast. All the anguish of the past two years welled up again, but this time it was, I realized, a bittersweet sorrow and one that was tinged with hope . . . with excitement? I did not dare guess. All I was sure of at that moment was that something within me I had thought long dead had come alive again.

When Edward left me at the open gate of the city, I dismissed Sabina's syce and allowed my mount to pick her way through the hillmen and their womenfolk who thronged the narrow street beyond. Many of them carried high wicker baskets on their backs, filled with the simple produce they were bringing to market. The occasional mule, laden high with firewood, plodded as a slowly moving obstruction among them, its load scraping against the overhanging walls, between which I glimpsed the tiny courtyards that were the center of a dozen unseen homes.

It was not until I had emerged into a small square of leather workers' shops—in reality no more than large cupboards let into the fronts of the houses—that I became aware of someone riding at my side. I turned, to find Adam McKenzie regarding me with smoldering eyes. Apart from a turban of scarlet silk, he was wearing European riding clothes, which for some reason made his tanned face look more Indian than ever.

I said, "Good morning, Khan sahib," and smiled, but received no answering greeting in return.

"Where is the princess, my sister?" His voice was harsh with anger. "They tell me in the stables that she rode out with you this morning."

More than a little put out by the brusqueness of his approach, I said coolly, "She and her syce joined Captain Ashworth and me—yes."

"But she did not return with you?"

"No," I agreed. "She complained of feeling unwell and said she would ride back to the palace. I offered to accompany her, but she refused."

The khan moved neared to me, so that the shoulders of our mounts were almost touching. He spoke quietly, so that even had he not been speaking in English, it would have been difficult for passersby to overhear. Nevertheless his anger was so apparent that I saw more than one of his subjects draw back in fear, a hand raised instinctively in a clumsy salaam of greeting.

"You are presumably aware that my sister goes nowhere unaccompanied. *Nowhere!*"

"I'm very sorry," I told him equally quietly but keeping my voice firm, "but as a matter of fact I was not aware at the time of any such rule. And in this case she could hardly have come to any harm. When she left us, she could not have been more than a mile or so from the city gates. She must have been there in a matter of minutes."

For an instant I actually thought that he would strike me, such was the fury that blazed from those blue eyes. But at the last moment he controlled himself. Nevertheless his tone was still implacable as he berated me further. "I would remind you, Mrs. Hunt, that the extent to which my instructions are disregarded is not the point. Kindly remember in the future that the overseeing of my orders is just as much a part of your duties here as giving lessons in French. I appreciate the fact that you are new here, although the same can hardly be said for Sabina's fool of a syce."

"It is hardly fair to blame the groom," I protested. "He had no wish to leave his mistress, but he could hardly have disobeyed her direct order."

"*Her* order?" The khan gave a grim smile. "I see that you have indeed a good deal to learn, Mrs. Hunt. The only orders that count here are the ones that come from me."

"I am not sure that I shall ever learn that, sir!" My eyes blazed with a flare of temper I did not even attempt to repress. "Strange as it may seem to you, I am not accustomed to taking orders from anyone." I stopped. It was the expression on his face that checked me. Astonishment and incredulity seemed to have banished anger.

For moments on end we glared at each other while our horses sidestepped restively and shook their heads against their tightly held reins. When the khan suddenly threw back his head and laughed—his teeth starch white against the dark skin—the color of my cheeks burned higher.

Furious, I spurred my mare, wheeled, then rode as fast as the gaping onlookers would allow up the slope to the palace gates.

I was still shaking with anger when I reached my room and managed to compose myself only when Suva, the little sloe-eyed maid who had been assigned to me, brought me breakfast of juicy mangoes and plantains, the tiny moist bananas that grew so profusely in this country. There was freshly baked bread and wild honey and the delicately scented tea that came from the hills.

But as I ate, my uneasiness about Sabina returned. Had that headache been genuine? And if it had, why was the girl so insistent that the syce stay with Edward and me? She must have known the man could be in deep trouble if discovered disobeying orders from the khan.

As soon as I had finished, I asked Suva to take me to Sabina's quarters. I half expected an empty room, but I was wrong. Sabina lay in the center of a white ornately carved bed, sleeping like a child. I did not see her again for the rest of the morning.

When it was time to change, I told Suva that I would be attending the audience and asked what I should wear. She told me that tomorrow the tailor would be seeking an appointment with me so that I might choose new gowns from the cloth he would bring to show me. The lawn dress was not suitable, so I must wear the other sari that the princess had found for me. This one was in warm, subtle shades of palest green and gold and seemed to make my hair shine like burnished copper.

When Suva had arranged the final folds of the rustling silk, she bowed and left the room as silently as she had come. I turned and studied the result of her careful ministrations in one of the many ornate mirrors that covered the walls of my room. Edward had told me he would meet me in the courtyard of the Hall of

96

Audience at two o'clock and I wanted to look my best. This morning Edward had told me I was beautiful.

The face that looked back at me was still too thin from the weeks of worry and strain, but I realized the fear had left my eyes, leaving them once again the clear leaf green that had always been my greatest asset. As I stared I wondered what other eyes had looked searchingly in that selfsame glass over the years.

Without warning I shivered violently, as though an icy wind had blown through the heat of the room. Instinctively I looked behind me, but there was no one there. Nevertheless I was aware of a curious sensation of no longer being alone, as though the past occupants of that room were watching me—slim, dark-skinned girls with enormous kohl-rimmed eyes that looked at me from the other side of the grave.

Abruptly I shook my head, as though to dismiss my ghostly companions, and was conscious almost at once of a lightening of the heart and an awareness that I was alone again. It was, I thought, all too easy to become a prey to strange fancies in such surroundings, and I made my way quickly down the wide marble stairs and into the dazzling sunlight to join the steadily growing crowd whose destination could only be the same as my own.

Edward had told me that the Hall of Audience was set apart from the rest of the palace, and indeed it could not be missed. The heart of the palace was the ancient fort that Adam's father had pulled apart and refurbished in its own, curiously decadent style, part Mogul, part Hindu. Outside the fort itself, cut sharply into the living hillside, someone had caused to be laid out a great paved courtyard, from the edge of which it was possible to look down over the town below. At the far end of the courtyard, alone and uncluttered by any other buildings, stood the Diwan-i-Am—the Hall of Audience itself—from which the khans of Khudistan pronounced their judgments.

As I approached it I could not help thinking that it stood in almost ludicrous contrast to the palace itself, for whereas the latter was purely functional from with-

97

out and ostentatious within, this building was a fragile delight in marble and rose-tinted sandstone, the work of some master craftsman of a past age who had been allowed to work with no more instructions than to produce the best.

It was a building that I judged capable of accommodating perhaps five hundred people, and it was entirely without walls, the delicate cupolas of the roof being supported only by a forest of slim pillars. What divisions there were consisted of marble screens, so pierced as to resemble lace, which gave an impression of such gossamer lightness that the whole structure seemed capable of being blown away by a puff of wind. The only truly solid feature was a massive central plinth, upon which stood the gaddi, or throne.

Edward came toward me out of the press of people making their way into the hall, and I felt the color mount to my face at the unhidden admiration in his eyes.

"This morning, Harriet, I told you that you were beautiful. This afternoon you quite take my breath away. You make me most proud to be seen with you."

I smiled as he took my arm. "Thank you, sir. I might well say the same for you." He was no longer wearing his customary dust-colored riding wear but the scarlet and gold of his full regimentals. He had worn that scarlet at the ball, I remembered. That first time I had danced with him, more than two long years ago.

Edward grinned back at me. "And damned hot this is, just the same. I've a good deal of sympathy for fellows who claim troops fight better in drill than serge in the hot weather. But one must look the part today, I suppose. Do you mind sitting on a cushion? No chairs, I'm afraid. Marble for the hoi polloi, cushion for the gentry, if they're lucky."

"No," I said, "I don't mind a cushion in the least." I had already learned that the hidden folds in a sari allowed for reasonable decorum. "Are we to be allowed to sit together, or do I have to go to the womens' place?"

"There will be few women here at all. The peasant

farmers don't encourage their women to come farther than the courtyard. Sabina may be here—if so, she will sit below the throne. Her mother, the begum, hardly ever leaves her quarters, and you and I, being unbelievers, won't offend anyone by sitting side by side."

Edward took my arm and led me into the astonishing cool of the marble hall, already three parts full of what seemed to be a cross section of the population of the whole valley, sitting cross-legged and solemn-eyed, wearing their best clothes and staring at the empty throne. Almond-eyed men from the far hills, hawk-faced soldiers of the khan's own guard, heavy, oxlike *bannias* from the local bazaars, they sat unspeaking, and their unwonted silence gave a curious sense of unreality to the occasion.

Edward had led me to a row of silken cushions directly in front of the throne when there was a sudden stir as everyone present stood up, and when I looked around, it was to find that Adam McKenzie had mounted the throne, followed, at a suitable distance, by his sister. He gestured, and the great congregation sank down.

I saw that on this occasion the khan had made no compromise in his apparel and was dressed formally, unadorned save for a swath of purple silk over the shoulder and a single great diamond that blazed from his matching turban. I could not help but feel almost mesmerized by the power he held so effortlessly over his people. His eyes raked his audience, taking in those present, I felt, in one sweep. He sat cross-legged on the broad seat of the throne, and across his legs he rested a curved sword in a scabbard of beaten gold.

Below the throne an official stood up and shouted, "Draw near, all who seek the justice of the great khan!"

Edward's description of what followed had been a commendably accurate one, and it was easy to understand its appeal to a simple people. For the most part the cases concerned the basic facts of peasant life—land and marriage settlements. The plaintiff simply stepped forward and stated his case, witnesses were called, then the defendant. Once the facts had been laid before the khan everyone appeared to be quite happy to abide by his decision, which was, as far as I could judge, most probably the correct one. Watching the applicants as they stepped forward, I guessed that the khan used his judgment of people to support him in cases where the evidence was thin, and from mutters of approval the watchers seemed to agree.

Not all the plaints were directed against other people. Among the first few petitioners was an old woman who claimed that her daughter had been killed by a tiger while filling a water vessel at the well.

The khan listened to the record of killings attributed to the animal, then, when the story drew to a close, he asked, "What is it, then, that you ask, woman? These matters are in the hands of God. We cannot bring your daughter back again."

"Lord, I ask only that you give orders that the tiger be killed, for we are a small village, and there is none among us who owns a gun."

"It shall be done."

All this time, Sabina was sitting on a chair of carved teak, a little below the throne, and I noted that on this occasion she wore a sari, part of which she had drawn modestly across the lower part of her face. As far as I could judge, she appeared utterly uninterested in the proceedings until an old man pushed his way forward and asked almost curtly for a remission of taxes on his village.

"Why?" the khan asked brusquely.

"Lord, there is much sickness in the village. There are no young men with the strength to tend the fields and because of this the crops will fail. That is why there will not be enough money to pay the taxes this year."

"What is this sickness of which you speak?"

"It is a bad fever, lord."

In India almost anything was a 'bad fever.' Apparently the khan thought the same, for he glanced away from the petitioner and toward a good-looking young man seated below him. To judge by his clothing, he appeared to be a person of some consequence, and he stood up with an air of authority as his khan addressed him.

"Dr. Gupta, can you be more exact?"

"Yes. The village is suffering from a severe outbreak of typhus. It is as the man says."

He sat down, and as he did so I saw him glance swiftly toward Sabina. Although half the girl's face was still covered with the corner of her sari, I could not help but note the sudden look that flamed between them. It lasted for only the barest instant, yet it was enough to convince me that here was a secret friendship about which the khan knew nothing. My mind raced back to the morning "headache." Had I unwittingly found the answer to Sabina's sudden disappearance? The more I thought about it, the more certain I was.

I glanced toward Edward, sitting cross-legged at my side, but his eyes were on the proceedings and it was clear he had noticed nothing out of the ordinary. Once again I found myself paying attention as the commanding figure on the throne spoke again to the village headman.

"The taxes are remitted. Take your sick to a place distant from your village, where they shall die or recover, as God wills. Those of you who are healthy shall leave your possessions within your homes. Then you will slaughter your cattle and burn your village and all in it until there is no mark of the place save its ashes. None shall live there again, and an officer shall inspect the place to make sure that this has been done."

"Oh, no . . ." The sheer ruthlessness of the edict shocked me so much that I had spoken the words aloud before I realized it, half rising as I did so. Just for a moment I saw the khan's eyes flicker coldly in my direction, but he said nothing and a moment later Edward's hand had clamped on my arm, pulling me back onto my cushion.

"For God's sake, Harriet—be quiet!"

I relapsed into angry silence while the headman fell on his knees, wailing for mercy until court officials dragged him away. There was a buzz of interest from the assembled throng, although whether it was of approval or otherwise I could not tell.

I glanced toward Sabina, wondering what her reaction was to her brother's pronouncement, but her eyes were once again on the young doctor, finally convincing me that I had discovered her secret.

"Does anyone else claim justice?" The khan's voice was flat and unemotional. Then, when there was no reply, "Let the syce Imam Bux be brought forward."

There was a little stir and a moment later the red-bearded groom who had accompanied Sabina this morning was thrust forward with a guard on either side.

"It has come to my notice that you allowed the princess Sabina to ride unguarded this morning. Is that true or false?"

Probably the wretched man knew well enough that to protest that he had done so only under his mistress's direct order would have done him more harm than good, for he said simply, his head bowed, "It is true, huzoor."

"It is truly written that by chastisement is the foot of folly placed in the stirrup of repentance. Two dozen lashes."

I saw Sabina's head jerk upright and then sink again in hopeless acceptance. "This is barbaric," I whispered hotly to Edward. "Why in God's name should that man be flogged for something that was not his fault?"

"Because ultimately I suppose it *was* his fault. Presumably he knew the khan's orders."

"But you can't just sit here and let this sort of thing happen. You were there, too. Aren't you supposed to be the British agent in this place?"

"My duties are to protect the interests of my fellow countrymen," Edward informed me quietly. "Imam Bux does not happen to be one of them. And I must remind you that this is the way justice is done here. You are not in a magistrate's court now."

"That," I agreed, "is only too apparent."

"The audience is over, in any case." Edward rose,

giving me a slight smile. "I suggest you return to your quarters until your anger has abated somewhat. No one has ever been known to defy the khan and not suffer either banishment—or worse."

"I most certainly shall go," I said savagely. "I have seen all I wish to of your white khan of Khudistan for some considerable time."

Yet it transpired that I was to have no say in the matter, for no sooner had I returned to my room than a woman was knocking at my door.

"The khan sahib sends his greetings and his hopes that you will dine with him tonight."

For a moment it was on the tip of my tongue to suggest that the khan could well dine on his own, for all I cared, but I knew at once that this would be unforgivable. He was, after all, my employer and nobody was keeping me in Khudistan against my will. If I was not prepared to leave, there was little point in antagonizing the country's most powerful citizen.

"Please thank the khan sahib," I said formally, "and say that I shall be happy to do so."

Dinner with the khan was an event that I would learn to anticipate on two or three evenings each week, usually in company with Sabina and sometimes with Edward as guest. The begum, I gathered, always ate alone. The setting was one that never failed to fill me with wonder, and even on this occasion I still felt a thrill of pleasure at a room that might easily have been no more than vulgarly ostentatious but was in fact a dream of delight.

The dining room of the palace provided a staggering display of mirrored walls and superb crystal tableware that threw back the candlelight of a magnificent chandelier in thousands of tiny reflected fairy beacons that flickered magically. The table, an amazing expanse of pale pink marble, was supported by legs covered in countless thumbnail-sized mirrors that formed a glittering mosaic, and the black marble floor, polished like glass, put the whole fantastic setting in dramatic contrast. I sat with my host at one end of the table, a white-coated and turbaned bearer rigidly at attention behind each chair. The khan was dressed in a plain suit of white silk, buttoned high at the neck, and without his customary turban his thick, dark hair was shining in the candlelight. Then, as my eyes went to a line of uniformed servants entering bearing what seemed to be almost countless silver serving dishes, he said quickly, "As you know, I usually prefer English food in the evening, but I thought we might dine *daisi* style for a change. Is that acceptable to you?"

"I love Indian food," I assured him, and indeed it was true.

"Excellent. I don't think you will have cause for complaint."

I had enjoyed the dishes of many regions during my years in India, but never had I experienced anything to match the meal that was laid before me that night. It had often amused me that newcomers to the country took it for granted that Indian cuisine consisted solely of one mouth-searing dish of something known by the general title of curry, and I wondered what its uninformed critics would have made of the exquisite flavor of the chicken cooked in almond cream that was placed before us that night or, for that matter, of the glazed roulades of lamb known as *parcha yakhni* or of the *machchi dumphokat*—fish steamed with the rare black mushrooms found only in the mountains of the North.

For a while we ate in silence, and it seemed as though the khan's thoughts were far away. But as the crystal bowls of scented water were brought around to cleanse our fingers he turned his piercing blue eyes on me and said quietly, "From your interruption I conclude that you did not entirely approve of the proceedings this afternoon."

There was neither criticism nor concern in his voice, nothing that served to guide me in any way. But since my father had always instilled in me the absolute need for truth, I said, as steadily as I could, "You are right—I did not. I thought your decision to destroy that village was not only needlessly harsh but ..."

"Go on. Outside advice does not always come amiss."

The color rose in my cheeks at his sarcasm, but I forced myself to continue. "I was going to say unwise."

"And why, may I ask?"

Possibly more sharply than I intended I said, "I should have thought the harshness was obvious enough. But unwise because the next time there is typhus in one of your villages the people who live there will probably go to considerable lengths to conceal the fact. With a contagious disease that can hardly be a good thing."

"So . . . Mrs. Hunt, I was right to listen to those who said that you are an intelligent young woman. In this country we do not see many such. Nevertheless you will have to learn to curb your tongue. The truth can be a dangerous weapon. I will answer your criticism. I do not think your second point is a valid one, though your reasoning is probably correct. The next village that discovers it has sickness will still report the fact for the simple reason that I will so order it. But if you honestly think I dealt harshly with that unfortunate old man, then tell me what you would have done."

"I'd have asked your doctor for advice, for one thing," I said boldly.

"Young Gupta's title is strictly an honorary one. In any case he is skilled only in the traditional Vedic medicine, based on religious and herbal cures, which can do nothing against typhus, although I admit it can be surprisingly effective in other ways."

"Then," I suggested, "you could have called in a British doctor. Captain Ashworth would have arranged for one to come."

The white khan stood up abruptly, looking very tall in the cluttered room. He said shortly, "My dear Miss Rogers, you do not seem to realize that a man in my position does not call in the British lightly. Once they came, they would find some reason why it was for the good of my people that they stay. And as you must know for yourself, even the best of European medical

105

men are useless when it comes to curing typhus. Their advice would be the same as mine: Burn the village down."

It was true, I realized, and suddenly I felt a fool.

Ignoring my discomfiture, the khan went on. "I admit that it may seem unnecessary to destroy not only the homes but their contents and livestock as well, but I have a personal theory that typhus may be carried from one person to another by fleas. Certainly it seems to thrive in more than usually filthy surroundings."

"I suppose it is possible." Indeed, I could remember an army surgeon saying much the same and being much derided in consequence.

"You encourage me," Adam McKenzie observed dryly. "And if it is of any comfort to you, the people of the village will be adequately compensated. Does that set you more at ease?"

"Yes," I admitted frankly, "much more. Only in the case of your sister's syce—"

"Your opinion on that case was not asked."

"Of that," I said hotly, "I am well aware. But apart from the injustice to him, Sabina must feel . . . well . . ."

"I trust she feels a proper degree of remorse for having caused someone to be punished for her own self-indulgence," he told me curtly. "Now, unless you wish to offer yourself as an expert on matters in Khudistan after two days here, we may consider the subject at an end."

I bit my lip. I had gone far enough. "Very well." I stood up, ready to go, but he motioned me back to my chair with an imperious hand. "And now," he went on, "to turn to a different subject. You heard the old woman complaining of a rogue tiger. We shall hunt it tomorrow. Would you care to join us?"

I had never taken part in a tiger hunt, nor, for that matter, had I ever had any desire to. But I sensed a challenge in the khan's manner and suspected it would afford him no small satisfaction should I make some excuse. So, in spite of my apprehension, I answered him readily enough.

"Thank you. I shall look forward to it."

106

"Excellent. You must allow me to select for you a suitable weapon."

Perhaps it was not challenge that I read in his eyes as he heard my acceptance. Perhaps it was amusement. I did not know, nor, at that moment, did I greatly care.

7

I had been curious about Sabina's mother ever since I
had heard the story of the arrival in Khudistan of her
husband, Duncan, yet it seemed presumptuous on my
part simply to ask if I might see the begum McKenzie,
so when later that morning I received a direct invitation through Sabina to visit this formidable lady, I felt
a certain satisfaction, even though I was conscious of a
twinge of apprehension at the same time.

There was an air of restraint about Sabina that
morning, and I thought grimly that in the circumstances it was not altogether surprising. Nevertheless
she made no reference to her escapade and instead led
me toward the back of the *zenana,* or women's quarters, in which my own rooms were situated. It had
come as something of a shock when first I had realized
that I was to live in a part of the palace where no man
other than the khan himself might tread and that by
only a small stretch of the imagination I could count
myself as an inmate of an Eastern harem. But I had reminded myself sharply that the arrangement was logical enough. The khan's subjects could be expected to
have little respect for a ruler who failed to provide the
customary privacy for his own women folk and it
would be taken as a slur on my virtue were I to live
elsewhere. Nevertheless I was unprepared for the magnificence in which the begum McKenzie lived. As Sabina led me through a black-lacquered door inlaid with
mother-of-pearl I had taken it for granted that I should

be entering no more than a private suite of rooms kept for one old lady's exclusive use. But the surroundings in which I found myself bore no relation to the needs of one person. As the door shut soundlessly behind me I saw that I was standing in a square marble-floored courtyard that was open to the sky. It was enclosed by a cloistered walk surrounded by slender marble arches, each pierced and repierced to form the endless, exquisite convolution of a stone vine. In the shadows of the vaulted ceiling of the cloisters I glimpsed the wonderful, matchless blue of Persian mosaic, and from somewhere behind carved wooden doors, black with age, a voice rose and fell faintly in a plaintive song.

I must have caught my breath, for at my side Sabina said, "Yes, it's beautiful, isn't it? The rest of the palace is really rather awful, but this—"

"This was made by craftsmen brought by my husband from Delhi. It was two years in the building because much of it had to be carried over the hills one piece at a time."

I had seen no one enter, but when I turned, I saw that we had been joined by an Indian woman dressed in a simple white sari, without ornaments of any kind save for a vermilion *bindi* in the center of her forehead. She could have been little more than five feet in height and so slight of build that she had a look of what I suspected was a deceptive frailty, for she moved toward us with the grace and ease of a young woman. My first impression of the begum McKenzie was that she was old but still beautiful, with a quiet, timeless beauty that had little in common with the sloe-eyed women immortalized by painters down the years, but then I noticed that her eyelids were without the cosmetic that Indian women commonly use, although the eyes themselves were regarding me with a keen intelligence. Familiar though I was with the rapid aging of women in an unforgiving climate, it came as something of a shock to realize that Sabina's mother was unlikely to be even sixty years old.

"*Namaste, Begum sahibah.*" I did not know why I instinctively chose the Hindi greeting for one who bore

109

a Muhammadan title, but she returned it readily enough, with a hint of amusement in her eyes.

"Yes, it is confusing, is it not? I took the title only to please my husband's troops, who followed the Prophet. But you are right, of course. By birth I am Hindu, and how can anything alter that?" She paused for a moment and then added, "Can you understand what I am saying?"

"Thank you. Yes." The begum was speaking Hindi, probably more slowly and clearly than usual for my benefit.

"Good. I have not spoken English for many years and I think it would be difficult to express myself fully now, although I understand it well enough." She gestured to the wide rim of pink marble that surrounded the fountain. "Come, sit here. And you, my daughter, wait for Mrs. Hunt outside."

"Very well, Mother."

I felt a moment's amusement at Sabina's unquestioning obedience, so much at variance with her customary manner, and I was interested to note the authority the older woman obviously still wielded from behind the scenes within her own home. When the girl had gone, the begum said quietly, "Look into the water beside you."

I did as I was told. The surface was broken not only by the droplets that fell from the fountain but also by what appeared to be a thousand glittering points of fire that flashed and flickered in the sunlight as though the tiny lake were alive. I looked up at the begum questioningly.

"The bottom of the fountain is studded with diamonds." She made the statement as an explanation, not in the manner of one striving to impress.

"It is very beautiful."

"Yes. When my husband was a young man in Delhi, he saw the pavilion that Jahangir made in the Red Fort, with running water everywhere, and he wished to make the same for me."

I remembered reading the inscription set in that

110

room, high up on the wall, and I said softly, " 'If there is a heaven on earth, it is this, it is this, it is this.' "

The begum looked at me quickly. "Ah, you have seen?"

I nodded. "Yes. But the diamonds in the water courses are there no longer. The British soldiers dug them out with their bayonets during the Black Year."

"You mean the Mutiny?"

"Well . . . yes."

I knew that things had happened during 1857 of which neither side was particularly proud, and many Indians preferred not to use the word.

The begum made a tiny gesture with her hands. "The Mutiny was the Mutiny—you do not have to spare my feelings. My husband would have fought for his own people, but they would not trust him." She looked slowly around the courtyard with a kind of quiet pride. "He was a great man. When he took me to wife, there were a dozen women in these apartments, beautiful as gazelles, all of them."

Nobody had told me that Adam's father had had other wives, but I realized it was likely enough. In the days when England had been a six-month voyage away and there were few white women in the country, it was accepted that most British officers kept an Indian woman, and it was not unusual for powerful officials to keep a zenana on an almost Oriental scale.

The dark, wary eyes were studying me narrowly. "That does not shock you?"

I shook my head. "No." Curiously enough, it didn't. "It is the custom of the country."

"It *was* the custom of the country. Now it is changing, like everything else. But it is true that after the Englishwoman who was my husband's first wife died, he took many women into his household. Then, after me, they were given pensions, one by one, until only I was left." A sudden spasm twisted the once-lovely face. "I, who never gave him a son."

I said quietly, "You must remember that sons are not so important for our people. When a Christian

111

dies, there is no need for a son at the funeral ceremony."

"So I have heard," the begum agreed. "In many ways their customs are not ours. When the father of my daughter died, I wished to become suttee, so that I might die honorably on the funeral pyre, but he had left instructions that it was not to be so."

The matter-of-fact way the begum spoke of burning herself alive gave me an involuntary thrill of horror, and there must have been something of that feeling in my voice as I said, "But widows do not burn themselves these days. Suttee has been forbidden for many years."

"So the raj speaks and all India obeys?" Real amusement played about the old woman's mouth. "You are not a fool, young miss. You know enough of this country to know its ways, and women still burn themselves with their men in a score of places where your rule has no meaning. And as far as I am concerned, I care not a fig for any law that stands between men and their gods. No, I live on, a widow, jewelless, in mourning clothes, because my lord would have it so." She paused for a long moment and then went on. "I wished to speak with you because I am of the old ways, and their time has gone. You will teach my daughter the things she should know in the world today?"

"Yes," I said, "that is understood. And I promise you that I shall do my best."

"But there is something else."

"Yes?"

"The khan, my husband's son. He would live the life of his father, ruling justly and without fear. All that is good. And yet it sometimes seems to me that I, who live behind the curtain, see the future more clearly than he, who lives in the world outside. The old kings are dead, and now I hear that even the great company is no more. If you have the opportunity, I would have you remind him of this, so that he does not spend his life building a house that will only fall down with the first of the monsoon rains."

I said quietly, "I am afraid, Begum-ji, that the khan is not likely to pay very much attention to my advice on a subject like that."

"Perhaps not. But one must take one's opportunity when it comes." The begum rose and walked slowly toward a table on which stood a small box, its surface covered in seed pearls. When she turned back to me, she said, "Now, miss from far away, do you know what a *nizar* is?"

"It's a gift," I said. "A formal gift that one offers to an important person. Very often the gift is refused, but it should be offered just the same." I hesitated a moment, suddenly uncertain, and then went on. "Forgive me. I should . . ."

"It does not matter," the begum said. "In this world that is turning upside down it is perhaps right that I should give the nizar to you. And in case you should be wondering, I tell you now that this is not one that you are expected to refuse."

I took the box she proffered me and opened it, and as I did so I caught my breath, for the diamond that lay within blazed light at me from dozens of perfectly cut facets. It was a thing of exquisite beauty as well as of enormous value, and such was my bewilderment that I said in English, "But I couldn't possibly . . ."

"You despise my gift?"

I felt myself flush with embarrassment. "Of course not."

"I have been told that British officers are ordered never to accept gifts lest they be corrupted by bribery. It is permitted to take only a little fruit or some such thing that has little value. Is that true?"

"Yes."

"Then content yourself that what you hold is of no more value to me than a basket of mangoes. It is no bribe. Why should I deal with you like a banyia seeking trade for his shop? It is a gift from one woman to another. In the meantime, you have my permission to go."

"Then thank you." I knew instinctively that as far as the value of the gift was concerned, what the old

113

woman said might be right, and just as instinctively I knew that what I had taken was in fact a bribe, although for what I was not sure. All I did know was that if I insisted on refusing, I should be making myself an implacable enemy, and that was something I had no wish to do, so I made the conventional salutation, only to find that the begum had already turned away.

Sabina was waiting for me on the other side of the door and regarded me curiously.

"Was she nice to you?"

"Yes, very nice."

"What did you talk about?"

Truthfully I said, "She said that she hoped I would be able to instruct you usefully." And then, before she had time to question me again, I added, "And that is something I can do only if we are frank with each other, don't you agree?"

We were walking back to our own part of the palace and I felt Sabina's pace quicken slightly. Cautiously she said, "Of course."

"Are you quite sure you have been frank with me so far, Sabina?"

"I don't know what you mean." All at once she was no longer a lovely young woman but a schoolgirl sulking at my side.

I said briskly, "I think you do. For one thing, you didn't really have a headache this morning, did you?"

She tossed her dark hair impatiently. "Does it matter very much whether I did or not?"

"It depends. I think it matters a good deal if you use a nonexistent headache as an excuse to get away and do something that is . . . well, forbidden. And if it causes a servant to be punished for something that was not his fault, then I think it is quite unforgivable."

Sabina eyed me rebelliously. "Whom have you been talking to?"

I frowned. "I don't understand you. If you want me to be your friend, you must trust me. Can't you see that?"

For a moment I thought that Sabina was about to dismiss my words with no more than an angry retort, but instead the mercurial girl flung her arms around me impulsively.

"Forgive me, Harriet, but I'm so used to having everyone against me that I can't get used to the idea that I've actually got someone on my side."

"Against you? In what way?"

"Against Ram Gupta." By now we were walking across the courtyard before the Hall of Audience, and white doves swooped down on us, tumbling and sporting in the air. There was something so gay and carefree about the birds' antics that I gave a little exclamation of pleasure, but the girl beside me gave my arm an impatient shake. "Harriet, please pay attention."

I said contritely, "I'm sorry, but they look so pretty. . . ."

"The poor birds are not really playing, they are simply bred that way and cannot help themselves." Sabina smiled wistfully. "Cannot you see that I am very like them? Just someone to be admired because I look pleasant? Nobody really cares if I am happy or not."

I felt a pang of remorse, because it was not difficult to imagine the loneliness of a rich and beautiful girl who was in no position to choose her own friends and could indeed do little more than behave prettily in the manner expected of her, as mindlessly as the tumbling birds. I said earnestly, "I do care, Sabina. But you cannot expect me to help you deceive your family. But tell me about this Dr. Gupta. What has he done that has put your brother against him?"

At the mention of her admirer's name, Sabina's expression changed magically and her eyes shone with something that I recognized with a sense of foreboding was all the wonder of young love, and I found myself hoping desperately that it might bring her joy instead of the desperate unhappiness I feared for her.

"Oh, he hasn't done anything. Of course Ram's family isn't like ours, but it's perfectly respectable. His father is one of the local *zamindars*—landowners— with several farms, and quite well off. At least he could afford to let Ram study medicine at one of the monasteries up in the hills."

115

I said gently, "Wouldn't it have been better if Ram had studied in a proper hospital?"

"Yes, of course it would," Sabina admitted readily enough. "And that's what he wants to do one day. But he says that the people in the valley won't have any confidence in him unless he shows that he understands Vedic medicine first, and his parents are very old-fashioned. They'd be horrified at the idea of his going to live alongside the British in India. One day they'll understand, Ram says, but not yet."

"How did you meet him?"

Sabina laughed. "I suppose if I had been brought up in Calcutta, I'd have met him at a ball. That's where one makes friends usually, isn't it?" She paused for a moment and then, without waiting for an answer, went on. "We don't have that kind of entertainment in Ranipur, and even if we did, I don't imagine I should be allowed to attend it. No, about six months ago I accidentally knocked over an oil lamp and burned my hand. Ram was called in to treat it."

I raised my eyebrows in surprise. "Without a chaperone?"

The girl blinked at the unaccustomed word. "A what?"

"A *khadsin*."

"Oh, I understand. Yes, my old nurse was present, but Ram and I spoke English, which she doesn't understand. I think we knew from the start that we weren't—just going to be friends."

It wasn't altogether surprising, I thought. Indeed, it was easy enough to imagine the effect of a young, good-looking man on a hot-blooded young girl eager for life yet bound about by people who watched her every move.

I said with a smile, "And of course it took a long time before the burn was properly healed."

Sabina smiled in return. "Oh, Harriet—I knew that you would understand! Yes, the burn proved very troublesome indeed. Ram had to make a good many visits to the palace before I was quite fit again."

"But," I protested, "if this young man is of good

116

family and is well educated, I still cannot see what your brother can have against him. After all, he must accept the fact that you will marry somebody someday."

Sabina said bitterly, "Of course. But you don't know Adam. As far as he is concerned, my marriage will be to a prince or nothing."

I did not find that hard to believe, for I suspected that Adam McKenzie's devotion to Khudistan was sufficient to make it essential, in his eyes, that his sister should marry and eventually have children by someone who was of acceptable lineage.

Sabina stared into my eyes appealingly. "You've got to help us, Harriet. You've just got to. What can you do to make Adam understand?"

I said with probably more honesty than she appreciated, "Frankly, Sabina, I don't know. But I'll do my best for you, that I promise."

"You're a darling!" Impulsively the girl kissed me. "Oh, I'm sure you'll make everything all right in the end. I just know you will."

"Well, if I am to succeed," I said dryly, "there will have to be no more of this business of your having convenient headaches just so that you can spend an hour with Dr. Gupta."

"I promise, Harriet, I really do!"

"In that case," I told her, "you had best come and attend to your studies."

"Studies?" Sabina stared at me in horror. "But, Harriet, we can't have lessons today. Have you forgotten? It's the tiger hunt!"

As it happened, I had forgotten, and I admitted as much.

"Have you ever been on one before?" Sabina asked.

"No." A formal hunt would have been considered curiously ostentatious in the world in which I had lived with my father. "But I saw one killed once. It came into the village near where we were living."

"Who killed it?"

"My father." I found myself remembering the silence of the village and myself pressed up against the

117

wall of the shoemaker's house, watching the stocky figure of my father making his way toward the little temple where the animal had been last seen. The sudden flash of black and orange in the shadows and the echoing crash of my father's rifle. There had been a great celebration in the village that night, and some of the men had skinned the dead animal and presented the trophy to us. We had used it as a rug for a while, but it had rotted because the villagers hadn't known how to cure it properly.

Sabina asked, "Your father—was he a great hunter?"

I shook my head and suddenly my eyes smarted with unshed tears. "No," I said. "No, he wasn't a hunter at all. In fact he hated killing things, but the villagers were frightened and there wasn't anyone else there who owned a rifle."

Rather unexpectedly Sabina said gently, "You must have been very proud of him."

"I was."

"I should have been, too. I expect Adam will kill the tiger this afternoon, but he's a *nausher* anyway, so it's not really the same thing."

Nau meant "nine," *sher*, "tiger." I said, Do you mean he's really killed nine tigers?"

"A good deal more than that, I should imagine. You'll see how good he is at it this afternoon."

I was not altogether certain that I relished the prospect of being present at a ritual killing designed to enhance the reputation of the khan. But when, that afternoon, I found myself seated uncomfortably in a plain hunting howdah on the back of a vast elephant, I realized that my first impression of the expedition had been a good deal divorced from the truth.

"We are here just in case there is more than one tiger," Sabina, who shared the howdah with me, explained as we rocked through the coarse grass toward the tree line that hid the village where the man-eater had been terrorizing the local farmers. "If this were no more than a sporting expedition, we should have started at dawn, when the animals are hunting. But as

118

this is for one particular man-killer, the villagers will beat the forest to drive him out from where he will be sleeping."

I glanced sideways at the other members of the party; there were three elephants in all, carrying Indians who I presumed were important officials of Adam McKenzie's court and who were entitled by rank to be present on what was essentially an informal occasion. Each great beast was guided by an almost naked *mahout*, who sat cross-legged on his charge's neck, just behind the great ears, and each, as with Sabina and myself, carried a native hunter, who squatted on the forward edge of the howdah, presumably as a guard. Our own *shikari*, a youngish man wearing a khaki-colored turban and an ancient, rather high-smelling drill jacket, spat the crimson juice of betel nuts in the general direction of the ground, chatting unconcernedly to the mahout in some unknown tongue. His rifle, a heavy double-barreled Manton ten bore, lay propped up beside him. Adam, alone and on foot, walked a little ahead of us, his own weapon held casually beneath his arm. Abruptly, and for no apparent reason, the three elephants stopped, and a sudden silence fell.

I said to Sabina in a low voice, "Is Dr. Gupta here?"

"Yes, he is on the far elephant on the right." She did not turn her head but continued to stare into the trees, from which the shadows were slowly beginning to lengthen as the sun continued its journey across the sky.

"You mean the khan invited him?"

"He is the doctor. We should hardly come without one." Then, "We are waiting for the beaters to begin. They make a lot of noise so that the tiger will wake up and come toward us."

I held my breath, for there was something strangely menacing about the silent trees, the quiet breathing of the elephants, and the hot sun beating down on the roof of the howdah. About a hundred yards to the rear of us, the khan's horse, held by a groom, threw up its head against the flies and its harness jingled like a distant bell.

Filled with a sudden urge to break the almost unbearable silence, I whispered, "Are tigers always driven by beaters?" I was trying to imagine what it must be like for the men concerned, unarmed, pushing their way through the jungle undergrowth with no more than past experience to tell them that their quarry would run before them.

"In the days of the Moguls all game was hunted like this," Sabina answered. "Hundreds, sometimes thousands of animals of all kinds were driven in a circle toward a *kush*, or killing ground. Today it is not considered very sporting, but it is permissible because a man-eating tiger *has* to be killed." She added with a touch of pride, "It's also quite all right to shoot a rogue tiger from a tree or the back of an elephant. It's just Adam's custom to face them on foot."

Without warning one of the shikaris cried out in a long, wailing call, and all at once there drifted from the jungle an extraordinary jangle of drums and gongs, interspersed with the voices of unseen men. Neither the elephants nor the waiting men moved as the sound drew steadily nearer. Birds, startled and outraged, shot up from the branches into the sky, settled indignantly, only to be scared into flight yet again.

Suddenly I was aware that I was looking at the tiger. At first it had seemed no more than a barred shadow, then it had moved and sunlight dappled the orange fur. Beneath me the elephant shifted its stance uneasily and the great trunk rose up uncertainly as it scented its ancient enemy, then, at a murmur from the mahout, fell again.

I gripped Sabina's wrist. "It's there!"

"I know."

I realized that everybody knew, for all at once the whole world seemed to hold an air of expectancy. Adam, motionless, was holding his rifle easily across his body in both hands. Something had been pricking at the back of my hand for a long time, and I saw that it was a mosquito, gorged on my blood. I pressed it almost absentmindedly with a finger and a crimson smudge appeared in its place.

Abruptly the tiger charged, low-bellied, traveling toward Adam at what seemed incredible speed, and in that moment the tableau came to life. I saw Adam's rifle swing up to his shoulder with a smooth, confident movement and then, unbelievably, the beast bounded on, and I knew instinctively that his weapon had misfired. I think Sabina guessed what had happened, too, for I felt her body stiffen beside me, and then there came the crash of a shot as Adam fired the second barrel.

The tiger gave a coughing roar and rolled over as the heavy lead ball smashed home, but in an instant it was on its feet, mad with rage and pain. I sat, motionless, frozen with horror, waiting for the tiger to take its revenge on the now-unarmed man, who was standing still with his back to us. But the wound seemed to have driven all thought of the tiger's original enemy from the maddened creature's mind. Twisting and biting at the ground, it turned suddenly and hurtled toward the elephant upon which Sabina and I sat, covering the intervening distance at incredible speed in a series of bucking jumps. Then, without even pausing to gather itself, it leaped straight up the elephant's neck toward the petrified mahout.

I have no means of knowing the speed with which the tiger came toward us, but at the time, it seemed to move as effortlessly as something in a dream. The mahout had thrown himself forward onto his mount's forehead, where he clung easily enough as the elephant screamed with rage and flung up its trunk, vainly trying to strike at the thing that was tearing at its neck. The shikari who had been perched on the edge of the howdah jerked backward as a great, taloned paw slashed down within inches of his leg, and at the same moment, the elephant flung up its head. The man gave a sharp, startled cry and fell ten feet to the ground. The next moment the tiger's great ruffed head came level with the side of the howdah and I was staring into mad, yellow eyes and feeling the hot, stinking blast of the creature's breath. And as though someone outside myself were acting for me, I reached for the gun

121

dropped by the vanished shikari, dragged back the hammers, and fired both barrels point-blank into the gaping mouth.

For a moment I thought that I, too, was to be thrown from the howdah, for the combined recoil of both barrels of the ten-bore hurled me backward off my feet, so that my head struck the woodwork behind me with a resounding crack. Desperate and sick, I struggled to my feet, clinging to the side of the howdah as I rocked wildly on top of the frenzied elephant. The tiger had vanished, and as I glanced down I saw it, motionless, on its side, and writhing in pain and terror beside it, the wretched shikari who moments earlier had been thrown to the ground.

The elephant clearly cared little that the tiger was dead. In all probability it did not know. All it undoubtedly was conscious of was the fact that the animal it feared and hated most was at its mercy. With a shrill squeal of triumph it swung around and one huge pad smashed down upon the striped body, stamping into the soft ground a patch of bloody pulp and missing the helpless shikari by inches. I heard the man scream in pure terror, and for an instant I found myself staring down into his fear-crazed eyes. He lay on his back, one leg bent at an impossible angle, powerless to move, while five tons of maddened animal literally danced over him. In a moment, I knew, he would be trampled on as the tiger had, smashed and obliterated into an obscene mess, and yet for some reason I seemed to have lost the power to close my eyes. Perhaps it was as well, for as I watched so helplessly, Adam McKenzie appeared below me, running forward as though his life depended on it.

I heard Sabina scream, "Adam, no!"

He could not have heard her over the trumpeting of the elephant and its companions' answering cries, and he would certainly have paid no attention even if he had. Heedless of the great pads that were stamping down beside him as the elephant sought to wreak still further vengeance on the tiger's unrecognizable remains, Adam ducked beneath the gray belly and

122

gripped the fallen shikari by the shoulders. Looking down, I saw the muscles of the khan's back knot beneath the silk of his shirt as he half lifted, half dragged the whimpering man to safety at the same moment that our mahout hooked his *ankus* into a sail-like ear and by main force dragged his charge's head away from the pulverized tiger.

"Hut! Hut! Hut!"

Breathing heavily, the elephant turned slowly, and as its driver shouted and beat it unmercifully with the heavy iron goad it stopped and lurched down on its knees, and all at once eager hands were reaching up and helping me to the ground.

"Congratulations, Mrs. Hunt. I'm sorry your elephant has so thoroughly ruined the skin of a very gallantly killed tiger." I looked up, light-headed with relief, to find the khan standing before me, breathing heavily. His eyes searched mine for a brief instant, as though questioning. Whether or not he found his answer I had no means of knowing, but he smiled suddenly, showing white teeth against his deeply tanned face. Then, as I swayed a little, he reached forward and steadied me, his hand upon my wrist. The touch should have been impersonal, no more than a courtesy to one in need of help, yet the contact seemed to go through my body like a galvanic shock. I stood as though rooted to the ground, dimly aware that I could not have moved if I tried. Then the khan let me go and I heard him asking, "You are not hurt?"

Somehow I managed to smile and shake my head. "Thank you, no. If one does not count a bruised shoulder." It must have been a reaction from what had just happened, I thought. No more than that.

"Firing both barrels at once has bruised stronger shoulders than yours, so I am not surprised," the khan told me. "But there is blood in your hair if I am not mistaken."

I put my hand to my head and brought my fingers away, now dappled red. "It's only a slight cut," I told him. "I struck my head on the edge of the howdah when the gun knocked me over."

"I had best make sure."

I felt his fingers part my hair and all at once, without warning, I was aware of a strange tingling in my blood, a sense of awareness that I had never experienced before. His fingers, as they touched and probed, were unexpectedly gentle, yet in some inexplicable way they seemed to take possession of me. It could not have been more than a few seconds, yet it seemed an age before he stepped back and nodded briefly. "As you say, only a slight cut. I'll get Gupta to clean it for you."

I said huskily, "You could have been killed." Shaken though I was, I found it hard to rid my mind of the picture of Adam McKenzie bending over the injured shikari while the maddened elephant had stamped and trumpeted directly above him. It was not, I realized, the fact that he had shown high physical courage—for someone with his background it was only to be expected. What had surprised me had been the readiness of one who seemed no better than a feudal autocrat to risk his life for one of the humblest of his subjects.

"Killed?" The khan looked puzzled for a moment. "You mean by the elephant?"

I think I was embarrassed that I had spoken at all, for I felt the color come into my face, yet I could not ignore his question. "Well—yes. He could easily have trodden on you."

"He could even more easily have trodden on that fool of a man. It would have served him right for falling, but . . ."

"Noblesse oblige?"

He smiled slightly. "Of course. Did you imagine that rank does not carry its own obligations? But we're wasting time. I must call Gupta."

He turned away, and I saw his back stiffen. Looking past him, I felt a sudden twinge of dismay. Oblivious of all else, Dr. Ram Gupta was deep in conversation with Sabina.

"Madam, do I have to remind you once again of your duties as far as my sister is concerned?" The khan

124

swung back to me and I saw that his face was pale with anger.

The sheer unfairness of the rebuke stung me to a sharp retort. "Since we have been speaking together for the last five minutes, it should be abundantly clear that I cannot be in two places at once." Even as I spoke I noticed Dr. Gupta leave his companion's side and run to where the injured man lay. Apparently aware that she was being observed, Sabina came toward us.

"The shikar's leg is broken," she said a little defensively. "I was suggesting to the doctor that we might put him on one of the other elephants to get him back to the city."

"That is a matter for Gupta to decide, and I imagine he is quite capable of making the necessary decision for himself." The khan's voice was so low that nobody apart from the three of us could have heard what he said, but the venom in it startled me. "I have made my views clear on this matter to Mrs. Hunt and I shall now repeat them to you. Under no circumstances are you to have any communication with Dr. Gupta. Do you understand that?"

For a moment I detected a flash of rebellion in Sabina's dark eyes, and she said in a low voice, "I can see no harm—"

"I am not interested in whether you see harm in this matter or not." The khan's voice cut like a whiplash. "I am ordering you to have no more to do with this man. If you continue to disobey me, I shall see that he pays heavily for your indulgence. With his life if necessary."

Sabina lifted her head. "So if I disobey you, it is Ram who will suffer for it?"

Her brother nodded shortly. "Exactly. You may indulge yourself if you will. But if you do, kindly remember that his life will be in *your* hands.

8

During the days and weeks that followed I found myself settling into a pattern of life that was curiously sat-
isfying. It was not just that Sabina was a quick and
rewarding pupil whom it was a pleasure to instruct but
also that while teaching her I found that it was comparatively easy to put the less agreeable aspects of my
new home out of my mind. In my heart I might know
that the problems of Sabina and Ram Gupta were always present, yet for the purposes of everyday living
the matter did not intrude. In fact, had I but given the
matter more thought, I might very well have wondered
at the docility with which the girl had accepted her
brother's arbitrary decision. As it was, I enjoyed both
my work and its surroundings, and my spare time
seemed to pass increasingly and pleasurably in the
company of Edward.

We had taken to riding together in the cool of the
evening, sometimes cantering through the lush grass at
the foot of the hillside but more often than not allowing our horses to make their own way along the winding watercourse that marked the lowest point of the
valley.

They were short, those evening rides, for the
darkness fell all too swiftly when the sun went down,
but there were other times when Sabina was involved
in family matters about the palace when it was possible
for the two of us to set off together for a whole day.
On such occasions the expedition would serve a dual

purpose, for Edward would make use of the opportunity to visit some outlying village where perhaps some old soldier from the company's army had settled or some question as to the size and population of the place had to be checked. But for me such days were pure enchantment, for not only was I able to see parts of Adam McKenzie's kingdom that I would not otherwise have been able to explore but I had a whole day of Edward's company that I need share with no one.

It was just before the Hindu festival of Holi that Edward and I set out on one of these day-long expeditions, one on which I was to meet Dr. Ram Gupta for the first time. Edward had said that as we had a fair way to travel, we had best ride at a less leisurely pace than usual, and accordingly we cantered our horses through the low-lying countryside briskly enough before striking up a winding, barely discernible track that climbed steadily toward where the great peaks of the Hindu Kush reached up before us until they seemed to touch the pale, clean blue of the sky. We were not going there, I knew, for although the snow on their upper slopes looked almost close enough to touch, I could guess that there was little likelihood of their being less than fifty miles away.

Nevertheless I stared up at the incredible range with a wonder that never palled, forcing down a sense of disappointment that on such a day we could not linger but had to reach a specific destination. Had it been my choice, I should have wandered unhurriedly through the lower meadows, bright with mountain poppies, gentian, saxifrage, and edelweiss, well aware that I was in an alpine paradise that seasoned travelers from Europe would stare at almost in awe.

Yet as we climbed up among the spruce, pine, and red-berried kharpal I began to see that the higher world was no less brilliant, for the woods were splashed with blue irises and huge crimson, pink, and yellow rhododendrons so that at times it seemed as though we were riding through an enormous, never-ending botanical garden. Nor was it only the profusion of plant life that kept me rapt in wonder. Every few minutes I became conscious of some form of wildlife either above me or moving at my side. Possibly the remoteness of the region or the limited hunting practiced by the local villagers had resulted in the denizens of the valley feeling but little fear of man, for a langur and her family barely moved from our path as she went on with her business of teaching the young monkeys how to discover the succulent young growths, and even shy chital deer peered out at us from behind trees without undue concern. There must have been wild pig there, too, for although I did not see them, I twice heard their crashing progress through the undergrowth and a distant squeal of rage as two hot-tempered boars came face to face.

Fascinated by it all, I asked Edward how it was that the villagers ignored what must have been a very real temptation to supplement their simple diet.

"Probably because they don't particularly wish to," he told me. "You may have noticed that up here there's a good deal less emphasis on religious differences. People of different faiths even respect one another's festivals and make no attempt to interfere with them. When I first came, I put it down to greater tolerance, but it isn't really that. In these parts everyone sooner or later becomes a sort of Buddhist, because that's the real faith of the hills, and whether they're Hindu Buddhists or Muslim Buddhists they all share the Buddha's respect for life." He turned in his saddle and pointed across the valley to where a shambling black shape moved through the shadows just below the tree line.

"Bear?" I hazarded.

Edward nodded. "Yes. The Himalayan black bear. Now, the chaps around here will chase *him* if they get the chance, because he can do a lot of damage if he takes it into his head to start investigating crops in search of food. But he's about the only thing on four legs that needs to worry and even then not much. Precious few villagers own a musket, and the average bear is quite capable of outsmarting them."

Something in the tone of his voice made me look at him quickly. "You like bears, don't you?"

Edward shrugged his shoulders. "They're pleasant creatures to draw."

The horses slowed to a walk as the track vanished beneath a scatter of recently fallen boulders, then opened to a lush meadow, blue with gentians. I said, "Why did you go into the army? You'd have been happier painting all this. Painting anything, for that matter."

"Because I hadn't the money to lead the life of a dilettante." There was that bitter edge to his voice again, I noticed. Abruptly he changed the subject and pointed to a huddle of a village built against the slope of the valley. There were perhaps a dozen huts, some half obscured by the typical hillman's stumpy haystacks, and a whitewashed mud shrine, bedecked with flags that I guessed as commemorating some local holy man. Far away in the distance some diminutive, hairy cattle grazed and the only sign of human life was that of an old woman frozen at the sight of our arrival in her business of drawing water from the village well.

Apparently Edward was well known, because the crone relaxed as soon as she recognized him and, in the fashion of the simple people of the hills, made no attempt to veil her face. She listened attentively while Edward questioned her in a dialect I could not understand, then broke into a voluble reply, gesturing higher up the valley.

Edward frowned for a moment, then turned to me in explanation. "It seems Dr. Gupta has got most of the men up that way, doing something to the lake. We'd better go and see what it's about. So far as I know, there isn't any lake for miles, but the word the old woman used could just as easily mean a pond. Anyway, the headman is there, and he's the chap I want to see."

It was indeed a pond that the old woman had meant, for there were several small patches of water at the far edge of the meadow, and as we rode over, the little group of men there turned toward us and salaamed.

The headman, a grizzled peasant of middle age, presented himself to Edward, who dismounted, tossing the reins to the nearest boy. Turning to me, he said, "Karrapa here has got something he wants to show me. I shan't be long. But you might like to find out from Gupta what's happening."

I nodded, dismounting in my turn, for I had identified Gupta as one of a group who had been standing knee deep in the water. He came toward me at once, with a look of pleased surprise on his face.

"Good day, Mrs. Hunt . . ." He paused and looked a question. His English was slow but surprisingly good in view of the fact that he could have had little opportunity to speak it. "You must excuse my asking. It is correct that I call you that?"

I smiled. "Why not, Dr. Gupta? It is my name."

"That is so, but perhaps I should say memsahib? I do not wish to seem lacking in respect."

"I think I prefer Mrs. Hunt." He was, I decided, an exceptionally good-looking young man. As he was pale-skinned, I guessed him to be the product of a local beauty and some high-caste Hindu who had arranged a union of his own choosing rather than someone of his own caste. If that were so, his mother's origins showed in the slightly almond eyes and broad cheekbones, and his father's blood had given a delicacy to the bone structure and an indefinable air of breeding that contrasted markedly with the heavy-featured, slow-moving men around him. Rather, I thought, as though one had identified a blood horse grazing with a group of hacks.

Now he nodded and said simply, "Thank you. It is a great pleasure to meet you here. Sa— the princess has spoken often and most highly of you."

"I'm glad."

"It would be a great pleasure if I might offer you some tea. Over there, in the shade, it has been prepared. It will also be more comfortable for you to wait until the captain returns."

I said, "Thank you. I should like some tea very much."

130

Together we walked to a place at the edge of the tree line where a charcoal fire glowed. A young boy poured scalding, milky tea into brass tumblers and vanished into the shadows.

"What are you doing here, Dr. Gupta?" I handled the tumbler warily, marveling as ever at the Indians' ability to avoid injuring themselves with the hot metal. I nodded toward the ponds and the men grouped around them. "You must have most of the village working here."

"Yes, indeed." Ram Gupta smiled in shy agreement. "You see me indulging my . . ." He glanced at me in query. "You are knowing what is a *shouk*, Mrs. Hunt?"

"Yes, I know."

"I should be grateful for the English word, if you please."

It struck me for the first time that there was in fact no English equivalent. I said, "I suppose we'd call it an all-absorbing interest or an obsession, perhaps."

"Ah, I see. I have been indulging my obsession. Thank you very much, Mrs. Hunt."

I smiled. "But you haven't told me yet just what your obsession is, Dr. Gupta."

"It is fever, Mrs. Hunt." Ram Gupta looked at me quickly, as though more than half expecting me to laugh. "Hill fever. What you call on the plains malaria."

"I'm sorry," I said, "but I don't understand."

"Oh, it is probably a foolish dream of an ignorant medical man who has not even been trained in the proper way. But I should very much like to put a stop to it."

"Cure malaria? But the greatest doctors in India have tried for years to do that, Ram Gupta! And millions of people still die of it every year."

The young doctor said quickly, "I am not speaking of *curing*, Mrs. Hunt. I am speaking of stopping. So no one catches the fever in the first place."

"But nobody knows how the fever is caught," I protested. "The best doctors think that in some places

131

there is bad air, but what sort of bad air no one really knows."

"I am thinking," Ram Gupta said, "that perhaps it could be carried somehow by mosquitoes. Would that sound very fanciful to you, Mrs. Hunt?"

I said blankly, "I—I don't know. How could such a thing happen? What makes you think that such a thing could happen?"

The young doctor sighed. "I am thinking that the only reasons I have are very foolish ones, but as you say, nobody is knowing where the fever comes from. But it must come from somewhere, and so I have thought about the matter very much." He looked at me keenly. "Mrs. Hunt, we know almost nothing about this sickness apart from the fact that it kills hundreds of your people and millions of mine. All that is certain is that it kills all over India but in some places more than others. Why should that be?"

"Dr. Gupta," I said, "this is not a subject about which I have any knowledge. I just do not know. Perhaps there is more bad air in some places than in others."

"I do not believe in this talk of bad air," Ram Gupta said. "We have the hill fever in this very valley and everyone knows that our air is clear and good. But always I speak to men who have traveled much in India, and when I hear them say that such-and-such a place has much fever, I ask them, 'What else did you notice about this place?' And three times men have said, 'It was a bad place, for all the time I was bitten by mosquitoes.'"

Mystified yet fascinated, I said, "That could have been no more than coincidence, Ram Gupta."

"True, and yet it is something, is it not? And if it were possible to banish these insects from a place it would be even more interesting to discover if fever becomes less." The young doctor gestured toward the water glinting at the edge of the meadow. "Did you know that mosquitoes breed in such water, Mrs. Hunt?"

I shook my head. "No. To tell you the truth, I've never thought about where they breed."

"Neither had I, but I watched, and it is clear that they do. And so it seemed to me that if we stopped the breeding, we would be sure that next year there would be no mosquitoes. Who knows? It may work." He spread his palms outward in a typical Oriental gesture.

"I simply don't know," I confessed. "But supposing that you are right . . ."

Apparently reading my thoughts, he said quickly, "Supposing that I am right, Mrs. Hunt, fever could become a thing of the past. I have had all the men from this village working down there since this morning, and by nightfall we shall have taken away all the water that stands in that meadow. Then next year we shall see if there is as much fever here as before or less."

I said slowly, "I don't know whether it will prove successful or not, but I'm sure it is tremendously *worth* doing." I found myself wishing very much indeed that someone who understood such matters could hear the young Indian's theory. It might be proved nonsense, as I was well aware, and yet it was difficult not to share his obvious sense of conviction. I had heard that many great medical advances had come about in just such a way, and if by any chance Ram Gupta had stumbled on the cause of malaria fever, it was not hard to imagine the fame and respect it would bring him. A man with such work to his credit might even be considered sufficiently eminent on Adam McKenzie's terms to pay court to Sabina.

Again as though he had been reading my thoughts, Ram Gupta said abruptly, "Mrs. Hunt, can you tell me something about proper medical training? Is it possible to become qualified in India?"

"I—I don't know." Taken by surprise, my mind became suddenly blank as I sought to recall anything that I might have heard on the subject. I said apologetically, "Ram Gupta, all the doctors I have met have been in government service, and they were already qualified in Europe before they came out here."

133

"But is there such a thing as an Indian doctor? Have you ever met one?"

"Yes—one." I felt sudden relief as an anonymous brown face swam up for me out of the past. "There was one in Banipore—a civilian. But I never actually met him and I certainly can't remember his name. And for all I know, he may have qualified overseas."

"But could you find out?"

"Yes, of course."

Ram Gupta said slowly, "I wish very much to become qualified in the European or American fashion. For simple people Vedic medicine is very good, because they believe that the wisdom comes from the Scriptures, and there are many things I can treat quite well. But then again there is much more that I need to know."

"Do you think," I broke in, "that once you were qualified the khan might not object to your friendship with his sister?"

Ram Gupta looked at me quickly, his eyes wary. Then he relaxed and smiled. "Of course. It is unlikely that Sabina would have any secrets from you. But, no, I was dreaming of all this for my own satisfaction. Apparently my company no longer amuses the princess, for I have had no word from her since the day of the tiger hunt." He added bitterly, "It is not surprising. A very ordinary student of Vedic medicine has no right to lift his eyes to those of the high born. Better to think only of my work, then, when I marry, it shall be to someone of my own class."

I said quietly, "Listen to me, Ram Gupta. That is not the reason you have not heard from the princess."

"No?" He raised his dark eyes to mine with sudden concern. "Then what is it, Mrs. Hunt? She is not ill?"

"No," I assured him, "she is perfectly well. It is just that the khan has forbidden her to communicate with you in any way. And she has been told that if she disobeys, it is you who will suffer and not her."

I was startled by the sudden anger that blazed in the young Indian's eyes, and he jumped to his feet with a quick, pantherish movement that seemed curiously out of character for so naturally quiet and self-effacing a man. In a voice harsh with emotion he said, "Mrs. Hunt, it is outrageous that the khan should be able to have such power over his people. If he wishes to say that his sister shall have nothing more to do with me, that is his right as a brother. I myself have sisters, and should they behave in a way that I considered unfitting for my family, then it would be my responsibility to correct them. But for the khan to threaten my life . . ." He broke off abruptly and looked down at me. "Because that is what he *is* doing, is it not?"

I said slowly, "Yes, Ram Gupta, I am afraid that it is."

"That is the way things happened in the old days. Or the way things still happen in little backward states where little princelings have too much power." The doctor's voice was tense with feeling. "I tell you, Mrs. Hunt, that a time will soon come when things will have to be changed here." He broke off suddenly as footsteps crunched on the dead leaves beneath the trees behind us and I turned to see Edward coming toward us.

"I must return and finish the draining," Ram Gupta said abruptly. "Thank you, Mrs. Hunt, for listening to me. Perhaps another time . . ."

I wanted him to stay and tell Edward what he had told me, but instinctively I knew that he either would not or could not. Probably as a woman and Sabina's friend I was in no way a forbidding person, whereas Edward, however sympathetic, could not be other than what he was—an officer of the British raj. And indeed as we rode away from the village I felt something of the same thing myself, for Edward said suddenly, "I couldn't help hearing what young Gupta was saying to you when I joined you just now. About it being time for a change."

"He was angry because the khan has forbidden Sabina to have anything to do with him," I explained. "I don't think he was exactly preaching rebellion."

"Probably not."

There was something in my companion's tone that made me look at him curiously. "Would it matter if he

135

had been—well, speaking against the khan?" I asked. "After all, this isn't British territory. I can't imagine it would matter very much officially if an internal rebellion did succeed."

"On the contrary," Edward informed me, "it would almost certainly matter very much indeed. For one thing, whatever one may think about the way he rules his sister's life, he does keep law and order in his own province. If someone else took his place, there's no knowing that he'd be anything like as good a ruler, and the government might find that—well, inconvenient. You see, it's not as though this were some small state in central India; it's a small state on the most northern frontier of all." He gestured toward the distant head of the valley. "On the other side of the mountains there's just a narrow strip of the Lodak, which isn't a country that's powerful enough to get in anyone's way, then—Russia."

Russia. It was a word that I had heard spoken in just such a way many times over the years—the subject that always seemed to be raised whenever military men met and spoke of the future. And the reason was not far to seek. In many parts of northern India it was possible to stand high on one of the great mountain ranges and literally see into the huge and rather frightening country that stretched limitlessly beyond. It was through passes in those mountains that the ancient invaders of India had come, from Alexander to the Mogul khans. And it was the way many feared invaders would eventually come again. I looked at Edward quickly. "Do you really believe there's a danger from there?"

"Not so far as Khudistan is concerned, because we've an unbroken range of mountains between the Russians and ourselves. But farther west, where there are passes—yes. We know their agents come in all the time with the traders coming down from Tibet. Just as ours go north to see what's going on with them."

I remembered the phrase I'd heard to describe the secret war that was being played out every day in remote places. "The Great Game?"

Edward laughed shortly. "So people like to call it."

There was something in the way Edward had spoken that did not encourage further questioning on the subject, but all at once I found myself thinking that perhaps this was the real reason for his presence in Khudistan. I had wondered from the start at the necessity for appointing a British officer as resident to safeguard the interests of his fellow countrymen in a land where they rarely appeared, but if Edward himself was part of the Great Game, everything was clear. I pointed to the distant north and asked, "Is there any means of knowing who comes into the valley from up there?

"Nobody does," Edward said shortly. "It's a blind valley, probably glacial, and it ends at the mountains. There is no way through." He nodded toward the stream that wound its way along the valley floor a quarter of a mile away. "That rises up there like a great spring, straight up through the ground. It's that tremendously holy place I told you about, where nobody is allowed apart from the priests who look after the temple. I should imagine that's why old McKenzie chose this for his kingdom in the first place. It's at the end of the world and there's only one way into it."

We spoke little for some time after that but rode back along the way we had come in companionable silence, passing from one little isolated farm to another only half aware that they were there, while the deep purple shadows crept down the mountainside and the woodsmoke from the cooking fires stretched out long and low above the ground.

"Do you remember the 'cold line' in the Punjab?" Edward asked suddenly.

I nodded, because that was what we called that straight ridge of smoke in the part of India we both knew best. "One never saw it until after the monsoon was over," I recalled.

"About October. The sign that the season of cool nights had come around again." Edward smiled reflectively. "Up in these parts you get it all the year round."

There was something good about having shared

137

memories, I thought. Aloud I said, "This seems to be like a world of our own." I slipped from my saddle and bent to pick from a little clump of gentians. After a moment Edward joined me and stood studying one of the bright little flowers before turning to look searchingly at me. He was smiling as he said, "It would be a pretty compliment to say that your eyes are this color, but they are not. They are green." Gently he took me in his arms and kissed me. His lips were firm and warm on mine, and suddenly, just for a moment, the memory of what I had thought lost forever surged up in me and blended with the quiet happiness of the day. The last and only time Edward had held me in his arms I had been a girl lost in the wonder of first love, unawakened and unaware. But those days were long spent, and although, God knows, I had experienced little pleasure in Garfield's bed, his embraces had left me with the beginning of understanding of what such love should be. And as I stood there with Edward's arms about me I found myself longing suddenly for something more and I thought fiercely that I had already waited too long to feel not the dusty drill of his tunic but his smooth body, hard and alive under my own hands. In a moment of revelation I understood suddenly that I wanted not gentle kisses but a man, this man, to take my love and my body at one time. And then, for no good reason that I could understand, I found myself aware that in my mind it was not Edward but Adam McKenzie who was holding me, his mouth exploring mine.

The shock of the revelation must have made me draw back for an instant, for Edward released me immediately.

"What is it, Harriet?"

I shook my head. "I . . . I don't know." And in truth I did not know what strange whim had taken possession of me. What kind of power did the khan have that he should be able to command my body like some demon lover even when I was in the arms of another man? I did not understand what had happened and perhaps just then I did not even want to. But between

138

Edward and me the spell was broken for the time being, and both of us sensed it. I turned back to my horse. "It's getting late," I said, and my voice shook. "I think you had best take me home."

9

It was while she was brushing my hair the next morning that Suva observed that it would be as well if I stayed indoors for the rest of the day.

"It is the festival of Holi, but only low-class people observe it. The young men throw colored powder about and sing vulgar songs."

I said, "That doesn't sound so very terrible. What does the festival celebrate?" In fact I knew well enough; Holi was a fertility rite, pure and simple, and usually unmistakably so. I had grown up with it, but I knew that newcomers to the country were often startled by its forthright imagery.

"It is a festival because it was in the month of Phalgun that the Lord Krishna killed the demon Putana," Suva informed me reluctantly.

"I see." I thought with amusement that the girl would most probably have been deeply shocked had she known that I was well aware that in many out-of-the-way places farming folk shut their eyes to a sexual freedom for their wives and daughters that would have been unthinkable at any other time. And yet as I stared through the window of my bedroom and saw the sharp outline of the distant hills I realized that I had a friendly feeling for people, bawdy or not, who lived on the land and found time to rejoice at the change of the seasons. Flowers seemed to blossom throughout the year on the sheltered slopes of this hidden valley, but now I noticed that the streams were filled to overflowing with snow water from the higher slopes and the sun was beginning to blaze down with more than its customary intensity. There was a freshness and a feeling of new life in the air and I was surprised to find that I was more carefree than I should have thought possible only a few short weeks before.

My mood continued throughout the day, and even Sabina's increasingly frequent absentmindedness at her lessons did little to diminish it. I had to admit that in the circumstances the sheer irrelevance of French grammar was hardly conducive to any sustained effort on her part. After a little while I suggested that we converse in French instead, but her thoughts were clearly far away.

"Perhaps," I suggested, "it might be better if we left this until another day."

"Am I that poor a pupil?"

"Not poor. Preoccupied."

Sabina smiled wryly. "Would you not be if you faced the prospect of being forced to marry someone you did not love?"

I suppose her feelings had been obvious enough, and in all conscience I found it hard to blame her. Yet as I was well aware, my own loyalty was to the man who had brought me to this remote place. Sympathy I might feel for the girl before me, but it was not my place to say so.

"Harriet?"

"No," I confessed reluctantly, "I should not like it. Yet on the other hand arranged marriages take place every day all over the world and most of them seem to be happy enough. How many brides in India have even *seen* their husbands before the wedding day? Surely you're not going to tell me that they all lead miserable lives?"

We were sitting on the private roof garden outside Sabina's apartments, and the girl sat silently for a moment, watching the palace pigeons endlessly tumbling above her head. Without looking at me, she said, "The girls you speak of have never had the opportunity to find anyone for themselves. But I have."

141

"And you are not just an ordinary girl," I reminded her. "Like it or not, Sabina, you are a princess. And a princess has responsibilities."

The girl sitting opposite me made a gesture of impatience. "You sound as though my brother has been speaking to you about me."

I shook my head. "No, that's not true."

"Then I must admit I'm surprised." Sabina gave a bitter little laugh. "He's a man who is used to having his own way, and he's not likely to take kindly to the idea of his young sister having a mind of her own."

"I give you my word that I'm on your side," I told her. "But, my dear, you must be realistic. If the khan insists on your marrying someone of his choice, what can you do? I suppose you could run away, but if what you tell me about your brother is true, he'll most certainly find a way to bring you back, and he seems quite capable of doing something dreadful to your Dr. Gupta."

Sabina turned toward me, her eyes huge. "I tell you this, Harriet. My brother may have a will of his own, but so have I. I'm not a fool. I know that he can prevent me from marrying Ram. But I swear I'll give myself to some peasant in the bazaar rather than take a husband I don't want." A sudden smile flickered about her lips as though she were savoring the khan's reactions to such an act. "If I did that, my dear brother would have considerable difficulty in finding *anyone* to marry me."

I said shortly, "That is foolish talk. You know that you would never do such a thing."

"Don't you be too sure." There was something of the defiance of a small child about Sabina at that moment, and yet the eyes that blazed at me held all the passion of a woman in love. I felt a twinge of apprehension, as though I had sensed something of the dangers to come. And then, all in a moment, I dismissed my fears. The day was too lovely a one for care. As soon as our halfhearted lesson was at an end, Sabina made some excuse and slipped away, and for once I was not sorry to see her go. Usually her gaiety

142

and quicksilver mind delighted me, but on this occasion I allowed a selfish impulse to get the better of me. There had been little enough reason for me to feel lighthearted myself during the past few months, and with the newfound knowledge of spring in my heart I was reluctant to stifle it with the troubles of a lovesick girl, well though I might like her.

I do not remember exactly how I spent the next few hours, for I was in no mood for any very serious occupation. I remember reading for a little while and later wandering idly about the palace grounds. I stared down at the empty tiger pit, where it was said two snow leopards had been kept in the old khan's day, and for quite a long time I watched a handful of the palace officers playing a scratch game of polo on a ground that would have put most British stations to shame. They were playing in the old Manipuri manner, riding long-stirruped on tiny, shaggy ponies that looked barely strong enough to carry a man at all, let alone gallop with him. Finally the players rode off and I made my way to the elephant lines, where a diminutive mahout was trimming the nails of his vast charge with a heavy file.

"Salaam, Piri Lal." I remembered the mahout's name, because Sabina had once pointed him out to me, remarking that his name, which meant "Red Fairy," could scarcely have been less appropriate for a professional rider of elephants.

"Salaam, memsahib." The little man straightened his back with a grin, then raised his arm to the mighty beast that towered over him. "Greet the memsahib, Moti, my jewel." He added a command in the unintelligible private language in which mahouts traditionally spoke to their charges, and the elephant raised its trunk obediently and trumpeted loudly.

"Thank you, Piri Lal." I had often watched elephants working in timber forests and marveled at their intelligence, but I had never seen one either so enormous or so well cared for as this one. There must have been a time when most of the principal officers of the old khan's court had been mounted on elephants, judg-

143

ing by the row of stables that stood almost empty. Moti was apparently one of the last survivors, the ruler's personal ceremonial mount. I gave his rider a coin, and Piri Lal spun it in the air approvingly.

"With this I shall buy beer for my heart's delight. He grows old, and like many old men, he is a great drunkard."

I smiled. "He doesn't care for sugarcane?"

"His mate did, but she is gone with the others. When the great khan died, there were a score of elephants at the parade that marked his passing. The earth shook with their tread. Now those days are long past." For a moment the old man looked lost and desolate, but then a thought seemed to come to him, for he brightened and added, "Yet we shall be present at one more *tamasha* before I die. I hear talk of a marriage between our princess and a young man from one of the great houses of the South. That will be a day worth remembering."

I stared at the old man, by no means sure that I had heard aright. "You have truly heard of such a marriage?"

"The memsahib must know it is common talk within the palace."

It was, as I well knew, easy to dismiss the talk of bazaars and kitchens as groundless gossip, but I knew from my own experience that nine times out of ten it was true. I said good-bye to the mahout and his charge and walked back toward my apartments with a troubled heart. It was, I realized, a situation over which I had no control, and indeed it was none of my business whom Sabina married. Yet there had been an expression in her eyes that filled me with unease, and as dusk fell and I bathed and changed I found myself unable to recapture the feeling of lightheartedness that had been mine earlier in the day. In an effort to set my mind on other things I walked to the edge of the palace gardens and looked down through the pierced marble of the wall down to the city that lay below.

The steady babble of sound that drifted up from the already crowded streets confirmed that the Holi festival was gathering momentum. During the day little would have been happening apart from the rather simple jokes that would be played on the gullible. But now, judging from the raucous chanting from some of the side streets, the toddy shops were doing good business and already a good deal of red powder and colored water were being thrown around, leaving bright splashes of color on the whitewash of buildings and the clothes of the revelers. As far as I could see, it was still harmless fun, but I could guess that in only a little while the fun would take a turn that would scandalize any watcher who was not prepared for it.

I turned away and walked slowly toward the shallow flight of steps that led to the terrace in front of my room, and then suddenly something white in the gathering shadows caught my eye. I glanced toward it and saw at once that it was someone dressed in the all-enveloping tentlike boorkah worn by women who lived their lives in purdah. Indoors, behind the "curtain," they would be seen only by members of their family and the occasional privileged woman friend. If they went out at all, it could be only in this fashion, totally covered, with no more than an embroidered slit before the eyes. The grotesque figure hesitated for an instant as I approached and then hurried on its way, and I smiled to myself, wondering which of the palace servants it was who was already on her way to take part in the coming orgy. Perhaps, I thought, that was one of the reasons Holi was so popular. However ill favored the woman beneath that boorkah might be for the rest of the year, she would find no shortage of partners tonight.

I went into my bedroom to fetch my gloves and found that for some reason the memory of the boorkah-clad woman persisted. I had seen nothing of her features, not even a glimpse of her eyes, and yet there had been something disconcertingly familiar about her. What had it been? Some trick of movement perhaps? I did not know, yet suddenly I caught my breath because in that instant I realized beyond any shadow of doubt that the woman beneath those concealing robes had been Sabina.

"Sabina!" I actually spoke her name aloud and turned toward the spot where I had last seen her, only to realize at once that any such action was useless, for the ghostlike figure had long vanished into the shadows leading to the town. For a moment I stood very still as I recalled Sabina's words to me such a short time before. *I swear I'll give myself to some peasant in the bazaar rather than take a husband I don't want. . . .*

At the time, I thought numbly, I'd taken those words as no more than bravado, but now I was not so sure. If the elephant driver had been telling me the truth, it was quite possible that the news of the planned marriage had just reached Sabina and in a moment of frustration and despair she had decided to carry out her threat.

I cannot ever remember feeling quite as helpless as I did in those few fleeting seconds while I wondered in vain what to do. Then all at once it came to me that Sabina herself was not purdah-nashin and therefore had never had need of a boorkah. In that case someone must have obtained the garment for her, and my mind went at once to the girl's personal maid, a good-looking young woman named Parvati, who I could guess would be prepared to assist her mistress in any kind of wild escapade.

Sabina's rooms were close to mine, but there was a mild stir of surprise among the attendants when I hurried in without ceremony and sought out Parvati, who was innocently engaged in folding a pile of clothes.

"Parvati," I said crisply, "where is your mistress?"

The girl met my eyes calmly enough. "I do not know, memsahib."

"You must know if the princess is within the palace or not."

Parvati shook her head. "No, memsahib. I do not know."

I supposed that it was hard to blame her for being loyal. She had probably served Sabina since she was a child and for all I knew her family had been part of the household since the days of the old khan. There was no reason whatever why Parvati should betray whatever secrets she might have to me, a stranger of another race, who for all she knew might care nothing for her mistress.

I said desperately, "Please listen. The princess Sabina could be in great danger. You *must* tell me what you know."

"And you *will* tell."

Neither Parvati nor I had heard Sabina's mother come into the room, but suddenly she was there. I turned toward her but the begum ignored me. She was a tiny woman, but as she walked past me I was aware that she dominated both Parvati and me because there was something in her face that held all the authority not only of her adopted family but of her own people for not tens but hundreds of years. She could, I realized, so easily have been one of those indefatigable Rajput women who in the days of the northern invasions had lined the walls of Chitor and Amber to cheer their men to victory or perish with them in the great fires made ready in the labyrinths deep beneath the ground. She was everything that centuries of warrior women could make her, and her voice cut like a knife through the silence of the room.

Parvati's eyes widened as she saw her and the honey-colored face paled. She whispered, "Begun-ji . . ."

The old woman looked at me. "Why are you so sure that my daughter has left the palace?"

"I am not sure. But I saw a woman leaving for the bazaar in a boorkah and there was something about the way she walked that . . ." I paused, for suddenly I knew with absolute certainty why when I had seen that cloaked figure Sabina had come into my mind.

"Well?"

I said slowly, "I remember now. The princess was limping this morning because she had sprained her ankle. The woman in the boorkah was walking in the same way."

"You have heard what the memsahib has said." The

147

begum turned back to Parvati. "You gave your mistress a boorkah?"

Speechless, the girl nodded.

"And where has she gone?"

For a moment I found myself wondering whether the girl shared my own apprehension as to Sabina's intentions but then dismissed the idea, for such a confidence would have been unthinkable. And I had to confess to myself that it was not a matter that I had any great desire to broach to Sabina's mother. As it was, I could see a cold fury beginning to burn in the old woman's eyes that I had no wish to see directed at me. Indeed the naked fear in the face of the wretched ayah was sufficient to fill me with a sick sense of foreboding.

In a shaking voice the girl whispered, "Begum-ji, my mistress did not tell me where she planned to go."

"You lie." The frail old woman went up to the girl and for a moment I thought that she would strike her across the face. But instead she said almost conversationally, "You graceless bitch, are you presuming to dictate to me on a matter concerning my own daughter? *My* mother would have had your breasts hacked off and thrown to the dogs for less. She'd have staked you out with six inches of young bamboo up your *yoni* and left you there till it grew out of your head. She . . ." The begum stopped, as though to control herself. Then she went on softly. "Do not think that things are managed very differently nowadays. This is not British India, with a sahib at every crossroad to say what may and may not be done. Here, in this palace, my word still has some little meaning, and I swear by all the gods that if you do not tell me where my daughter has gone, no man shall look on you again except with horror."

Sick with revulsion, I said, "Begum, you cannot—"

"I cannot do what?" The old woman laughed harshly. "Little English miss, I can do whatever I wish within these four walls, and neither you nor your queen over the seas can do anything to stop me. If this matter

148

is too strong for your delicate stomach, then go from here. Meanwhile . . ."

It was no moment to point out that as an American I had no queen, for Sabina's maid was on her knees, her hands making the small, fluttering movements against the begum's feet in the traditional gesture of supplication.

"All, all I know is that the lady Sabina ordered me first to fetch for her a boorkah of the sort that common people wear. And also she said that I was to leave word with Kuda Baksh, the horse trader, that a mount was to be kept saddled and in readiness from six o'clock."

"Ready to go where?"

"I swear I do not know," the girl whimpered. "But it is possible that Kuda Baksh does."

The begum pushed Parvati aside with a tiny slippered foot. "Enough. Go. And speak to no one of this if you wish to keep your tongue in your head."

Gray-faced, the girl fled, and the old woman turned to me. Strangely, she no longer seemed so very terrible, only weary and very vulnerable. With something akin to despair, she said, "You have been her friend. What is it that the child has done?"

"It is possible," I suggested, "that she has heard the rumors of a marriage that has been arranged for her."

The begum narrowed her eyes. "And where did you hear such a rumor?"

"Since you ask," I said, "it was from a mahout in the elephant lines."

"And you are in the habit of gleaning your information from such sources?

"No," I told her quietly, "I am not. The story was spoken of as something that was common knowledge."

"Common knowledge!" Sabina's mother spat out the words contemptuously. "Common knowledge among the servants, I suppose."

"Probably," I agreed. "But even bazaar rumors have to start from somewhere. If Sabina heard it—or, even worse, if she knew for a fact that a marriage was being contemplated . . ."

The begum stared at me with eyes of stone. "If she did know, what would she do?"

I drew a deep breath. "Frankly," I said, "she might do anything. You are her mother. You must know that she wishes, very deeply, to marry someone of her own choice. Someone who is not acceptable to the khan."

"Marriage," the begum informed me coldly, "is too important a matter to be left to children."

"And an Indian woman understands this and accepts it because this is the manner in which she has been brought up. But Sabina thinks like a European. She *expects* to marry the man of her own choice." I sought desperately for some way of impressing on this implacable old woman the world of difference that existed between her daughter and herself. "Please," I said, "you must tell me. Has Sabina been told that a marriage is being arranged for her?"

For a moment there was silence, and then the begum nodded her head. "Yes. Her brother thinks he has found a suitable husband for her in the person of Prince Amrat Khan, whose blood is as good as any in the Punjab."

"And she has been told this?"

"Yes. This afternoon."

Below us, in the unseen city, someone was beating a drum. Its complex rhythm rose and fell with a kind of maddening insistence that precluded everything else. So it was very much as I had feared. Up till now it had been bad enough for Sabina to know that she was not allowed to marry the man of her choice. The additional news that she was also expected to take another man as a husband could only have a cataclysmic effect on a girl who valued her independence above all else.

"Whatever you know," the begum was saying, "you must tell me. This is no time for misguided loyalties."

She was right, of course. It was glaringly apparent that the begum and I would have to work together if Sabina was to be saved from the consequences of her folly. I said slowly, "All I know is that Sabina said that she would go out and give herself to the first man she met rather than marry someone she didn't love. When

150

I saw her going out just now in a boorkah, I thought that was what she had in mind. Fortunately it seems that I was wrong."

The begum smiled thinly. "As you say, fortunately. I know what happens on the night of Holi is considered to be sanctified among some classes, but I do not think that my stepson would be convinced by such an argument."

"No," I agreed, "I don't think he would."

"But clearly as she has made arrangements for a horse, she has no intention of playing the whore in our own bazaar." The old woman eyed me narrowly. "Do you know where she would be most likely to go?"

I shook my head. "Frankly," I said, "I have no idea. But it would seem that wherever it is, it will be with Ram Gupta. The boorkah would be no more than a disguise to conceal her while she passed through the bazaar. It's possible that . . ." I hesitated, reluctant to put my guess into words.

The begum finished the sentence for me. "You were about to say that it is possible the two are running away together."

"It's possible," I agreed. "But I don't really think it all that likely. Ram Gupta is an intelligent, sensible man. He must know that he would stand little chance of crossing the border. Even with a night's start the khan's men would catch him long before he could reach it. And besides . . ."

"Yes?"

"I think Dr. Gupta would be reluctant to take such a step in any case. He is an orthodox young man of good family, and the idea of running away with the woman he wishes to marry would be against everything he believes in. Sabina might be willing to go with him, because she thinks more like a European than an Indian. But whether Dr. Gupta would agree is another matter." The more I thought about it, the more likely that seemed to be true. On the other hand, there was another possibility that could not be ignored. I said slowly, "Princess Sabina may think that if she stays with this man all night, she . . ." I hesitated because I

151

had no idea how one said "she would be compromised" in Hindi. Instead I ended rather lamely, "She would be shamed if she did not marry him."

The begum made a gesture of impatience. "The girl must be mad to think that she could command her brother in such a way. I do not know what he would do to her, but I can imagine what would befall the man." She raised her dark eyes to mine. "I could send out horsemen to scour the countryside, but I have no great wish to let this matter be known among the servants. Yet someone must bring her back, and I think, dear miss, that it must needs be you."

I suppose I had known from the start that the task would be mine, although at that moment I had very little idea as to how I should go about it. I managed to smile with confidence that I did not feel. "I'll do my best. But she could be anywhere."

"You had best take money with you. It opens the door to most secrets."

I suppose that had I been faced with such a task on my own, I should have immediately dismissed it as being beyond anything I could reasonably be expected to do. I had only the hours of darkness before me and no idea where to commence my search. Yet such was the personality of the old begum that I had already changed into a riding skirt and was on my way to the stables before I realized the magnitude of the task before me. To take my own horse would be an act of madness, for I knew that the khan made a practice of visiting his stables every evening and although he would not normally query the absence of my horse, the fact that I had left the palace during the night of Holi was bound to lead to inquiries. Clearly that was why Sabina had hired a mount from the city and why it was only prudent for me to do the same. Prudent it may have been, yet I found myself hesitating as I turned away from the stables and headed instead for the north gate. I had been amused by my maid's insistence that I avoid the streets on the night of Holi. Now I had to admit that I did not relish the prospect, and I felt more than a twinge of embarrassment at the surprised looks that were directed at me by the two uniformed guards. They were Muhammadans, and I understood well enough that they would never have allowed their own womenfolk to expose themselves to what they considered a shameless and pagan festival. Well, I thought, now they had the evidence of their own eyes to confirm the widely held view that white women, with their uncovered faces and bold ways, were no better than they should be. For a moment I wondered if they would make some attempt to dissuade me from leaving the palace, but with instinctive courtesy they turned their eyes away and did their best to pretend that they hadn't seen me. So with my face flushed with an embarrassment I had not expected to feel, I passed through the gate, to be swallowed almost immediately by the raucous turmoil of the streets beyond.

Familiar though I was with the Holi festival, I had usually witnessed it only from a distance and then in the more sophisticated communities where the more explicit parts of the rites had been forbidden by the priests, who had no wish to have their religion judged unfavorably because of them. But I had barely entered the street before it became apparent that here in Khudistan the old ways still held good. The laughter and shouting that had been no more than rough and good-humored early in the day was now thickened with drink, and through a haze of red powder I glimpsed couples clutching at each other shamelessly in shadowed alleys while others, still with some sense of decency, hurried away urgently together in search of a little privacy. In the center of a cheering throng a man stained blood-red with dye capered with what at first I took to be some kind of flagpole, only to discover as I drew nearer that he was wearing strapped to his loins a grotesquely large male organ, carved from wood.

Someone cried out in a drunken voice, "Well done, memsahib! Welcome to our Holi!" And there was a shout of approving laughter as, with burning cheeks, I pushed my way through the throng. I was not frightened because, drunk or not, the men knew that I was no part of their festival and that whatever color

153

her skin, it was almost unheard of for a woman to be assaulted in India. Nevertheless I was conscious of a cold fury directed at Sabina for having been the cause of such an outrageous situation. However drunk he might be, there was not a man in the bazaar who would not remember in the morning that he had seen the English governess from the palace walking unveiled amid sights of wild debauchery. Normally I was not overconcerned as to what other people thought of me, but I could not pretend that I relished the prospect of being laughed at behind my back for as long as I remained in Khudistan.

In the circumstances it was fortunate that I did not have to ask the way to Kuda Baksh's stables. Situated as they were within a rough mud-wall enclosure just outside the main gate, they were a landmark as well as a source of local gossip.

Most of the stories about the Pathan horse trader I was prepared to dismiss as an understandable distrust of strangers, and Kuda Baksh was as foreign to the valley as myself, so I was conscious of a certain curiosity as I left the hubbub of the Holi revelers behind me and skirted the wall of the horse dealer's *serai*. The single nail-studded door creaked open under my hand, and in the moonlight I could make out the shadowy outlines of tethered horses and the glow of the stable boys' fire. There was also a light in the small building that served Kuda Baksh both as home and office, and as I made my way toward it I noticed a bay standing close by the door, his reins held by a ragged-looking boy. Even in the poor light the bay struck me as familiar, and I realized with a start of surprise that it belonged to Edward.

The boy scrambled to his feet as I approached and the big horse raised its head restlessly.

"My compliments to Kuda Baksh," I said. "Tell him I wish to have a word with him."

The boy held out the reins wordlessly to me and pushed open the door. Over his shoulder the interior of the room sprang up vividly in the light of its single oil lamp. I glimpsed a jumble of harnesses on the walls, a simple table, with Edward seated opposite the thick, heavy figure of the horse dealer and a bottle and two glasses between them. The boy said something to his master and the two men jumped to their feet with an alacrity that I dismissed as being due to nothing more than surprise. I tossed the reins back to the stable boy and went into the room without further introduction, narrowing my eyes a little at the light.

"*Stara ma shai, memsahib.*" Kuda Baksh greeted me with the formality of the frontier. "May you never be tired." He looked much like any other middle-aged Pathan I had ever met. Dark, heavy-lidded eyes, hooked nose, a straggling mustache meeting a graying beard.

It was on the tip of my tongue to say "May you never be poor" in return, but at the last moment something stopped me. Few white women spoke Pashto because there were no family stations in India's Far North. I could not have spoken it myself had it not been for the fact that as a child I had been cared for by an Afghan woman who, for some long-forgotten reason, had drifted south and found employment as an ayah in the cantonments of the British. Now, probably for no better reason than that I disliked Kuda Baksh on sight, I found myself keeping my knowledge of his language to myself. So instead I returned his greeting in conventional Hindi, then smiled at Edward, who was regarding me with not-unexpected disapproval.

"Good evening, Edward. I had not expected to find you here."

"I could say as much of you." Edward's tone did nothing to conceal his disapproval. "Damn it, Harriet, what are you doing here? And tonight of all nights! Surely you've been in this country long enough to know to keep out of sight during Holi?"

Kuda Baksh's eyes flickered between the two of us for a moment before he said in English, "Do not be too hasty, sahib. It is possible that there is an emergency."

It came to me that the horse dealer understood the reason for my presence well enough, and so I addressed him directly. "I believe you have been asked for a horse this evening. By a woman."

155

"It is possible."

"Where was she going?"

"Memsahib, that was not my affair."

Edward frowned. "I don't understand. What woman?"

Kuda Baksh said easily, "It was before you arrived Captain sahib. And truly, I did not see the woman's face."

I took out the purse I had brought with me and held it in my hand. "Frankly," I said, "I do not care whether you saw the woman's face or not. But I will pay you fifty rupees to know where she went."

"No, memsahib. Not even for fifty rupees."

I stared into the heavily lidded eyes and acknowledged the fact that the man was speaking the truth. He would not admit he had seen Sabina for fifty or even five hundred rupees. But it was possible that what money would not accomplish for me, fear might. So I said quietly, "Listen to me, Kuda Baksh. I know that the lady Sabina had a horse from you little more than an hour ago. Either you tell me where she was going or I shall have you taken before the khan for questioning. The choice is yours, but you must make it now."

"Harriet, have you taken leave of your senses?" Edward took a step toward me, then swung around on the Pathan and said in rapid guttural Pashto, "Are you mad? Did you see the girl or not?"

In the same language Kuda Baksh said sullenly, "No, as I have said. She wore a boorkah."

"But you knew . . ."

"Aye. But she paid me a hundred rupees."

"Fool! If the khan hears of this, you'll have no hands to count them with. Now, if you know where she has gone, say so."

There was a moment's silence, then the gray-mustached Pathan turned back to me and said harshly, "So be it. The woman was riding to Sabathu, the hill village where there has been sickness lately. The young doctor has some sort of hospital close by. I know this is so because the lady Sabina said that if any followed,

I was to send them elsewhere. I swear by the Prophet that is all I know of the matter, nor do I wish to learn more."

"There is no reason why you should," I told him. "In fact it would probably be as well for you if you forgot what you know already. But in the meantime I, too, shall be wanting a horse."

"Very well." The horse dealer nodded and went out of the door and a moment later I heard him shouting an order to his men. Edward came toward me with a sudden, swift movement and took me by the arm.

"Harriet, for God's sake! Is this true? Has that little fool run off to Gupta?"

I nodded. "She's heard that her brother's arranging a marriage for her. Now I think she has some crazy idea that she can avoid it be getting herself compromised."

Edward let out a low whistle of incredulity. "The girl must be mad. She can't try holding a pistol to the head of a man like McKenzie. She's signing young Gupta's death warrant, for a start."

"I know," I agreed. "That's why I've got to get to her tonight and get her back to the palace before her brother finds out."

"Do you think she'll take any notice of you?"

"Quite honestly," I confessed, "I've no idea. But I've promised the begum that I'll do my best."

"You mean she knows about all this?" I nodded. "Well," he said, "I hope you know what you're doing, because if things go wrong, you're going to find yourself in a good deal of trouble yourself." Edward hesitated for a moment and then asked abruptly, "This place where Gupta's working. Do you know where it is?"

I shook my head. "No. I was hoping you might."

Edward gave me a reluctant grin. "You're a persuasive woman, Harriet, but as it happens, I know the place well enough. I also know that the reason Gupta has got some kind of makeshift hospital there is because Sabathu, the nearest village, is rotten with cholera. Are you still sure that you want to go?"

In truth I did not want to go. Twice in my life I had been briefly explosed to the horrors of that disease and it was not an experience I had any wish to repeat. And yet . . . I did my best to make my voice sound casual as I said, "Whether I want to or not is rather beside the point. Who else is likely to bring Sabina back if we do not?"

Edward nodded reluctantly. "I expect you're right, so we'd best be going. We've a two-hour ride ahead of us."

He led the way out of the hut and with something that probably sprang from a twinge of conscience I said, "You have time to come with me? I have already interrupted your business with Kuda Baksh. If . . ."

"We were only discussing a horse I was thinking of buying." Edward dismissed the matter abruptly. 'Naturally I shall come. It would be absurd for you to make the journey unaccompanied." He offered me his hand to mount the Kabuli mare that Kuda Baksh had led forward.

"She is one of my own," the horse trader said, looking up at me.

"Thank you. I shall see she comes to no harm."

A stable boy had brought Edward's mount and he swung himself into the saddle with easy grace. Looking down at Kuda Baksh, he said in Pashto, "See that your brother renders his accounts to me without delay. I do not like to be kept waiting."

"On my head, huzoor."

Horses, I thought. With a young man's life in danger all either of them really worried about was a deal in horses. Impatiently I said, "Edward, we have little enough time."

"This way, then." He urged his mount forward and we rode out of the serai together into the moonlight and headed for the distant hills.

10

It was just after midnight by the time Edward and I reached Sabathu. It was a tiny hamlet built in the shadow of the great pine ridge that followed the line of the hills that enclosed the valley, and had it not been for the brilliance of the moon, I do not think I should have been able to distinguish the little huddle of thatched mud huts that seemed to be more a part of the landscape than something painstakingly erected by man. No light burned in the doorways, but as we reined in our horses an aged night watchman shuffled out from behind a rock, clutching a lantern and his staff of office. He salaamed respectfully but held his ground when Edward would have ridden past him.

"Huzoor, it is forbidden to go farther."

"Indeed?" Edward raised his eyebrows. "And by whose orders?"

"The orders of the doctor sahib. There is much sickness in the village. No one is allowed farther than this point even if they bring food. Everything is left here and the women of Sabathu collect it later."

Edward turned toward me. "At least that should contain the infection."

"Perhaps," I agreed, "although a good wind would be even better." I knew little of the treatment of the dreaded cholera, but I had heard army officers relating their experiences often enough, and the majority had always had faith in the ability of a breeze to blow the miasma away. Nevertheless it was universally ac-

159

knowledged as a sensible precaution to isolate infected areas, and I had little doubt that if similar steps had been taken all over the country, India would have been far less liable to disease than it was. I addressed myself to the *chowkidhar* and asked him where the doctor could be found.

The old man made a gesture to the south. "Half a *kos* along that track. He has had built there a place for the care of the sick, to which all may go."

"And has anyone else asked for him tonight? Another woman?"

"Surely. But half an hour ago. One who rode a gray horse and who carried a veil before her face."

Edward and I exchanged glances. It was unlikely that Sabina would have attempted to ride this far in her tentlike boorkah, but it was reasonable to suppose that she would have at least have held a scarf in front of her face to conceal her identity from someone like the night watchman.

"She must have ridden hard," Edward observed. "I'd hoped we might have caught up with her before she got this far."

We turned our horses and followed the track that had been pointed out to us. Half a *kos* was a little more than a mile, but I had little confidence in our informant's ability to measure distance in surroundings where a journey was more usually measured by the time taken to complete it. But as it turned out, I had misjudged him, for within a quarter of an hour we came upon what was clearly a hastily erected shelter with unglazed windows from which lamplight glowed. There was an open-ended tent standing before the door, beside which a gray horse was tethered to a piquet post. Without waiting for more, Edward and I slid to the ground and ran to the tent.

"Sabina!"

As I had expected, she was there; she was staring at me, dressed in her usual riding breeches, her long dark hair emphasizing the pallor of her face. Ram Gupta was standing beside her, separated only by a small folding table that was littered with books and papers.

160

The young doctor was wearing much the same clothes as his companion, and I found myself noting that this was the first time I had seen him in European dress. He looked weary and distraught in the lamplight, and I formed an immediate impression that he and Sabina had been engaged in angry words at the time of our arrival.

"Harriet, what do you mean by following me here?" The dark-haired girl's eyes flashed angrily as she came toward me. "And who told you—"

I said quietly, "It so happened that I saw you leave the palace, and I could hardly help recognizing you even though you were wearing a boorkah."

"But you couldn't have known I was coming here." Sabina broke off abruptly and bit her lip as she mentally reviewed my possible informants. Then she said bitterly, "I suppose that fool of a girl told you. I'll beat—"

"It's hardly fair to blame your maid," I told her coldly. "I can't imagine any servant having the courage to keep silent when being questioned in earnest by your mother."

"You mean that she knows, too?" An expression of dismay crossed the lovely face.

"Not only your mother but Kuda Baksh and, for all I know, half the bazaar," I informed her. "I should have thought that you knew this country well enough to know that it's hard for even ordinary people to keep their goings and comings to themselves, let alone a princess." And then, while she stared at me with disbelief, "For goodness' sake, Sabina, you're not a child! Do you really imagine that a Pathan horse dealer would hand over a horse to a nameless woman in a boorkah if he didn't have a very good idea as to who she was?"

Sabina said sulkily, "I don't see why not. I paid him a hundred rupees."

Behind me, Edward gave a short laugh. "I can hardly imagine that would make much difference. That nag over there must be worth at least three times as much. Besides . . ."

161

Rebelliously the girl turned on him. "Besides what, Captain?"

Edward nodded toward her feet. "I've no doubt the old rogue helped you to mount. And I can't imagine there are many purdah-nishan women in these parts who wear Calcutta-made boots."

For a moment I thought that Sabina was about to protest further, but instead she cast an appealing look in my direction. Her voice was little more than a whisper as she asked, "Does—does my brother know?"

"No," I told her, "and what is more, he won't if you return to the palace immediately. Why else do you think I came here?"

There was a moment's silence, then she said in her normal voice, "Harriet, I know you must think badly of me but you don't understand. . . ."

I said, "I understand that you're facing the possibility of a marriage you don't want. But I assure you there's nothing to be gained by compromising yourself. Cannot you imagine the consequences for Dr. Gupta? Do you seriously think that you can force your brother into following your own inclinations?"

Ram Gupta said stiffly, "Mrs. Hunt, I must protest. There is no question of the princess's being compromised by me or anyone else. The matter is unthinkable."

Edward made a small exclamation of disbelief. "Don't be an ass, Gupta. Nobody is insulting the princess. Mrs. Hunt is simply doing her best to help, and if I'm not mistaken, you yourself were expressing much the same sentiment just before we arrived."

Sabina shook her head vigorously. "But you don't understand! I didn't come here to be—compromised, as you call it. At least, not in the way you mean." She broke off unhappily and I saw that suddenly she was close to tears.

Instinctively I reached out and touched her arm. "Please, Sabina—we're trying to understand. Why?"

But it was Ram Gupta who provided the answer. "Perhaps, Mrs. Hunt, I should explain." He gestured toward the primitive building in the background.

162

"There is cholera in Sabathu, and I believe it is necessary to keep those people suffering from the fever away from those who are still healthy. To burn a village where there is typhus—yes, there is, I think, good reason for that. But with cholera I am not so sure. So this time I make the local people build this shelter as a hospital, and I am treating patients with good results."

"I'm sure you are," I said. "But I still don't quite see . . ."

Ram Gupta smiled wearily. "I am, of course, the only one here with any medical knowledge. What helpers I have are sweepers from the village and perhaps some member of the patient's family if there is one who is not sick."

"You must have friends back in the city," Edward broke in. "Couldn't they help?"

The young doctor shook his head. "Unfortunately, Captain, I dare not risk letting it be known that this place even exists. You know as well as I do that if word of it reached the khan's ears, he would at once order me to burn the village down, and I am most anxious that this should be avoided. If we are to learn . . ." Gupta broke off and smiled apologetically. "Forgive me, but this is not important. What *is* important is that the lady Sabina alone has known the work I am doing. And tonight she has come saying that she wishes to help nurse the sick."

I said involuntarily, "You must be out of your mind to allow such a thing. . . ."

"On the contrary," Gupta informed me, "I have *not* allowed it. First because it is too dangerous, and second because the lady Sabina has no knowledge of nursing."

"You don't need to know much about nursing if your patients have cholera," Edward observed with distaste. "The most you can hope to do is keep the poor devils clean."

"But don't you see?" Sabina raised her head quickly. "That is the whole point. I know what it means to look after those poor souls over there. It's filthy work—so filthy that even in proper hospitals they employ untouchables to do it. And once it became known that I had done it, my brother could hawk me from one end of India to the other without finding me a presentable husband!"

I studied Sabina, and she met my eyes with a stare that was rebellious but unflinching. "You really mean that you'd do that?"

The girl smiled at me grimly. "Oh, yes, Harriet, I shall do it, that I promise you!"

It was ingenious, that much I found myself admitting. Quite apart from the determination called for, Sabina seemed to have hit upon a way of rendering herself ineligible for her proposed marriage without in any way imperiling the man she loved. It was true that Adam McKenzie would be furious with Dr. Gupta for allowing Sabina to undertake the kinds of duties she had in mind, but these were feelings he would have to keep to himself. Only the very highest castes would be revolted when they heard the news. To the ordinary people, who made up the bulk of the population, Sabina's action would be regarded as highly meritorious, indeed almost saintlike in its selflessness. Not even the khan of Khudistan would dare to go against public opinion on such a matter as that.

As though mirroring my thoughts, Edward said crisply, "I congratulate you, Princess, on a well-thought out scheme. But now I suggest you get on your horse and return with us."

Sabina looked at him coldly. "It would seem, Captain Ashworth, that you have misunderstood me. Neither Mrs. Hunt nor yourself was invited here. Go if you wish. But as far as I am concerned, I shall stay."

I must confess that at that particular moment I had no idea how best to appeal to Sabina's good sense. There was something about her that suggested no reasoned argument was likely to have much effect, and short of dragging her back to the palace, there seemed no alternative. But, to my relief, Dr. Ram Gupta took the matter into his own hands.

"The lady Sabina will return with you as soon as you are rested," he announced.

164

The girl swung around on him, wide-eyed. "But . . ."

"There is no 'but' about it." Quite suddenly he was no longer a young man at a loss in the presence of the girl he loved. Instead the words came crisply from a man who had important work to do and who had already wasted more time than pleased him. In the pale yellow glow of the oil lamp I saw the dark shadows beneath his eyes and realized suddenly how desperately tired he was. How long had he been without sleep? I wondered. Nevertheless his voice was steady enough as he said to Sabina, "If you really *wanted* to look after these people, I'd have been glad to make use of you. But you don't. You're just prepared to put up with them to help you get your own way with your brother, the khan. That way you are belittling both yourself *and* my patients." Just for a moment I caught a flicker of a smile about the tense mouth, a touch of tenderness. "So go back now. While you are safe."

With a touch of her old spirit Sabina said, "I am the princess of Khudistan. I take orders from no one."

Ram Gupta laughed softly. "Then if you mean to spend the rest of your life with me, you had best learn." He reached out and gave her shoulder a gentle push. "Go now. I have much work to do. My time is not my own."

I found it hard not to smile at Ram Gupta's easy assumption of superiority over the woman of his choice and indeed at Sabina's ready acceptance of it. Would it have been any different if we had not followed her? I wondered. Somehow I felt that it would have been, because Ram Gupta's asserting himself in our presence was one thing, but I suspected that doing so on his own might well have been something else again.

I said to Sabina, "We'll wait by the horses. Don't be long."

I should have liked to have spoken with Ram Gupta, but it was clear that his mind was on other things. I think, too, that Sabina had realized that this was a very different man from the one she had expected. A man who might well love her but who was at this moment fully occupied with his work. It was not, I thought, that he rejected Sabina. It was simply that as far as he was concerned, she was not there.

It was a strange ride back to the city, and a silent one, for Sabina rode ahead with clearly little desire to communicate with anyone. And I must confess that I had little to say to her. When first I had learned of her escapade, I had been angry because of its sheer irresponsibility, but I suspected that Ram Gupta's reaction to it had wrought a sobering effect. For the moment, at any rate, Sabina was no longer the willful princess taking matters into her own hands but a subdued and chastened young woman who had been made to realize for the first time that she was not necessarily the most important thing in the life of the man she loved. In truth I felt more than a twinge of sympathy for the sadly dejected figure that rode before us, and in spite of the weariness caused by a long and fruitless ride, I felt content that the night had turned out well enough. The only sobering thought was that of Ram Gupta single-handedly fighting a lonely battle for which he could expect but little thanks from anyone save the villagers for whom he was risking his life.

I said as much to Edward when the distance between the two of us and Sabina made it certain that she would not overhear, adding that I could not see how the situation would resolve itself.

Edward shrugged his shoulders. "Sooner or later he'll scrape up enough money to go to India and that's the last Khudistan will see of him. Then either his place will be taken by some incompetent local *hakim* or McKenzie will have to face the inevitable and bring in a European doctor. As there simply aren't enough of the latter to go around, we may suppose this place will have to revert to the general ignorance and superstition that existed before Gupta came along." He glanced up at the sky reflectively. "It'll be almost light before we get back. How is the girl going to manage?"

"I imagine she'll get back to the palace the same way that she left it," I said. "She still has her boorkah. There's no reason why anyone should stop her."

"And what about you?"

"Me?" The thought that I might be noticed on my return had not in fact come into my mind.

"It's not impossible," Edward pointed out. "Suppose someone told McKenzie that you'd been seen arriving home at dawn."

It was probably relief that the night's events had ended more happily than I had expected that made me discount the likelihood of further complications. At any rate, I answered lightly, "Then I fear my reputation would have to suffer. But if the princess's companion chooses to spend the night in the company of a British officer, that is surely her affair. I cannot imagine anyone would be so indiscreet as to comment on it."

Edward's eyes dwelt on me for a long, calculating moment. "And if the British officer should suggest that such a flight of fancy might perhaps become more than—a flight of fancy?"

I laughed lightly. "I think I should say that he was taking advantage of a situation that he had invented in the first place."

"Harriet . . ."

I felt a twinge of remorse. It was not, I supposed, altogether fair to make light of such a matter, and indeed at any other time it was a remark I should never have thought of making in the first place. But there had been something about the whole night that detached it from reality. Perhaps, I thought, it was the influence of the age-old festival just ended that had prompted my rash words. Nevertheless it was I who was at fault and I did what I could to make amends.

"I'm sorry, Edward," I said. "I should not have spoken as I did. Please don't read more into my words than—was intended."

There was a moment's silence, then Edward laughed. "Of course not." He turned toward me in the saddle and I saw nothing but friendliness in his smile. "I did not mean to take advantage, my dear. But you cannot blame a man for snatching at any straw—however elusive it may prove to be."

Little enough remained of our journey and what there was we accomplished in silence. Only when we drew in sight of Kuda Baksh's serai did I urge my mount up alongside Sabina's so that I might ask if she would prefer us to enter the city together.

She shook her head decisively. "Thank you, Harriet, but I think it would be best if we went in separately. Nobody will look at me—a purdah woman going home late on the night of Holi. But in company with the English miss from the palace—that might make them think again."

I could not deny that there was sense in what she said, and so I nodded agreement. "Very well, then. Leave your horse at the entrance to the serai—Edward will see it is returned. And—good luck."

Sabina made an effort to smile. "Thank you, Harriet. And I'm sorry to have caused so much trouble—to you and everyone else. Perhaps we can talk about it tomorrow. That is, if you're not too angry with me."

"My dear," I said, "I'm not in the least angry with you. I just wish that things could be happier for you, that's all."

Sabina smiled fleetingly at Edward. "Good night, Captain Ashworth. Thank you for escorting Harriet."

Edward raised a hand in salute. "Good night, Princess. My pleasure. And do your best not to draw attention to yourself now that you are so nearly home."

"*Dilli dur ast?*" Sabina laughed softly as she quoted the old proverb.

"Yes, ma'am, it certainly is a long road to Delhi," Edward agreed, unsmiling. "Many a slip, as we should say. Which is all the more reason why you should watch yourself now that you're in sight of home."

A long road indeed, I thought as I said good-bye to Edward and went through the gate into the sleeping town. The greater part of the Holi revelers had long gone to their homes or were sleeping rolled in sheets on the roadside. A privileged cow nosed inquisitively at a heap of rubbish and from somewhere in the shadows I could hear the sound of a pack of dogs quarreling over a bone. The guard at the gate, huddled with a blanket around his shoulders against the chill of the night air, looked at me with curious eyes but made no comment

168

as I passed him and went on up the street that led to the palace, picking my way through the puddles of red dye and the scattered remnants of the recent debauch.

I glanced up at the outline of the palace built into the hillside above the town and caught my breath at the fairy-tale beauty of the buildings that seemed to hover, ghostlike, against the indigo blue of the sky. At that moment it would have been hard to find anything in more marked contrast to the sordid rubble that the night's excesses had left about the town, and yet it occurred to me that in the winding little streets of Ranipur there was a robustness and an honesty that would be hard to find behind the palace's marble walls. Doubtless the dawn would see many a still-befuddled peasant stagger off to work with an aching head, but at least he lived a life uncomplicated by malice and intrigue.

I ignored the broad sweep of close-fitting granite setts that led to the royal elephant gate of the palace, guessing that the guards on duty there were more likely to be alert than their companions in the town. Instead I made my way through the deserted bazaar to where a narrow pathway wound upward to the small picket gate used mainly by the palace servants. I guessed that Sabina had probably made good her entry by the same means only minutes before, but by the time I had shut it behind me the small courtyard that separated me from the back of the stable was deserted. There was a light glowing from one of the stalls and I skirted it cautiously in case one of the grooms should still be awake. The huge, ornate bulk of the palace loomed ahead of me and I could see the door that led to my apartment invitingly near. For safety's sake I moved forward by way of a deep pool of shadow, and as I stepped out of the moonlight my foot caught against a bucket that had doubtless been left there by a careless stable boy. It fell over with a clatter that seemed to echo around the courtyard, and I shrank back against the wall with a wildly beating heart.

From what seemed almost at my side Adam McKenzie's voice said, "If you wish to return unseen at this

169

hour, Mrs. Hunt, I suggest you take better care of where you place your feet. Any slut of a kitchen maid could give you a lesson in discretion."

I spun around with a sharp intake of breath that must have added to my general air of guilt. The khan must have heard my approach and come up behind me. Now he stood studying me with eyes bereft of expression but with an awareness that I was sure missed nothing. In spite of the hour he was dressed much as he might have been for a visit to his stables during the day, with a tweed jacket over ankle-length Indian-style riding breeches. The moonlight fell on him with the intensity of limelight in a theater, and I found myself taking in such details as the fact that instead of ankle boots he was wearing native slippers of soft leather decorated with threads of gold.

"Perhaps," Adam McKenzie said after a silence that seemed to have lasted an age, "I might be permitted to ask where you have been?"

I was so startled at his sudden appearance that my mind seemed unable to function, confused as ever by the strange magnetism of the man. Then, like a fool, I said the first thing that came into my head.

"I went down into the city to see the Holi festival." And then, with what show of indignation I could muster, "I hardly imagined that it was necessary for me to have permission to do that?"

"No. Not in the least necessary, although I should have thought that you had been in this country long enough to know to avoid that particular celebration." He took me suddenly by the arm and led me out into the moonlight, where he glanced down searchingly at my clothes. "At least I must congratulate you on your capacity to touch pitch without being defiled. Do you really expect me to believe that you have spent some hours in the bazaar without being splashed by a single drop of dye or smudge of powder?"

Feeling absurdly like a naughty schoolgirl caught out in some escapade, I looked down guiltily at myself. "I . . ."

"Please, Mrs. Hunt, don't embarrass yourself further. Had I not been up and about with a sick horse, I should have known nothing of this. As it is, I have already detained you too long. Good night."

I suppose it must have been the lightly veiled scorn in his voice that made my cheeks burn. I opened my mouth to form some kind of protest, I know not what, but before I could say a word, he had turned away and walked back around the corner of the stables. For a moment I hesitated, half wondering whether or not to follow him. But I stopped myself in time. What was there I could say? Clearly he had not believed my clumsy lie, but at least in dismissing it for what it was worth, he had refrained from probing further. Better by far that I leave matters as they were.

I went to my room and took off my dusty riding habit, grateful for the forethought that had led me to dismiss Suva for the night. But before preparing for bed, I hesitated, then pulled a robe about my shoulders. I had seen no sign of Sabina once inside the palace grounds, and certainly had her arrival been detected by her brother, he would hardly have concealed the fact. Nevertheless I was reluctant to go to bed without reassuring myself that all was well with the girl.

The long marble-flagged corridors were oddly quiet as I made my way to Sabina's suite within the ancient zenana. I was not surprised to find that Parvati's place had been taken by a much older woman, who was slipping silently out of the bedroom as I approached.

I said formally, "My greetings to the princess."

"But she is sleeping."

My face must have expressed some disbelief, for without further comment the woman pushed open the door again and stood aside. In the shaft of light that fell in the darkened room I could see Sabina's face against the silken pillows of her gilded bed. Ivory white against the dark hair, it was the face of an exhausted child and I realized that she must have thrown herself down immediately on her return and fallen asleep within the instant. For a moment I found myself wondering if perhaps her sleep was feigned, but there was something about her total abandonment that I very much doubted could be counterfeit.

The ayah looked at me curiously. "It is a matter of importance? You wish me to wake her?"

I smiled and shook my head. "No. It is a small matter that can wait until morning."

With a sense of relief I turned and retraced my steps, consoling myself with the thought that whatever else had gone wrong, at least Sabina's folly had remained undetected. But my relief was short-lived. Scarcely had I regained my own apartment when there came a sharp rap on my sitting-room door. For a moment I thought that perhaps Suva had heard of my return and had come to see if there was anything I might need, but as I opened the door it was to find myself face to face with the khan.

Without preamble he said curtly, "I find that there is something that still needs settling between us."

"Is it so vital that we have to discuss it tonight?" Rather to my surprise, my voice sounded steady enough, but there was something in his eyes that held me and would not let me go. Not for the first time I found myself wondering what strange quality this man had that he could impress his personality so strongly upon those around him.

"Yes, Mrs. Hunt. I think it is." Adam McKenzie's voice was pitched low but nevertheless it cut like a whiplash. "Obviously you lied to me about your visit to the town this evening. Quite apart from the fact that it was highly unlikely that you would wish to study Holi at close quarters, you could hardly expect me to believe that you would make such an expedition while dressed for riding."

He was right, of course. I cursed myself for my oversight, even though I could not imagine what else I could have said at the time. Unwilling to acknowledge my defeat, I said defiantly, "You have questioned me once about this already. . . ."

But the khan ignored me and went on remorselessly. "So you were, in fact, out riding." It was not a question but a statement.

172

"Yes."

"Without a horse?"

He had been in the stables himself. Obviously he had had ample opportunity to note whether or not I had brought a mount back. I remained silent because there was nothing to say.

"Exactly. And furthermore I am informed by the guard that you left both your mount and the company of Captain Ashworth at Kuda Baksh's serai."

My first reaction to his words was relief that the sleepy guard had apparently taken no notice at all of Sabina's earlier arrival and had noticed only Edward and me. But almost at the same time, I was conscious of a sudden wave of anger flooding over me. The fact that this man should question me like one of his servants was bad enough, but the thought of his questioning his guards about my coming and going was unsupportable.

I said coldly, "Your spy's report is perfectly correct. I was escorted back to the town by Captain Ashworth."

For the first time a look of bewilderment showed in the khan's eyes as he said, "But if you wanted to go out riding with Ashworth, why the devil didn't you take your own horse?"

He was so near to discovering Sabina's secret that I might well have answered as I did to put him off the scent, but in truth it was blind anger that spoke for me. I said harshly, "I hired a horse for the sake of discretion. Unfortunately it did not occur to me that I should have to submit to a boorish cross examination on my return!"

Adam McKenzie's face went suddenly white. "Damn it, madam, are you telling me that it was just so you could spend the night with Captain Ashworth?"

Well, I thought, at least I had warned Edward of the explanation I might have to give, even though it had been half in jest.

Adam McKenzie's voice was softer and even more dangerous than it had been before, and he almost whispered, "Answer me, madam!"

I said bitterly, "I should not have thought there was any need. Your powers of detection are flawless."

The khan drew a deep breath and angry though I was, I was frightened by the look in his eyes.

"Thank you. I am obliged to you for your frankness." For a long moment he stared into my eyes. Then he turned abruptly and walked out swiftly into the growing dawn.

11

I did not go to bed at all that night. The eastern sky was already growing pale by the time the khan left, but even with a whole night before me I doubt if I would have slept. I was filled with anger, it is true, but much of it was directed at myself. It had been a sordid, shabby episode and one that I wished I had been able to resolve with more dignity. Yet I found comfort in the thought that at least I had been successful in saving Sabina from the consequences of her own folly. That, at least, had been worthwhile.

I sat in a cane chair facing my window and watched the day break while my thoughts roamed over the happenings of the night. I recalled Edward with gratitude and at the same time found myself wondering what had really taken him to Kuda Baksh's establishment at that late hour. Whatever the reason, I now felt reasonably sure that it had nothing to do with a horse. That explanation had come, I felt, too readily to Edward's tongue. On the other hand, there were probably many aspects of his work about which I knew nothing and about which he would be reluctant to tell me. I had met sufficient of my father's friends to know that there were many strange tasks carried out in the remoter parts of India that were not talked about. Men came and went along the northern frontiers, and the information they brought back was, I had little doubt, harvested in many strange fields. The Pathan's presence was likely enough, because he came of a people who could

175

be found in the most unlikely places, bartering horses or setting up strange little banking enterprises that seemed primitive in the extreme yet were, had I been informed aright, surprisingly substantial even when judged against the infinitely better-known names of the West. Kuda Baksh, for all I knew, was a part of some tangled, semiofficial web, and I would serve Edward best by not querying that particular friendship too closely.

It was curiously easy to let one's thoughts wander at such a time, and I think it likely that I dozed now and then, for it was with a feeling of surprise that I found it was eight o'clock and Suva was by my side offering me an early morning cup of tea and doing her best to appear unconcerned at the fact that her mistress's bed had not been slept in.

I bathed and put on a dress of sprigged muslin, feeling relieved as I brushed my hair that the face that looked back at me from the dressing table's mirror showed no apparent signs of lack of sleep.

Her eyes on my dress, Suva said, "Memsahib is not riding this morning?"

I could well have said that memsahib had ridden all she wished during the last twelve hours, but I managed to smile and shook my head. On most mornings I rode early and on such occasions joined the khan and Sabina for the customary ten-o'clock breakfast that started the Indian day. But this morning I had no wish to make polite conversation with the khan over kidneys and bacon and *kedjeree*. Nor did it seem at all likely that Sabina would be there.

"No riding this morning," I said. "I'll have breakfast in the next room. Just tea and toast."

I took my breakfast in a leisurely fashion, consciously whiling away the time until the little ormolu clock above the fireplace chimed nine. In the circumstances it did not seem likely that Sabina would be in the study room on time, if indeed she arrived at all, but I made my way there just the same to find her awaiting me. Unexpectedly there were dark circles beneath her eyes, although I could vouch for the fact that she had enjoyed at least some sleep. She jumped up as I entered and came toward me.

"Harriet—I'm so sorry. I should have waited for you last night and instead . . ."

"And instead you went to sleep." I smiled. "I know because I paid you a visit."

"Now you make me feel even guiltier. So you had no trouble?"

For a moment I considered keeping what had transpired to myself but realized almost at once that it would certainly come out sooner or later. So I said as casually as possible, "As a matter of fact, I met your brother."

"At *that* hour of the morning?"

I said wryly, "Apparently he'd been up with a sick horse."

"Harriet, tell me! What happened?"

"I gave a rather stupid explanation, which, not surprisingly, he didn't believe." Then, seeing the expression on her face, "But you don't have to worry. Your name wasn't even mentioned."

Sabina reached forward and gripped my arm. "But, Harriet, I have to worry! I can't have Adam thinking—well, wrong things about you just so that he won't know what a fool I've been."

"And as far as I'm concerned," I told her firmly, "I have not the least intention of wasting all that effort last night. *You* got back without being seen and that's all that matters, and as far as the rest is concerned, I must confess I have grown rather tired of the whole subject." I sat down at the table and picked up a book, saying briskly, "It is our morning for French conversation, I believe."

Sabina sat down in front of me and regarded me with eyes suddenly misty with tears. She said in a small voice, *"Chère Harriet, vous êtes bien aimable. Vous avez fait une grande faveur."*

"Vous m'avez fait," I corrected her automatically. And then I smiled in spite of myself, realizing as I did so how truly fond of this wayward young woman I had become and warmed in the knowledge that at certain

177

times, at least, it was an affection that was returned. We were still working congenially together when a servant came in and said that the khan sahib requested my presence immediately.

Sabina looked at me with wide, apprehensive eyes. "Why do you think he wants to see you?"

"I haven't the faintest idea." I tried to make my voice sound casual but it was true that at that moment I felt a twinge of something that reminded me of similar occasions in the distant past when I had received a message that the headmistress wished to see me. And there was no reason, I told myself, to consider this summons to be any more important. Less, in fact.

Sabina bit her lip. "Do you think I should come with you?"

"Of course not!" I told her definitely. "It's sweet of you and I'm very grateful, but the less you have to do with your brother at the moment, the better. And besides, it's quite possible that he wants to see me about something that's got nothing to do with last night." Then I added, "And if you'll take my advice, it's high time you stopped being so scared of your brother. You're not a child anymore; you're a young woman with your own life ahead of you. The khan may lose his temper but there's nothing he can actually *do* to you."

Sabina smiled bitterly. "If you think that, Harriet, then I'm afraid you've a lot to learn, too."

It was probably because I had a very real desire to hang back that I forced myself to walk briskly across the courtyard to Adam McKenzie's office. Apparently I was expected, for the uniformed lancer at the heavy door swung it open unasked on my arrival. The khan, still dressed as he had been when last I saw him, was sitting at his great desk with a mass of papers before him. Even seated there was a kind of pantherish grace about him, but it was on me that his eyes fixed themselves as I entered, and there was an expression of smoldering hostility in them that made my heart sink. Why was it that he had this effect on me? I wondered resentfully.

178

"Please sit down, Mrs. Hunt."

"Thank you." I took the chair nearest to my side of the desk and composed myself in it with what I hoped was an air of assurance. "You wished to see me?"

"It seemed only fair to tell you that I have just returned from a visit to your friend Captain Ashworth."

"Indeed?" To conceal my dismay at the news was one thing, to hide my surprise quite another. I pictured the road to Edward's home in my mind and realized as I did so that it must have required an urgent feat of horsemanship on the part of the man before me to have completed the journey there and back since dawn. I said quietly, "And to what purpose, may I ask?"

"I should have thought that would have been obvious. As my sister's companion you are under my care and protection. I have heard from your own lips the news that Captain Ashworth has willfully compromised you, and so I visited him this morning to make it clear that I expected him to take the only honorable course open to him."

I stared at the man before me, scarcely able to believe my ears. "Honorable course? You mean *marry* me?"

Adam McKenzie said harshly, "Naturally. Does it strike you as so very strange in the circumstances?"

"You must be mad!" I burst out. "Hasn't it occurred to you that the fact that I happened to spend the night in his company doesn't necessarily mean that I was occupying his bed?"

"No?" The khan raised his eyebrows. "But you must admit that it was you yourself, madam, who made it very clear to me that you had been, as you so elegantly put it, 'occupying his bed.' You charged me with a certain lack of discretion regarding the incident, did you not?"

I felt the color rush into my cheeks. "Yes," I admitted, "but . . ."

Adam McKenzie ignored me. "I fear you lack a worthy champion in Captain Ashworth, Mrs. Hunt. He even refused me satisfaction when I called him out."

179

"You called him out?" I stared at the khan in disbelief. "You mean you challenged Edward to a duel?"

"Of course."

"But why?"

Adam McKenzie smiled suddenly, his teeth showing white against the sun-darkened skin of his face, and I was reminded sharply of a tiger. He said gently, "Surely, my dear, that is obvious? You are in effect my ward. He has dishonored you, yet he seemed unable to see the immediate necessity for marrrying you. So quite naturally we had to fight."

I drew a deep breath, forcing my voice to remain steady. "And did you?"

"I have already said he refused. I gave him the choice of sword or pistol, but he seemed to have little enthusiasm for either."

Quite suddenly I realized that the man was playing with me, much as a cat plays with a wounded bird. Whether or not his account of the challenge was true I had no means of telling, but some instinct made it clear to me that this was by no means the point of the story. There was more to come and so that it would have its maximum effect Adam McKenzie wanted it to come to me as a surprise.

"So what did you do, Khan sahib?" I inquired. "Shoot him down like a dog?"

"I assure you I would have taken very little prompting," Adam McKenzie informed me. "But as it happened, your gallant captain could hardly wait to explain to me that there had been a terrible mistake. That far from spending the night enjoying your favors, the two of you spent it aiding my sister in her folly."

So he knew, I thought. Perhaps I should have guessed. I said coldly, "It would be more accurate to say that we spent the night extricating her from it." I wondered what pressure this man had really brought to bear on Edward in order to wring the truth from him. I could not find it in my heart to believe that the admission had come willingly, and I could only pray that nothing too terrible would befall Ram Gupta now that it was known Sabina had gone to him.

"Please," I said, "you must believe me when I tell you that Dr. Gupta knew nothing of this. The princess's visit came as a complete surprise."

The khan stood up abruptly, towering over me. "Believe you? Why should I believe you?" His voice was harsh now and trembling with anger. "You have told me nothing but lies since the beginning of this business. You were well aware that I had forbidden my sister to see this man again, yet you were prepared to go to any lengths to help her to deceive me. It was I who employed you as my sister's companion and tutor because I thought your influence would be a good one. Now I find that the two of you have formed an alliance against me—that instead of being a steadying influence—"

"Your accusations are unjust," I broke in hotly. "Your sister has never to my knowledge done anything she has reason to be ashamed of. But if you insist on treating her as though we were living in the Middle Ages, you must expect a girl of spirit to rebel. The princess was quite prepared to obey your order not to see Dr. Gupta, unreasonable though it was. But when she learned that she was to be forced into a loveless marriage—"

"Be quiet, madam!" The khan's fist crashed down on his desk. "Get back to your rooms and stay there! If you attempt to leave them, I shall have you locked in and a guard put on the door."

I stared at him in disbelief. "Am I to be imprisoned?" I demanded. "Do you seriously intend to punish me by—by confining me to barracks, like one of your soldiers?"

"No, madam, I do not," Adam McKenzie told me savagely. "I propose keeping you under my eye until I decide what to do with you. Probably my best course would be to send you back where you came from, if I can spare someone to escort you. My chief regret is that you ever found your way here in the first place."

I found myself staring into his eyes. There had been a time, I remembered, when I had felt that there was much to be learned about this man and I had told myself that one day I might even understand the forces that drove him. But now, as our glances locked, I found myself faced with a cold hostility that was far more chilling than anger. I knew I should have resented it, yet for some inexplicable reason I found that I did not.

With what dignity I could muster I stood up and went back to my rooms, suddenly sick with apprehension as I realized just how precarious my situation had become. As far as Sabina was concerned, I was not particularly worried, for angry though her brother might be, the fact remained that she *had* returned. Moreover, he could hardly ignore the fact that Ram Gupta had had no part in the escapade and actually refused to let Sabina stay. But what filled me with very real dread was the thought that Adam McKenzie might well carry out his threat and send me back to India.

The day that followed seemed endless and was unbroken by work, for my inquiries regarding Sabina produced only the reply that she was not available. My meals were brought to my room and I had only reading to help me pass the time. Under normal circumstances I should have been happy enough with what few books I had borrowed, but now I found it almost impossible to concentrate on anything other than my predicament. It was almost a relief when, shortly after night had fallen, Suva came to me, wide-eyed and obviously seething with suppressed excitement.

"Memsahib, a man has come."

There was an air of conspiracy about the girl, an unnatural lowering of her voice, that made the very ordinary words significant. I looked at her usually guileless hill woman's face, still attaching little importance to what she had said. I was in no mood for servants' gossip, and so I asked with some irritation, "A man? What kind of man?"

"A black man, memsahib."

"Are you sure?" I knew that as far as Suva was concerned, a black man was not necessarily black, it simply meant that he was not white and, very probably, from beyond the borders of her own land. Had he been a compatriot, she would almost certainly have described him as a man of this or that village. And then the true enormity of what the girl was saying struck home. My rooms were in the women's part of the palace, totally out of bounds to any man who was not a blood relative. "You mean," I said in genuine astonishment, "that he . . ."

Suva nodded vigorously. "Yes, memsahib. He came to me secretly as soon as it was dark. He says that he has a message for you."

For a moment I found myself thinking that it might be a message from Edward, but I dismissed the idea as impossible. Edward was well enough aware of palace protocol for him not to risk the unforgivable, quite apart from the fact that he could perfectly well have had a letter delivered by a servant. No, the message would have to be from someone else, presumably someone who considered its contents worth the risk involved. "Very well," I said to the girl. "Bring the man to me, but do not go away."

I had not supposed that I would know the mysterious messenger, and certainly when he slipped furtively through the door, his face meant nothing to me. As far as I could tell, he was a very ordinary low-caste Hindu, probably from somewhere in the Central Provinces, about thirty years of age and dressed in a *dhoti* and an old tweed jacket that was probably a castoff from some Englishman for whom he had worked. He greeted me in Hindi and stood eyeing me doubtfully.

"You are Hunt memsahib?"

"Yes. If you have a message, give it to me."

The man felt in his pocket and produced a grubby envelope, which he handed over with the air of a man who had satisfactorily concluded an arduous mission. I saw at once that the envelope was unsealed and bore no address. It contained a crumpled telegraph form and a few penciled words written in a straggling hand. The writing was so faint and the form itself so crumpled and stained that I had to take it close to the lamp before I could make out its meaning, but as soon

183

as I had succeeded, I gave an involuntary cry and felt the blood drain from my face.

It was addressed simply to Hunt, c/o Matherson, Narranagur, and the message read:

Regret to inform you Rupert detained here due serious illness stop doctor advises your presence vital

WHITTLE

I glanced at the date and saw that the message had been sent from Calcutta three weeks earlier. Three weeks! For all I knew, Rupert might well be dead by now. And of what kind of serious illness? I clenched my hands and held them to my sides to stop their shaking. There was no point in giving way to panic, I told myself. Joseph Whittle was no fool, and he was well aware that it would take me a very considerable time to reach the capital. Surely he would not have sent such a message if he knew with any certainty that my journey would be in vain?

I sat down suddenly, uncomfortably aware that my legs were weak and shaking. And as I stared at the telegram form an obvious question presented itself. Mr. Whittle knew of my whereabouts, for I had written him to that effect, although with grave doubts as to whether my letter would ever arrive, but how his message had come to me was something of a mystery. There was, of course, no telegraph line to Khudistan, so clearly the message had been forwarded to me from its most northerly terminal. It had been addressed to me care of someone called Matherson, a name that meant nothing to me. How, then, had this unknown helper known of my whereabouts? And if he knew, was this knowledge shared by anyone else?

I looked toward the messenger. "Did you bring this message all the way from Narranagur?"

"Yes, memsahib. My name is Puran Das and I am the servant of Matherson sahib. He gave me the message and told me to bring it to you with great secrecy."

"And what is the business of Matherson sahib? Is he an officer in the army?"

Puran Das shook his head. "He is a very learned man of great age who draws maps and puts them into books."

Which meant, I thought, that he could very well be the kind of man Joseph Whittle would know and trust. Possibly there had been another message for the elderly mapmaker making the situation clear and stressing the need for secrecy. And yet it seemed strange that the telegram should have been forwarded to me without some kind of covering letter of explanation.

"Is there no other message for me?" I asked. "No letter from your master?"

"Yes, memsahib, there is."

I had forgotten that in India nothing could be taken for granted, and the fact that there was a further communication did not necessarily mean I should get it unless I asked for it. I said patiently, "Then give it to me, please."

Puran Das looked crestfallen. "Alas, it is lost. On the journey here I met with robbers who beat me and took all I possessed. The telegram they would have taken also had I not hidden it in my turban for safe-keeping."

Which would account for its stained and crumpled condition, I realized. I sat considering the matter for a moment, wondering whether to ask Puran Das to carry a reply, but on reflection I dismissed the idea. He had already proved the risks that were inherent in one man making a long journey on his own, and if I left at once with a suitable escort to the border, the chances were that I should be in touch with a telegraph station before him.

I asked, "Did anyone see you as you crossed the border?"

Puran Das smiled. "No, memsahib. Nor will anyone see me return."

"Then thank your master," I said, "and tell him that I will thank him myself as soon as I can. Now take this money and leave this place carefully."

The little man took the fifty rupees I offered and slipped away, silent as a shadow. I looked at Suva. "You are to tell no one that man came here. Do you understand?"

"I understand. I shall never speak of it."

"Then go and give my greeting to the khan sahib and tell him that I wish to see him as soon as possible on a matter of great importance."

When the girl had gone, I sat motionless for a long time, my thoughts in a turmoil. At first I reproached myself bitterly for ever having sent Rupert away, but after a while I realized that at the time, there had been nothing else I could have done, and I had lived in India long enough to understand that sickness could strike anywhere. True, Calcutta was notoriously unhealthy, nevertheless people lived as long there as anywhere else in a land where a snake, a marauding tiger, or a band of murderous dacoits on a lonely road could bring death even more swiftly than any pestilence.

I stood up and paced about the room, every fiber of my being rebelling against the passing of time. How long, I wondered, would it take me to reach Rupert's side? And would the khan provide me with an escort to the borders of his country with a minimum of delay? I cursed the ill fortune that had brought a rift between us at this particular moment and the necessity of asking his help at such a time. Yet if he wished to humble me, I thought, this was his opportunity. I was quite prepared to crawl to him on my knees just so long as he gave me what I asked.

I was suddenly aware that Suva had returned and was standing before me, her face full of concern for a trouble she did not understand.

"The khan sahib dines. He asks that you will join him after one hour."

I could have screamed at the delay, but there was nothing I could do, and in fairness I had to admit that

Adam McKenzie could have no means of knowing how urgent was my mission, and I nodded my consent.

"Memsahib will take her own food now?"

I could remember few times when I had felt the need for food less, but I realized I had best eat something, and in any case it would help pass the time. So I did the best I could, but even so it seemed a great deal longer than an hour before I found myself being escorted by a servant not into the crystal dining room but into an apartment I had never seen before. It was, by the standards of the palace, a comparatively small room, with a floor of blue and white marble and with a superbly carved wooden gallery on all four sides. There appeared to be no means of entering the gallery from the room itself, but at the eastern end a low arch led to a dais on which three musicians were playing an accompaniment to an equal number of dancers, two girls, in gold-embroidered bodices and the full, pajamalike trousers of the North, and a youth, crowned with jewels, who was going through the motions of playing to them on a reed pipe. As I entered, the accompanying music consisted only of a complex rhythm beaten out on small drums, and it blended mesmerically with the steady jingle of the tiny bells fastened about the girls' ankles. They were each rooted to one small circle of floor, yet their entire beings seemed to be borne up by the music, their arms, hands, and fingers apparently boneless as they followed the age-old movements of the dance.

In spite of myself I was so riveted by the beauty of the spectacle that I must have stared at them for a full minute before becoming aware of the khan, bareheaded but wearing a high-necked silken jacket and trousers, sitting on a pile of cushions and watching the performance much as Indian noblemen must have done for a thousand years. A priceless silver hookah stood before him, but the water pipe was apparently no more than a convention, for Adam McKenzie was smoking one of his inevitable thin black cheroots and holding a fragile teacup in his other hand. He turned his head and saw me, making no attempt to rise but gesturing to

187

the empty cushions at his side. I sank down on them obediently and took the tea a watchful servant immediately offered me.

The khan nodded to the dancers. "It's a very old story," he said in explanation. "Do you recognize it?"

"Yes. It's the dance of the Lord Krishna before the milkmaids. Strictly speaking, there should be more than two."

"There should indeed. Unfortunately this form of dancing is unfamiliar to the people of this valley, so we have to make the best of what performers we have." The khan's mouth twitched in an unexpected smile. "And incidentally, just as their performance is traditional, so is mine. They would be ill at ease with an audience who sat watching them in straight-backed chairs."

"I am sure that is so."

The khan laughed. "No, Mrs. Hunt, you're not really sure at all. If the truth were known, you are really trying to make up your mind as to whether I'm some kind of scoundrel taking advantage of a lot of simple peasants or if I'm simply a madman who thinks that time stopped a century ago." His smile faded abruptly. "But one thing, my dear lady, you must *not* think, and that is that you have only to flutter your eyelashes at me and I shall release you from your confinement."

"Frankly," I said, "it had not occurred to me that you might be sufficiently human as to make it worthwhile."

"Unfortunately I am as human as the next man. But don't worry, I haven't forgotten the embarrassment it would cause you if I sent you back to India. I promise not to send you home."

I drew a deep breath. "That," I said, "is my reason for asking to see you. I want—I *must* go back to India."

He stared at me for a long moment while in the background the drums throbbed as Krishna interminably wooed his milkmaids. Then Adam McKenzie said quietly, "Why?"

I held out the crumpled telegram. "Because this evening I got—this."

He read it swiftly, then handed it back. "And just how did this come into your possession?"

"Does it matter?"

"As presumably someone gained access to the women's quarters, it matters very much. It's the kind of thing that wouldn't be tolerated in the home of my poorest subjects, so if it happens in the palace it's not the kind of thing that can be overlooked."

I cried desperately, "I don't care if you overlook it or not. Don't you see that I must leave here immediately?"

"Don't be a fool. That telegram is just a trick to get you back."

I stared at him in disbelief. "But how can you say such a thing? How can you possibly *know?*"

The khan shrugged his shoulders. "I suppose because it doesn't make sense."

"Why not?"

"Because by all accounts Joseph Whittle is no fool. And only a fool would send a message like that knowing that by the time it was delivered, and supposing you set out immediately you received it, you could not possibly be in Calcutta for several weeks—even supposing you were not arrested on the way. By that time the boy would either have recovered or be dead and buried and your presence would be a waste of time."

"But," I protested, "you cannot forge a telegram!"

"For God's sake, Harriet," Adam McKenzie said, "you know as well as I do that you can buy anything in this country. I tell you the whole business is just a trick to lure you out of hiding. Forget it."

I think that on any other occasion I might have given very real consideration to his advice. Even the fact that he had been so moved as to use my first name was so unexpected that it would have called out at least some notice. But as it was, I felt nothing but anger at his blindness, his bland assurance that he was right.

I said tensely, "I shall not forget it. You are quite

entitled to think whatever you like, but this is something that concerns me, not you. If I wish to risk going back to India, that is my business, and I would be grateful if you could see that I reach the border as soon as possible."

Adam McKenzie shook his head. "I'm sorry, but I shall do no such thing."

I stared at him in disbelief. "But you cannot . . ."

"Cannot what? Cannot deny you anything?" The dark eyebrows raised slightly in surprise. "My dear girl, I'm under no obligation whatever to do anything for you. I didn't ask you to come here in the first place and my men are certainly not at your beck and call."

With a considerable effort I restrained an impulse to snatch up the silver hookah and hurl it at him, and it was in a commendably level voice that I managed to say, "Very well. Fortunately my horse is my own property, so I'll return to India on my own."

Adam McKenzie studied me thoughtfully for a long moment, as though assessing my capacity to make good my words. "I really believe you would try," he said at last, and I thought I detected a certain grudging respect in his voice. "But of course the question does not arise, since I have confined you to your quarters and you will stay there until I order otherwise."

I looked back at him in disbelief. "I'm sorry, but I don't understand."

"On the contrary, you understand perfectly well. You do not leave the palace—your own rooms in the palace—without my express permission. I made that clear this morning and nothing has changed."

"You mean," I said, "that you seriously intend to keep me a *prisoner* here?"

"Since it's clearly the only way to prevent your doing something you'll regret—yes." Adam McKenzie tossed away the butt of his cheroot. "And just in case you think you can disregard my orders, there will be a guard placed on the zenana with instructions that you are not to leave it."

The sheer termerity of his proposal took my breath away. I think I was too shocked to be angry, and certainly at that moment I did not believe that he meant to carry it out. To forbid me the freedom of the palace as a rather childish punishment for going against his wishes was one thing, but to forcibly restrain me from leaving his employment and returning to my own home was entirely different. I said quietly, "You know perfectly well that you haven't the right to keep me here against my will."

"On the contrary, I have every right. I make the laws here, and if necessary I can most certainly break them."

I said desperately, "Doesn't it mean anything at all to you that my brother may be dying—that every hour I spend here lessens the chances of my getting to him in time?" I threw my pride aside. "Please—I beg of you, let me go."

A muscle twitched in the khan's face, the first sign of any emotion on his part. But his voice did not alter. "You leave me no choice but to detain you. This is not a matter of that childish business over my sister. It is simply that I have no intention of letting you place yourself in danger. Give me your word that you will stay and you can have the freedom of the palace. But otherwise I shall just have to make sure that you do not do something I know you'll regret."

"You won't change your mind?"

"You should know by now that I never change my mind."

I stood up and went back alone through the archway that led to the women's apartments. When next I looked out of the window, there was a sentry there, the moonlight glinting on the polished steel of his lance.

12

By rights I should not have slept at all that night but exhaustion took its toll and in fact I slept like a log, waking to find Suva by my side with a message that the old begum wished to see me.

"My compliments to her. Say that I shall be with her as soon as I am dressed."

I was grateful for the summons, for at least it gave me something momentary to think about besides Rupert, and as I made my way to the old woman's apartment I congratulated myself on the fact that even the khan could hardly put a stop to meetings behind the walls of the zenana and that my imprisonment need not be one of solitary confinement.

The begum was waiting for me on her favorite seat beside the fountain and motioned me to join her.

"Mrs. Hunt, I am grateful to you for what you did on my daughter's behalf. I am only sorry that it has caused you some distress in consequence."

"It was unfortunate," I agreed. "Sabina has told you what happened?"

"Yes." The great eyes that dominated the still-beautiful face lifted to mine. There had always been a haunting sorrow in them, but now I thought I detected something else—something that was very like despair. "And now you have yet another trouble, another difference between yourself and my stepson. Do you wish to tell me what it is?"

"Yes," I said, "I should be glad to." I hesitated a moment, uncertain where to begin, "Begum-ji, you know how I came to be here and that I have a young brother."

The dark eyes did not shift from mine. "Yes, that also has been told me."

"Then you should also know that last night a messenger came to me to say that my brother was still in India and is very sick." I described the subsequent meeting between Adam McKenzie and me and ended, "I myself think that the message is real enough. But even if I doubted it, to stay here is a risk I cannot take."

The old woman nodded. "True. You cannot stay here, and yet you are forbidden to go."

"So the khan has said. I wondered . . ."

"Yes?"

"If perhaps you would speak to him on my behalf."

For a moment the begum did not speak. Then she said slowly, "I already have." And then, when I looked at her in surprise, "You must forgive me if I was curious to hear your version of what happened. But now I must tell you that the khan is quite adamant that you are to stay here."

"But why?" I cried. "What does it matter to him whether I go or stay?"

"That was something he would not discuss, other than to say that in his opinion you would be safer here."

"Am I to have no say in the matter?" I asked bitterly. "Begum-ji, what kind of man *is* the khan? Cannot he imagine how I feel about my brother? Doesn't he realize that my life is my own, to do with as I think best?"

A smile of infinite sadness illuminated the Indian woman's face. "Mrs. Hunt, I know my stepson better than you, but even I no longer understand him very well." She reached out a tiny hand and touched a frangipani blossom that floated on the water in the marble pool at her side. Then, almost as though speaking to

193

herself, she added, "No, that is not true. I understand him well enough. It is just that I do not agree with him anymore."

I asked gently, "What is it you do not agree with, Begum-ji?"

The old woman stood up slowly, "Come, child, I would show you something. And then perhaps you will understand as well."

"I don't think I care very much if I understand Adam McKenzie or not," I told her. "All I want is to find a way out of this place."

The begum touched me gently on the arm. "Do not give up hope, Mrs. Hunt. It may even be possible to do that."

I think that at that moment I was so desperate that I would have followed anyone without question. Nevertheless I felt a stirring of curiosity as I followed the begum up a winding staircase and waited while she unlocked a black teakwood door. It opened noiselessly at her touch, and the begum stood aside to let me enter.

"These are my husband's possessions. I have cared for them since he died."

I looked around me with some bewilderment. It was a small room that overlooked the stables, and it was furnished haphazardly with so many tables and glass-fronted cabinets that there was little room to walk between them. The polished wood of the furniture glowed warmly in the morning sunlight and the room was spotless, which suggested that it was cared for regularly, even though it was clearly no more than a storeroom.

As if reading my thought, the begum fingered an old book affectionately and said in explanation, "My husband's room was not here, of course. It would not have been fitting for him to have it in the zenana. But when I became a widow, I brought these little things behind the curtain so that they could be close to me."

It occurred to me that, apart from some trusted servant, I was probably the only person outside the McKenzie family who had set eyes on these relics of the old adventurer. I let my eyes wander around the room, taking in the personal toll of what one man had kept about him. There were shelves of leather-bound volumes in English and Persian, sheaves of papers and rolled maps. Weapons of every description were propped up in corners—Indian swords and daggers, round brass-bound shields, and long-barreled *jezail* muskets, inlaid with mother-of-pearl. There was a pair of superb high-pommeled Rajput saddles, infinitely delicate stirrups of pierced steel, a telescope in a leather case, and tiny, exquisite Mogul paintings, framed and stacked in piles. It was strange, I thought, that all this would add up to a man, as far as the begum was concerned, whereas to me, an outsider, they were curiously impersonal. They added up to a man who had fought for what he had gained, who had developed a taste for a certain school of painting, who read books in the court language of his adopted country and might well have left some writings of his own. But to form any real impression of what Duncan McKenzie had been like I suspected I should have to go through the piles of papers and investigate the contents of the leather mule chests stacked in a corner by the door.

I think some of my feelings must have shown in my face, for the begum gave a tiny laugh. "The toys of a man's life, Mrs. Hunt, and yet perhaps some rather more than toys." She pointed to a great claymore, suspended from a hook on the wall. "See, that is the great sword my husband brought from his own land. And this—this I found for you yesterday. Read it, Mrs. Hunt, and then give me your word that you will speak about it to no one."

I took the yellowed letter that the begum proffered and took it to the window, for the ink was faded and brown with age. At first glance there was something about the writing that struck a chord in my memory, and then, as I scanned the lines, I caught my breath.

In camp
near Meerut
August 23, 1858

MY DEAR FRIEND:

I am taking up my pen to write you a letter that may well never reach you in that Fair Valley you and I know as Khudistan.

None should quarrel with the decision of Duncan McKenzie to hang up his Sword and found a fair new State. That we found the site of this Brave Enterprise together will ever be a great Joy to me. Would that I might join you, but I have set my shoulder to my own Plow and each man had best drive his own Furrow.

I write in the main to inform you that I have had assayed the nugget of metal I brought with me from the most northerly pass, and it is indeed fine gold. With memories of the great quantities to be had there for the asking I would commend to you the thought that the Less said, the Better. Should the news of these deposits become generally known your new Eden would be despoiled within months by Greed and Avarice. Use what you will for the well-being and Independence of Khudistan, but *no more!*

It seems unlikely our paths shall cross again, for you have chosen your way and I mine. May God bless your project and may it flourish.

This letter I am entrusting to Risalder Man Singh, a Native Officer of your service who is returning to resume his duties with you. I know not whether he will survive the perils of the road, which are many for one man, yet should he succeed in making his way to you, I pray that you will accept the sincere greetings of your old friend and companion,

CHARLES ROGERS

As if in a daze I read my father's familiar signature. Despite the old-fashioned phrasing of the faded sentences above it, the words rang true. This letter had been written when I was a child. In those days my father must have known the legendary Duncan McKenzie and had been with him when he had first set eyes on the secret valley he was to make his own. And together they had found gold. . . .

Beside me the begum said gently, "My husband never forgot your father, Mrs. Hunt, and he followed his work with admiration. Once, through a trusted intermediary, he tried to press on him a little of the gold that they had found together, but it was sent back. Nevertheless when your father died, my stepson journeyed to pay his respects and would have proffered help to you had he not learned that you were about to be married."

With those words something that I had never understood suddenly became clear. So that, I thought, was the reason for Adam McKenzie's presence at the funeral! And indeed for his surprising readiness to find work for a complete stranger. Just as the secret wealth of Khudistan was the reason for its continued independence.

As though reading my thoughts, the begum said, "My husband took your father's advice. The place where the gold lay was in the most northernly part of the valley, and so he declared that the place was sacred to his own gods and that no man or woman should go there. A temple was built for these supposed deities and three trusted men were appointed priests. They lived near the temple, with their wives, and they and their families gathered the gold. These men are dead now, but their sons and their sons' sons carry out the work in their turn." The begum reached out a frail hand and touched the letter I still held. "Your father's words were wise and good. You have seen the land here, rich and fertile beyond all others, so that any man who works hard can live well. The knowledge of the gold would have brought nothing but greed and idleness and sorrow, so my husband used it only when it was vital.

Even today only a tiny trickle of gold leaves the valley."

I put into words the question that had been with me ever since the begum had started talking. "I understand the wisdom of mining it only a little at a time. But *how* does it leave the valley without anyone knowing about it?"

The begum smiled. "Because, Mrs. Hunt, it leaves by another way. Beyond the mine there is a narrow pass to the north. There is a way up the side of the pass by which one may reach a track through the high hills by which one may make one's way to India. By which *you* may make your way to freedom should you so desire."

I stared at the old woman unbelievingly. "You mean that you would allow me to go there, even though I have been confined. . . ."

The begum said impatiently, "Of course. Why else should I be telling you this?"

"But—the khan . . ."

"The khan will be away training his cavalry for two days. During that time I shall make it my business to visit the temple for . . . religious reasons. You shall travel with me."

"But," I protested, "I shall be recognized. The guards . . ."

"Nobody shall recognize you because you will travel in my own palanquin. My own servants are perfectly trustworthy, and one of them can ride your horse. Believe me, there is nothing to fear."

I said slowly, "I'm not frightened. It is only that I do not understand why you should do this for me."

The begum turned away from me and stared in silence out over the roofs of the palace buildings and the blue-hazed hills beyond. Then she said slowly, "I am not very sure myself. My stepson is khan and the ruler of this land, and never before have I gone against his wishes in any way. But when you came here, Mrs. Hunt, I listened to you talking and it seemed to me that the world beyond the borders of Khudistan is changing. I do not know if this change is for better or

198

worse, but perhaps that does not matter very much. What does matter is that here things are as they have always been. The khan is the father of his people, as was my husband before him, and yet sometimes I ask myself if this is enough. A father should know more than his children, should he not?"

"Yes," I agreed. "I think he should."

"I am not sure that Adam does. All he knows is that there is much poverty and much that is evil in India today, since the British government has stolen half the country and set one man against another. Now he thinks that because his peasants are fat and each man can appeal to him for justice, it proves that the old ways are best."

"And you doubt it?"

The old woman turned back to me with a faint smile. "Who knows? Perhaps it really was a golden age when Shah Jehan beggared India for his queen and built the Taj Mahal. I do not doubt that the men and woman of this valley are happy to be ruled by an Englishman who lives as though time stopped a hundred years ago. But one day a wind of change will blow through this land and I fear that many will be ill prepared for it. But meanwhile it is not right that a man should keep a sister from her brother simply because it pleases him."

I said gently, "Be honest with me, Begum-ji. Is that the only reason?"

"No, Mrs. Hunt, it is not. One day soon your accusers will trace you here and then they will ask themselves what is to prevent their riding in and taking you back. One day that wind of change may indeed blow through these hills, but not, I trust, at your bidding." The begum raised her eyebrows in query. "So what shall you do? Go or stay?"

I thought of Rupert. There could be only one answer. "I do not wish to stay, Begum-ji," I said. "When do we leave?"

"Today."

"There is . . . Sabina. May I say good-bye to her?"

"No." The begum shook her head. "Only the khan

and myself know of the gold. My daughter will be told when I die."

It was a curious procession that left the palace later that morning and headed north. I was not surprised by the begum's own transport, which I was to share, for it was the familiar elaborately lacquered two-wheeled *ruth,* or wagon, of a well-to-do woman, made safe from prying male eyes by a richly embroidered canopy with two domes, not unlike a double-humped camel. The inside was inevitably dark and airless but nevertheless comfortably cushioned, being drawn by two tough little hill ponies. A second, slightly less elaborate and open ruth carried tents for accommodation upon arrival, as well as food and cooking equipment, and trailed my own horse on the end of a leading rein. The drivers and their companions were all hill women, and I could hear them through the canopy, chatting interminably in the harsh local dialect, their conversation accompanied by a villainous squeaking of poorly oiled wheels.

Sitting there in the half dark, it was difficult to keep my thoughts on my surroundings, for they seemed to return, unbidden, to the palace. Illogically, I found myself wishing that I had been able to say good-bye to Adam McKenzie, and absurd though the whim was, I would have given much for the chance to explain my flight. Would he be angry when he discovered what had happened? I wondered. On reflection it seemed unlikely. Far more probable that he would simply give one of his short barks of laughter and then dismiss me from his thoughts forever. The thought gave me a stab of pain, for I well knew that I should never be able to banish Adam so effectively from my own life. For better or worse, the catlike grace, the harsh decisiveness of that extraordinary man, would never leave me now.

Once we were in open country, the begum ordered the canopy to be drawn back, evidently satisfied that any man we chanced to encounter would recognize the vehicles from a distance and have the discretion to make himself scarce. And I must confess that I was glad to feel the cool breeze of the hills on my face again and be able to watch the dazzling white palace with the huddled town at its feet grow steadily smaller below us as we climbed upward along a grassy track that wound its way through steep meadows bright with gentians.

In any other circumstances I think I would have felt ill at ease in the riding breeches and jacket of English tweed that the begum had apparently appropriated from Sabina's wardrobe and insisted that I wear as being more suitable for my proposed journey than a conventional riding skirt, but as it was, I had ample chance to get used to my novel attire, for the begum's women ignored my presence completely. Indeed I could perfectly well have mounted my own horse had it not been for the insidious comfort of the cushions in the ruth and a feeling that courtesy forbade my leaving my hostess. And in truth I enjoyed the opportunity to listen to her, for she seemed to enjoy talking, and I guessed it was something of a luxury for her to have someone outside her own family to whom she could recall and savor the past.

About the gold she seemed to know surprisingly little save that twice a year, whatever quantity it had been thought advisable to sell was handed over by the "priests" to someone in a village high in the hills beyond the valley and from there made its long-established way down to the plains, to end its journey in the hands of some trusted gold merchant in a back street of Delhi. That was the route I was to follow, the begum told me. Once I was at the head of the valley, one of the miner-priests would escort me to the village that marked the start of the gold route, and from there I should be handed from guide to guide until I reached a point where I could travel on my own.

I asked my companion how often the mine was visited and from the vagueness of her answer it seemed as though there was no established frequency. Either the khan or herself would make the journey perhaps half a dozen times a year, ostensibly to worship at the shrine or to pay respect to the old khan's tomb. No, the keepers of the mine were jealous of their position and would consider it shameful to steal gold for themselves, although, the begum added, it would matter little if they did, as there was more than anyone would ever want.

From what I could gather there were indeed extraordinarily rich deposits. Apparently there was a stream where, in Duncan McKenzie's day, sizable nuggets could simply be picked up from the sandy bottom. Indeed, they could still be found, although it was now more usual to chip them from the rock. At first I had assumed that the gold had been washed down from somewhere in the endless mountain peaks that rose, one above the other, for as far as the eye could see. But it seemed that the parent lode was here in the valley, waiting to pour out prodigious wealth.

We had two days' journey in the slow-moving ruth, the begum said, and when we camped that night and I looked up at the hard brightness of the stars and the moon-drenched peaks frosty white against a purple sky, I found myself thinking that if such untouched peace and beauty were mine, I might also try to hold back the clock in order to save it. Old Duncan would have had no such problems. He would have found his valley as a kind of safe haven after all the fury and disillusion of his buccaneering life, a place where he could fashion in miniature all the kingdoms he had sought and lost. Remembering his background, I found myself marveling at the personal discipline of a man who had spent his life in search of wealth and power and who could yet hold back when almost infinite wealth was his for the taking and lay it out, little by precious little, so that it might not corrupt either himself or the people he had made his own. And this was the man who had been my father's friend. This was the man who had trained his son to rule his kingdom after him and, it seemed, had trained him only too well. Khudistan was safe in Adam's hands. To the people of the valley he was the old khan born again—brave, kingly, just, and, above all, one who followed what had in such a short time become the old ways. But for how long? I wondered. For how long?

Next day the track became even steeper, and there

202

was a bite in the crystal-clear air that numbed the cheekbones and made one's breath quick and short. The floor of the valley up which we were climbing was now narrowing by the hour. From the palace gardens one could look east and west and see both sides of the valley across half a score of miles of meadow and cultivation. Now the two steep inclines were drawing in, so that it seemed as though we were traveling up into the bows of some vast natural boat, to a point where trees and rocks met and, as far as one could see at first glance, the valley came to an abrupt end against the vast barrier of the mountain range.

When we were within perhaps half a mile from what was for some reason a curiously forbidding spot, the begum gave orders for the ruths to be stopped and for camp to be set up in the shadow of a clump of towering deodars. In response to my look of query she said shortly, "The servants are never allowed nearer than this. You and I go on alone. Lead your horse."

We left the women putting up a tent with practiced skill and walked slowly onward, and as we did so I saw that there was a ridge ahead of us that effectively masked what lay beyond. I would have taken my companion's arm to assist her, but she strode up the sloping turf easily enough until we reached the top. There she paused and I was able to see our destination for the first time.

It was, in effect, a small village set in a clearing amid the great boulders and trees, the usual huddle of huts with pens for goats and firewood heaped against the cold of winter. Immediately before us stood what was instantly recognizable as Duncan McKenzie's tomb, a great oblong mausoleum of whitewashed stone, crouching on roughly fashioned clawed feet and its top a curious parody of the roof of a Greek temple. It was not unlike the kind of sturcture that could be found marking the graves of dead Europeans all over India save that this had a curiously Eastern flavor and one that succeeded in making the old khan's last resting place not unlike the shrine of some Muhammadan saint. I could see from the small clay pots that marked its extremities that lamps would glow about it each night, and here and there the whitewash threw up the colors of flower petals, scattered everywhere.

By the side of the tomb rose a structure of a very different kind. The walls were made of split wood, and it was narrow and tall, so that its thatched roof was high above the other buildings in the clearing. There was only one window that I could see and a high door reached by a broad flight of wooden steps. It did not need the dozens of tiny flags to tell me that this was the temple. Fixed at head height along one wall there was even a row of prayer wheels, presumably introduced by one of the miners who had inherited memories of his forefathers' Buddhist ancestry.

"It looks," I said, "very like a real temple."

The begum said simply, "It *is* real." And then, in reply to my look of mystification, "My husband told me that it was impossible to explain to these people that he had built a temple only for its appearance. The people who live in these parts are naturally religious."

"What do they pray to?"

"Since he died, they have prayed to my husband. I do not know whom they prayed to before."

Well, I thought, at least it had the merit of being a very rational religion. The first white khan had created their country, dispensed justice, and guarded them from their enemies. In times of trouble he would still be the natural person to turn to.

"Leave the horse here," the begum said. "We had best let ourselves be seen. Usually someone passes the word that we are coming so that they can be ready to greet us. As there is no one here, it is possible that they have sickness in the village."

Together we walked down toward the clearing, and as we did so I could see for the first time that the valley did not in fact end abruptly. As the begum had said, there was a narrow cleft among the rocks that was clearly a pass that led onward through the hills, almost certainly the path of some long-vanished glacier. A chance outcrop of granite hid the entrance, so that from a distance it was quite impossible to see that it was there at all.

"At least," my companion said, "there is a cur to greet us."

A great brindle dog had evidently heard our footsteps and emerged growling from the open doorway of one of the huts and for a moment I thought it was going to attack us. Fortunately it changed its mind at the last moment and padded away, intent on its own affairs. I glanced into what was apparently the animal's home and at that moment a woman appeared in the doorway, holding a child in her arms. She was a typical woman of the hills, high-cheekboned and almond-eyed, dressed in a simple cotton shift, her dark hair roughly braided and hanging forward over her shoulders. For a moment she stared at me uncomprehendingly, then her eyes shifted to the begum and she said something in a low voice and moved to one side to allow a man, who was presumably her husband, to emerge from the shadows of the room and take her place.

Behind me, the begum said sharply, "Well, what are you doing there?"

"*Namaste, Begum-ji.*" Young and sharp-featured, the man hurriedly joined his hands in greeting, staring at the imperious old woman by my side with something I could only take to be apprehension. He wore a saffron-colored robe as his only garment, and not for the first time I found myself wondering at the open-handed way the people of the white khan's country borrowed indiscriminately from different religions and apparently saw nothing incongruous in a priest wearing the dress of a Buddhist monk in order to care for a temple dedicated to a freebooting Scot.

"Forgive me, Highness," the man was saying. "We did not know that you were coming."

"How could you not know we were coming?" The begum eyed the unfortunate man coldly. "We have been in sight for the last three hours."

"Nobody was watching, Highness. The fault was ours."

I became aware that other saffron-robed men and

their families were emerging guiltily from their homes. Each made hurried obeisance to the grim old woman who stood facing them and I was not surprised to note the fear in their eyes. Yet there was a strangely furtive air about them that I could not place. Neither, it appeared, could the begum, who did not seem prepared to overlook the breach of ceremony.

She said abruptly, "Is it not the custom to have a child keeping watch on the valley to see if anyone comes?"

"Yes, Highness," someone muttered. "It is the custom."

"Then why was the watch not kept?"

"The child grew weary, Highness, and slept."

High in the steel blue of the sky an eagle drifted silently overhead, wings motionless, borne up by some unseen current of air. It seemed almost as though it were eavesdropping on the man's discomfiture.

"Which child?" The question came like a whiplash.

"Highness, I . . ." The priest looked desperately about him as though seeking inspiration. "Highness, it was . . ."

"You do not know who it was because no child slept." The begum dismissed the excuse as unworthy of attention. "What is more, the matter of greeting me in a fitting manner is a matter for the head priest alone. I do not see Nattu here. Where is he?"

The little group stared back at her in dismay, and the dismay was so total that it communicated itself to me. For some reason that I could not fully explain I could sense the intensity of that feeling, and it had nothing to do with shame at not having offered the fitting courtesies to their visitor.

"I think they're frightened," I said in a low voice. "I think they are really frightened about something."

"Then why cannot they tell me?" The begum demanded impatiently. She raised her voice so that it carried far beyond the ring of troubled faces around her. "My children, stop this foolishness and tell me what has happened. Fetch Nattu, wherever he is, and tell him to come before me!"

There was a long pause, during which no one said anything. Then a man emerged from behind the farthest hut and came toward us with long, loping strides. I heard the begum draw in her breath with a little hiss, but I paid little attention, for I was too busy studying the newcomer. He was of medium height and his clothing could scarcely have been more dissimilar to that of the villagers around him. Instead of a saffron robe he wore a loose, baggy blouse of gray serge, drawn in tightly at the waist with a leather belt. Matching trousers were stuffed into the tops of high black riding boots and on his head he wore a cap of black astrakhan. I had never actually seen anyone wearing such clothes before, but I had seen them in pictures so often that I barely needed the confirmation of the darkly handsome olive-skinned face to recognize the stranger's nationality.

The villagers drew back from him as he passed, but he did not spare them a glance. Instead he came up to the begum and me, and the lips below the pencil-thin mustache parted in a smile. "I am sorry that the old priest was unable to welcome you." He addressed the begum in fluent but heavily accented Hindi. "He is unharmed, but he and his family are for the moment being cared for by my men."

In a steady voice the begum asked, "Who are you?"

"I had hoped that this meeting would not have to take place. But . . ." His shoulders lifted slightly. "But since it has, my name is Zarkov." I think I must have made some slight sound, for his dark eyes turned to meet mine and I felt a sudden chill as I looked into depths that were pitiless and cruel. Abruptly he concluded his introduction in English. "Captain Zarkov, of the army of His Imperial Majesty, the czar."

13

———◆———

Having introduced himself, Captain Zarkov continued to stare at me with narrowed eyes, and it was easy enough to guess that he found himself somewhat taken aback by my presence, and indeed his next words confirmed this.

"I had not expected to find a white woman in these hills. What are you doing here?"

"Surely," I said, "this is a question I should be asking you. It is not I who has crossed the border into someone else's territory."

"No." Captain Zarkov smiled faintly. "I concede you the point, Miss . . ."

"Mrs. Hunt."

"Thank you. And your companion?"

"She is the mother of the present khan of Khudistan and has come to worship at the temple."

The Russian raised his eyebrows. "And you have come for religious reasons, too? Come, Mrs. Hunt. I find that hard to believe."

"No," I admitted. "I simply came to keep the begum company. I am employed as tutor to her daughter."

"So." The captain relaxed a little and glanced toward the begum. "And does this lady understand what we are saying?"

"I am the begum Amrita Devi of Khudistan." The lined face lifted a little. "And, yes, I do understand English if it is spoken slowly."

Zarkov bowed slightly. "That is convenient. My

Hindi is the result of somewhat recent study, English I have spoken from childhood." He paused and then went on. "You must not blame your people for what has happened. When we saw you approaching, I did not realize you were an honored guest, so I told them to carry on their work as usual in the hope that you were just a casual visitor who would soon go away. I had my men take the old priest and his family as hostage in order to ensure that nobody revealed our presence. As it was . . ." He made a deprecating gesture and smiled.

The begum asked quietly, "And where are your men, Captain?"

Zarkov nodded toward the rocks that hid the entrance to the pass. "They are keeping themselves out of sight over there." Then, as a thought struck him, "And your escort? Where is that, may I ask?"

I said casually, "The begum does not have an escort for a religious journey. The women who brought us have gone to stay in a village a few miles away until we send for them." There seemed only a very slight chance that one of the begum's servants might discover what had happened and return to the city for help, but for the present it seemed the only chance.

The explanation seemed to satisfy Zarkov, for he dismissed the subject and turned toward the saffron-robed priests and their families. "Carry on as usual, do you understand? Remember that nobody is allowed to leave the village. My men will shoot anyone who tries." There was a low, scared murmur of assent, and then the Russian turned back to the begum and me. "And now, ladies, perhaps you will take some refreshment while I decide what is to be done with you."

It was all totally unreal, I thought. Since early childhood I had heard my father and his friends talking among themselves of "the Russian menace" and the possibility that one day the hordes from the north would sweep down through the passes into India. It was for just that reason that passes such as the Khyber and the Bolan bristled with fortifications and the Great Game of spy and counterspy was played by Russian and Briton alike in an effort to discover any suspicious movement of troops. For me, at least, there had been a certain unreality about it all, and more than once I had found myself suspecting that the threat was nonexistent and the whole thing no more than an elaborate charade designed to keep the military on its toes. Never for one moment had I really believed that Russian troops would actually set foot on Indian soil, and yet now I was not only seeing a czarist officer with my own eyes but was about to be entertained by him.

The begum and I were silent as we followed Zarkov through the village and toward the rocky defile that formed the mouth of the pass. Looking about me as I went, I glimpsed further buildings set a little apart from the village and guessed that these marked the site where the gold was mined. Obviously the Russians had already investigated it. For all I knew, it might well be the reason for the intruders' presence here.

"My comrades in this small adventure!" Zarkov rounded a mass of granite and with a sweep of his arm indicated a dozen men dressed much as himself, each standing at the head of a small, shaggy pony. I noticed carbines held in saddle holsters and pistols at the men's belts, and then my eyes had gone on beyond them and up the craggy defile that wound its way through the hills behind them.

Zarkov noticed the direction of my glance. "Yes, that is the pass by which we came. It is amusing to reflect on the fact that the government does not even know that it is there." He rapped out an order in Russian and his men began to disperse, having apparently been told that it was now safe for them to show themselves. Then, as another, younger officer came up, "May I present Lieutenant Vasili, who has been supervising the preparation of our evening meal. Let us trust that his men foraged with some success."

The young lieutenant said apologetically that the village had yielded surprisingly little. "There are some goats we can butcher for tomorrow, but for the moment there is only what these people were having for themselves."

I could guess at the typical hillman's evening meal of lentils and coarse *chapatti* bread, and indeed as we gathered around just such an offering laid out picnic fashion on a blanket I could understand it being disappointing fare for a soldier. Zarkov regarded it without enthusiasm.

"Poor hospitality, I fear. Alas, it seems to be the best we can offer."

"Since it is stolen," I observed, "perhaps it would be best not to offer it at all."

"The soldier must needs live off the land." Zarkov tore a chapatti in two and munched reflectively. The old begum sat like a statue, ignoring the food, but after a while the pangs of rather unexpected hunger drove me to follow the Russian's example.

After a while Zarkov said suddenly, "We shall not harm you."

"There appears no reason why you should," I said, trying to keep my voice steady, although I was aware of a tremor of unease. For some reason the thought of actual personal danger had not occurred to me, although apparently it had to our captor. To change the subject I said, "Perhaps you can tell us why you and your men are here at all."

Zarkov raised his dark eyes to mine. "Do you know what is at the far end of that pass, Mrs. Hunt?"

"Afghanistan?"

"I fear your geography leaves something to be desired. Actually it is Lodak, a remarkably small province, Mrs. Hunt, and one that my country has laid claim to for some time. To its north is, of course, Russia. Its southern frontier is—where would you suppose?

I did not know but hazarded a guess. "At the far end of that pass?"

"It is possible," Zarkov conceded, "although according to my government, that particular frontier line has never been officially confirmed. There is a case for claiming that it runs not to the north but to the *south* of Khudistan. Now, you must admit, Mrs. Hunt, that such a proposition has interesting possibilities, has it not?"

I did not have to consider the matter long to realize that what my captor said was true, for the possibilities were not only interesting but frightening in their implication. If Russia pressed its claims to Lodak, Lodak would have little choice but to concede them. And if in turn Adam McKenzie's little kingdom was swallowed up as part of Lodak, the Russians would have established a broad highway into the very heart of India. . . .

"But supposing," I said, "that the British government denies that the frontier extends so far south?"

Zarkov gave a short laugh. "Is there not an English saying, Mrs. Hunt, that possession is nine tenths of the law?"

I forced myself to laugh in turn. "Come, Captain Zarkov, you would occupy this country with a handful of men?"

The Russian spread his hands. "Indeed no. I am here only to carry out a reconnaissance. My report goes back a day's ride to the main body, which can be here in forty-eight hours."

Listening to the cold, factual sentences, I found it hard to remember that this man was not joking and that he meant every word he said. I asked quietly, "And what kind of report do you intend making, Captain Zarkov?"

"That the pass is open. That there is no opposition . . . and that the region appears to be rich in gold into the bargain." The Russian gestured idly toward the mine. "I must admit that the gold is an added incentive for the operation. An unexpected bonus, so to speak."

"You realize," I said, "that the action you are proposing could start a war?"

Zarkov shook his head. "I hardly think so, Mrs. Hunt. We are not invading Indian territory—we are simply going to occupy land that we consider ours by right. Oh, there will be protests and discussions in high places, I grant you, but not war. And when the talking eventually stops, we shall still be here."

"Ideally placed to invade India itself when it happens to be convenient."

The Russian captain plucked a gentian from the grass beside him and studied it absently. "Mrs. Hunt, I fear that you exaggerate."

"Do I?" Suddenly I was no longer afraid of this softly spoken, quietly menacing man. Indeed, the only emotion I felt was one of anger that fate should have thrust someone like me into this situation. Then another thought struck me. "Captain Zarkov, why are you telling me all this?"

"I thought it might amuse you."

"Surely it is classed as a matter of military security? Do you discuss your country's security with everyone you meet?"

Zarkov leaned back in the short mountain grass and folded his hands behind his head. "My dear lady, of course it is a matter of the very greatest secrecy. On the other hand, you will never be able to make use of your knowledge, because tomorrow you and your friend will be on your way to Russia."

At those so casually spoken words my heart seemed to miss a beat. To Russia! This apparently affable young officer was cold-bloodedly proposing to kidnap the begum and me! It was hard to believe, but the more I thought about it, the more it came home to me that unless he was prepared to kill us, Zarkov had little choice. If released, there would be nothing to stop us carrying the news of the coup back to India, whereas once we crossed the Russian border it would be diplomatically impossible for us to be returned. The begum and I would simply vanish and no amount of official inquiry would ever pick up our trail.

I drew a deep breath. "Captain Zarkov . . ."

"No, Mrs. Hunt." The dark, fathomless eyes regarded me without pity. "There is no other way. Do not embarrass me by asking the impossible."

I glanced at the begum, who was still sitting motionlessly, apparently absorbed in her own thoughts. "But what will happen to us in Russia? The begum is an old woman—she could never stand the hardships of the journey."

"We are not barbarians, Mrs. Hunt. She would be given every consideration when traveling."

"And when we arrived?"

"I do not know what would happen then. You would be handed over to the proper authorities."

I looked up at the sky. Already the day was ended and the lower slopes of the valley were full of deep shadows and the last rays of the sun were tinting the summits of the hills in a fantasy of swiftly changing color as the fleeting northern dusk swept down. Suddenly I felt overwhelmingly weary.

"Very well," I said. "Where do you wish us to spend the night?"

The Russian considered the matter for a moment. "It becomes cold at night. You had best spend it in the temple, and I'll see that you get a blanket each."

By the time the blankets had been found and we had been escorted to the temple, night had fallen completely and only the thin sickle of a new moon threw a faint, cold light upon the village. Inside the temple the oil lamps flickered yellow on either side of a crude clay representation of a man astride a horse. Save for the fact that the upper part of the rider's body had been painted red, there was nothing about the figure to identify it with the first khan of Khudistan. A garland of withered flowers had been set about the horse's neck and the base of the statuette was smeared and streaked with *ghi*. It was not difficult to imagine that a time would come when the people of the valley would forget all about Duncan McKenzie and simply worship here at the shrine of a strange god on a horse with a name unknown in the Hindu pantheon.

Vasili, the young lieutenant, pointed to a ladder that apparently led to an upper room above the shrine. "I would suggest that you ladies rest up there. It is a kind of storeroom and a good deal cleaner than the floor down here."

I glanced down at the floor and saw that he was quite right—the place was thick and slippery with a

214

thousand votive offerings of clarified butter and its rancid smell made me feel suddenly ill. Grateful for his consideration, I thanked the young officer and received an apologetic smile in return.

"I hope you will not be too uncomfortable. But also Captain Zarkov says that he does not recommend any attempt to escape, as he has posted sentries all around the village. He says it would distress him greatly were he forced to restrain you in a more undignified fashion."

"Thank you, Lieutenant," I said. "We shall do our best to remember. Good night."

"Good night, madam."

It was dark in the room at the top of the stairs, but in the light of a lamp borrowed from the altar it was possible to take stock of our whereabouts reasonably well. As Lieutenant Vasili had said, the place appeared to be a storeroom, for there were boxes everywhere and at least a dozen earthenware *chattis* that on investigation turned out to be filled with oil and still more ghi.

"It would seem," the begum observed, "that the priest is keeping more of the offerings than he uses. He must be finding his position profitable."

I looked at my companion with admiration. Through all that had happened during the day she had shown no sign of fear or distress of any kind and even now appeared to be capable of showing her own brand of tart humor. I asked her if she would not sit down but she shook her head.

"It is not a time to take our ease."

"Perhaps not, but there seems very little else we can do." I myself felt suddenly desperately weary, and I dropped down on one of the blankets the Russians had left us.

I do not think my companion heard me, for she was standing at the small window, staring out unseeingly into the night. After a while she said, "It is strange, is it not, that whatever happens, the old ways end here. My husband's son thought that they would go on forever."

I had a sudden mental picture of Adam McKenzie, seated on his throne in the Hall of Audience. Adam, gorgeously uniformed, at the head of a squadron of mounted men. It had, of course, all belonged to the past. He had known it and gloried in the fact.

"I think he knows Khudistan can't go on as it is forever," I said. Soon, I thought, I would be part of Adam McKenzie's past, too. Someone who had suddenly come into his life and then, just as suddenly, gone away. Would he remember me? Common sense told me that he almost certainly would not. Perhaps in the years to come something would jog his memory and he would say to Sabina, "You had an American girl to teach you once, didn't you? What was her name?" Something inside me cried out for more, but I knew that if he remembered that much about me, it was all I had a right to expect.

Why should it mean so much to me? I wondered. Why was it suddenly unbearable to realize that I should never again experience the extraordinary sensation caused by his hand touching mine? So small an intimacy. And yet I remembered the excitement of it far more than anything that had passed during the long nights spent in my husband's bed. I had given myself to Garfield as fully as I had been able, but nothing he had wrought on my body had left anything but a memory of pain and degradation.

"Without us, Khudistan will die tonight." The begum's voice broke in on my thoughts. "The old ways may have to change, but there is no reason why they should be replaced by those of a rabble of Russians. You had best warn my stepson of what has happened so that he can take action while there is still time."

"*I* warn him?" I stared at the fierce old woman in disbelief. Perhaps, I thought, I had been wrong in my assessment of her. Perhaps, after all, the strains of the day had proved too much.

"Yes, girl, you! Who else?" The begum rounded on me. "Or are you content to be carried back by those foreigners like some trophy of war?"

I said steadily, "I would willingly seek out the khan

216

and warn him what is happening," I said, "but it has been made plain that we are prisoners here. With luck my horse is still tethered where I left her, but you yourself heard the officer say that the village is surrounded by his men. They will be on the lookout for just such an attempt. What chance have I got of making my way past them?"

"None," the begum agreed, "unless something directs their attention elsewhere. Does nothing spring to mind?"

I shook my head in mystification. "No . . ."

"Fool! Take those chattis of oil. The building is no more than thin wood and thatch. Pour out the oil on the walls and floor. Soak everything well."

All at once I understood her meaning. Soaked in oil, the temple would explode into flame like a torch at the first touch of a light, and such a conflagration would surely rivet the attention of every Russian within the village. Where we ourselves would be at the time was uncertain, but it seemed possible that one of the huts would give us momentary shelter while we waited for the guards to run to the flames.

"How long must I wait?" the begum demanded. "Hurry, girl! You are wasting time."

I did as I was told, slopping the greasy contents of the earthenware vessels as far as I could reach. Oil trickled down the walls and formed into pools on the floor, dripping between the rough-cut boards down onto the shrine below. When I had emptied everything I could find, I went to the window and looked down at the dark outlines of the nearest building. There was one no more than twenty paces away, with deeply shadowed outbuildings behind it, more than adequate to shelter us. Beyond it was the ridge that lay between the village and the valley itself, and I could make out the figure of one of the Russian soldiers standing watchfully there, leaning on his carbine.

The begum said quietly, "Go now."

I shook my head, knowing that of the two of us it would take her longer to descend the ladder. "It is bet-

217

ter if you go first. Leave me the lamp and I will start the fire."

"No, that is for me to do."

There was something in the old woman's voice that made me look at her quickly. She was standing very still, holding the guttering little lamp in her hand and although her head was turned toward me, I had the feeling that she was not seeing me at all. Unbidden there came into my mind something that she had said to me when first I had spoken with her by the fountain in the women's quarters, of the old khan's death, the emptiness of her life without him. And the widow's pyre that had been denied her, though it had been hers by right.

I said hoarsely, "No, Begum-ji, you cannot..."

"And who are you to deny me?" Suddenly the steady dark eyes were upon me, seeing me again. "I know now why my khan forbade me the flames, for on his deathbed he would have seen clearly that there would be a more fitting time. Now is the time appointed."

"You mean to die here," I whispered. "You mean to make this your suttee...."

"Go quickly, child, and do what has to be done."

"No." I shook my head. "It's horrible. I won't go unless you come with me."

Abruptly the gentle voice hardened. "What do you know of these matters? The world that I saw built is ending, and I say that it is right that it should be so. For years I did not understand because the truth was hidden from me. Now I see that all is accomplished and here in this place I shall make suttee. Thus I say that there shall still be a new and honorable beginning, and tonight I shall be with my lord."

"Please ..."

"You have my leave to go."

I did not mean to go, but in that moment, among the flickering shadows of that room, I realized that the begum Amrita Devi of Khudistan was no longer with me, that already she was treading some path known only to herself and that neither I nor anyone else could make her step aside now. Only half knowing what I did, I backed away from that slight, regal figure, and like someone in a dream, I made my way down the steps and to the temple's open door.

At ground level the night seemed even darker, and I had to accustom my eyes to it until I could make out the outbuilding that was to be my refuge. There was no one about; even the guard I had observed earlier was hidden from view behind one of the huts. I held my breath and ran.

It was no more than twenty paces to the deeper shadows that I sought but it seemed far more, and by the time I had flattened myself against the rickety goat pen and its adjacent pile of logs my heart was beating painfully, but apart from its steady pounding there was no other sound. And then, from between the ill-fitting wall boards of the building I had just left, there came a flicker of light. Had I not known otherwise, it could well have been no more than someone carrying a lamp, but then the light steadied and grew. Next instant, with the suddenness of an explosion, the temple burst into flame.

I had never had reason to picture the conflagration that would follow the touching off of an oil-soaked wood-and-thatch building that had stood long years in the Indian sun. The place must have been like tinder, and as the fire took hold I heard a muffled roar a fleeting instant before great gouts of yellow flame poured between the open spaces in the walls, licked greedily at the dry wood, and then leaped to the thatch of the roof with a crackling like rifle fire.

Someone shouted behind me and the guard on the ridge behind me rushed toward the building. From all sides men came running, villagers and Russians alike, to pull up short as the heat struck them. And then, even above the sound of the flames, I thought I heard a kind of sigh of horror go up from the watchers. I raised my eyes and for what seemed to be an endless moment I saw the figure of the begum standing at the window, clearly outlined against a background of fire. It was beyond all belief that anyone could have survived even that long in such an inferno, yet she stood apparently unscathed, her eyes not on the men below her but on the great white pile of her husband's tomb and I saw that she was smiling. A small, proud smile, like a bride's at her wedding. Then she turned away from the window and went back into the room as with a great tongue of fiery sparks the roof fell in with a crash.

Blindly, with hot tears running down my face, I ran unseen to where I had left my horse.

I remember little of my ride back down the valley. I do know that I rode all night and the journey that had taken two full days in the ruth had almost been retraced by the following morning, when, no more than an hour's ride from the city, I came upon Adam McKenzie at exercise with a squadron of his cavalry. They drew up at the sight of me and I think I would have halted, too, had it not been for the fact that I was so numb with fatigue I had not the strength to rein in my mount. Slumped forward in the saddle, I could barely see where I was going and would have ridden right through the column of horsemen had not the khan seized my mount's bridle and pulled me to a stop.

"It seems that I am fated to meet you when you are in trouble."

I heard his words as if in a dream as I allowed myself to be helped from the saddle. As soon as my feet touched the ground I would have fallen had it not been for strong arms that gripped me and held me up. Even in my dazed condition I felt the well-remembered magical tingling in my blood at the contact between us. I tried to speak but my mouth was so dry and full of dust that I could only croak.

"Don't try to say anything. I'll get you something to drink."

Adam McKenzie lifted me as though I were a child and carried me to the shade of a nearby mulberry tree, where I lay with my back against the trunk. In a daze I listened to him call for water and then tell his men to stay with their horses and leave us alone. The rim of a metal cup grated against my teeth and ice-cold water trickled into my mouth. I drank greedily and the blissful shock of it jerked me to my senses. The khan was kneeling by my side holding the cup, his face taut with concern.

"You look as though you've been riding all night. Where the devil have you been?"

I suppose that without consciously thinking about it I had taken it for granted that he had discovered my flight. I said with difficulty, "Then you didn't know we had gone?"

"I know nothing. I've not been back to the palace. Tell me."

"The begum is dead."

The kneeling body stiffened but that was the only sign that he had heard. He put the silver cup down gently on the ground, but the voice was suddenly harsher as he said, "Where? How do you know?"

"I know because I was there. The Russians . . ."

"Harriet!" The whiplash of his voice pulled me back from the brink of hysteria. Then, when I looked at him, he went on swiftly but quietly, "What about the Russians? Take your time. Tell me exactly what happened, and don't leave anything out."

"The begum was going to show me how to get back to India, so she took me to the gold mine . . . to your father's tomb." The words came more easily and the khan listened in silence, his eyes fixed on my face. Only when I came to describe the Russian intruders did he break in with an occasional question as to their numbers, arms, or dress. When I finished, he bowed his head for a moment.

"What was it my stepmother said before she died? About something ending?"

I said, "I think she said, 'That which my husband built is ending.' "

"She was right. I'm beginning to think she was always right." Adam McKenzie smiled bitterly. "Strange how one can sometimes do the wrong things for the best reasons. My father built a kingdom where there was peace and justice and a chance for the people to live their lives in the old ways, without a foreign gov-

221

ernment corrupting everything with what they choose to call progress. I tried to carry that work on and now I have to choose between handing over Khudistan to the British or risk opening up the whole of India to the followers of the czar."

"And since you have to make a choice," I said, "what is it to be?"

His face twisted in a wry smile. "That's the devil of it, Harriet. There isn't any choice, is there?"

I shook my head. "No, Adam. There isn't."

He pulled himself upright, as though throwing off a mood for which this was neither the time nor the place. When next he spoke, it was with his old assurance. "Are you fit to ride a few more miles?"

I moved my legs cautiously. My whole body was stiff and aching to the point of agony, but it would still answer to my will. "Yes," I told him, "I can ride."

"Then get to Edward Ashworth as quickly as you can. Tell him what has happened and that I'm riding for the pass immediately. If I can catch the twenty-odd Russians you saw before they can get back to call up their friends, everything may be all right. . . ."

"There's no reason why they should hurry," I broke in. "They'll have taken it for granted that I died in the fire, too, so they won't be expecting you." In my heart I knew that I was reluctant to let him go, to watch him ride off to danger and possible death.

Adam said grimly, "Perhaps not, but I can't take the chance. Edward will have to ride south as though the devil were after him. I'm told there are a couple of regiments of British redcoats on maneuvers somewhere just over the border. He has my permission to invite them in."

I caught my breath. "But if you once ask the British government for help . . ." I began.

"It's the first stage of handing over the country." Adam finished the sentence for me. "Yes, I know. But I haven't got the men to hold the main force of the Russians if they come." He leaned forward and touched my hand. "Don't worry, Harriet. Edward will know what to do. After all, he's a British officer. As a man he may not like the idea any more than I do, but he'll know where his duty lies."

"Very well, if that is what must be done." I hesitated, wrenched by a sudden vision of what the immediate future might bring. "What will you do if when you get up there you find the Russians have already gone back for reinforcements?"

"Follow them, I suppose. If we're lucky, we shall catch them before they get that far."

"And if you're not lucky?"

Adam smiled faintly. "Then we shall find out what it's like to fight half the Russian army."

"You don't have to throw your lives away unnecessarily." I had to say the words, even though I knew he would disregard them.

"Defending one's own country—even a little one—isn't generally considered to be throwing one's life away," Adam informed me shortly. He stood up and gave me his hand to rise. "Good luck to you, Harriet. And while I remember, you don't have to worry about that young brother of yours. The messenger *was* lying."

I caught my breath, half afraid to believe the news he gave me was true. "You mean you know for certain?"

"I assure you there is no doubt at all. Somebody wanted you back where the law could get at you, I imagine. Telling you that the boy was sick was as good a way as any."

I said angrily, "But you never said that you knew definitely. You let me think it was just your opinion. And anyway, how *could* you be that certain?"

This time, in spite of the tension of the moment, he threw back his head and laughed in genuine amusement. "Good God, woman, how do you think? My guards caught your slippery little messenger as he left you and brought him to me. He wouldn't talk at first, so I explained to him that the ancient punishment for men who broke into the women's quarters was to be trampled to death by an elephant. I don't think he believed me, because it wasn't until I'd had him chained

223

to old Moti's front foot that he changed his mind and told me what I wished to know."

I formed a vivid and horrifying picture of the wretched man being bound to the pad of the great beast I had seen in the elephant lines. Why did this man have to evoke first love and then revulsion in me? If the man had not confessed, would Adam have carried out his threat? I did not know and some native caution made me hesitate to ask. Besides, this was something that belonged to the past. Even the sheer, blissful relief in the knowledge that Rupert was alive and well could wait. Just for now, there were other things that had to be done.

A little huskily, I said, "Good-bye, Adam. And good luck."

"Good-bye, Harriet." The white khan raised his hand in a brief salute, and a small smile lurked at a corner of his mouth. "I've been a fool to fight you for so long. I should have loved you while I had the chance."

I did not wait to see Adam and his men go. But my head was in a whirl over Adam's startling parting words as I mounted and rode south to Edward. And above all was the inevitable question: Would I ever see Adam again?

It is curious that in facing an anticipated crisis, it only rarely bears any similarity to how one imagines it would be. And so it was to transpire in my meeting with Edward Ashworth, the man I had once loved and almost willed myself to love again.

Just what I had imagined that moment would be like I find hard to put into words. I had known pain with Edward in the past, pain and disillusion, yet at the same time I had known great happiness and all the bittersweet wonder of first love. Our parting had seemed like the end of everything for me and when I had got over the worst of the heartbreak, I comforted myself with the thought that whatever happened down the years, I was free of Edward and he had lost his power to haunt me.

I had been wrong, of course. I had known it that

first day when Sabina, all unknowing, had introduced us at the palace. And yet, in some kindly way, those lost years had made a difference. To me Edward was no longer a knight in shining armor, able to do no wrong. I saw clearly now the want of security that lay behind the gaiety, the artist behind the soldier, and could well imagine the bitterness of the lonely agent who worked almost forgotten in the back of beyond when other men of his age were making brilliant names for themselves. Perhaps it was with this new understanding something had become rekindled that I had long thought dead. So as I made my way to Edward's bare little bungalow I was conscious of the fact that I was about to give him a task that could hardly fail to make his name known. It could be said of few men that they carried the alarm that saved a kingdom, but now, it seemed, Edward was to be one of them.

It was as well that he was at home when I arrived, for I should have been hard pressed to look further. After one startled glance at my condition he lifted me from the saddle and bore me indoors. Stretched out in a Roorkee chair and sipping brandy and water, I jerked out my story in short, disconnected sentences, paying but little attention to the effect it was having on my audience. "And so," I ended, "it must depend on you now. Adam says that there are British troops within a day's ride of the border, so get to them as best you can and call them in. God knows if they will be in time to save him, but at least the Russians will be stopped before they get a foothold in the valley."

Edward was standing with his back to a window, so I could not clearly see his face, nevertheless there was a note of despair in his voice when he spoke that jerked me upright in my chair.

"He knows I cannot call in the army. The man must be out of his senses!"

"Adam understands well enough what he is doing," I told him sharply, suddenly angry that he should be so slow to understand. "He knows that once he asks help of the British government it's the end of the old

Khudistan. But you must see that he hasn't any choice."

For a long moment Edward stared down at me, then he turned away and said slowly, "It's not so simple as that. If McKenzie wants to call for help, that's his affair. But he cannot expect to send me."

I cried out in agony, "But Adam has done all he can, and for all we know he and his men may be dead by now! What is to stop your setting out while there may still be time?"

Almost as though he were speaking to himself, Edward said, "Yes, there may just be time—at any rate, for you and me." With a swift movement he bent over me, the knuckles of his hands showing white as he gripped the arms of my chair. "Listen to me, Harriet, there's still time. Come with me and we'll leave this place together. Forget about India. We'll go and live in Europe—America, even." Edward's hands shifted to my shoulders, lifting me so that his face was close to mine. "I'm a rich man, my dear. I'd hoped to be richer, but I've more than enough to give you a life that's better than anything you've known before. Only if we're to have it, we must leave this place . . . now."

There was a desperate urgency in those eyes that were staring into mine—urgency and something very like fear. "Edward," I cried, "what are you talking about? What are you trying to run away from?"

He dropped his hands from my shoulders suddenly and turned away from me toward the side table that held the decanter of brandy. He splashed spirit into a glass and tossed it down in a curiously futile gesture that stirred in me a kind of pity. I said gently, "Whatever it is, you'll have to tell me. But please be quick. . . . God knows what is happening up at the pass while we're talking here."

Edward laughed mirthlessly. "Ah, the pass! Can't you imagine the consternation in high places when I gallop up to report that the Russians are riding into India through a pass that nobody even knew was there!"

"But surely," I said in bewilderment, "you can hardly be blamed for that?"

"Of course I can, you little fool!" Edward turned back to me bitterly. "Don't you understand? For three years I have been the British government's representative in Khudistan. It has been my duty to learn all there is to know about this little kingdom—to map it and assess its potential for trade and defense. What else would I be sent here for? How do you suggest I explain that my reports have never mentioned the highly important fact that there is a previously unmapped pass with almost direct access to Russia? And, for that matter, how is it that by some extraordinary oversight I've completely forgotten to point out that the mountains are overloaded with gold?"

I said slowly, *"Did* you know about that pass?"

Edward made a quick, dismissive gesture with his hand. "No, of course I didn't. My dear Harriet, I may be a rogue but I'm not altogether a fool."

"But I don't understand." What was happening? I asked myself. All of a sudden my world was falling to pieces about me. Adam was already risking his life in a desperate venture, and now Edward was hinting at something that was not just reckless but shameful. . . . I went over to him and gripped him by the arm. "You knew about the gold. How could you have known that and not about the pass?"

"How do you think?" He smiled at me with something of his old humor. "Adam knew well enough when I was posted here what my job was and that it wouldn't take me long to discover the pass *and* the gold. After all, Khudistan is small enough. He realized that the moment I passed that tidbit of information back to headquarters the British would annex this little garden of Eden in about five minutes flat. Obviously I couldn't be expected to buy the sacred-grove story, so he decided to offer me an . . . arrangement instead."

Edward moved away from me, his hands thrust deep into his pockets. He said quietly, "All my life, Harriet, I've been short of money. For some men this doesn't matter all that much, just as long as they have enough to get by. A commission in a second-rate regiment, a couple of rather badly cut uniforms, and some usable

227

nag and they're reasonably content. But not me. For my sins I've been cursed with tastes above my station. Oh, I don't want money to drink or wench or gamble. I just happen to like good pictures and decent furniture. I want the means to go to a decent tailor without worrying about the bill. To be able to drink good wine instead of country rotgut and write a banker's draft without having to wonder if I've the funds to cover it. Well, by the time I came up here I'd decided that I'd been poor long enough—damn it, if I'd been of any consequence, they'd never have posted me to Khudistan in the first place. So I accepted the arrangement Adam offered me with thanks."

For a moment I stared at him, hardly understanding. I had come to know that Edward was weak, but this . . . Then, "What was the arrangement?" I asked.

"Gold." Edward stared back at me in surprise. "What did you expect? He gave me gold on the understanding that I would never report its existence or go to look at where it came from. I passed it back to India and quietly banked it away. And now, my dear, having betrayed my trust, I am a comfortably wealthy man." He paused and looked around the bare little room with distaste. "I must say it's time to go. I was getting damnably tired of living like a pauper just for show."

Much that had puzzled me but that I had put aside became suddenly clear. The superb horse, the bronze head, the Purdy guns. Edward had done his best to curb his tastes but certain indulgences he had been unable to resist.

I asked dully, "How did you get the gold to India and bank it? Why didn't anyone find out?"

"It wasn't difficult," Edward told me. "Why do you think I'm on such good terms with a lousy old horse dealer like Kuda Baksh? He takes my ill-gotten gains out with his horses, and as you know, many Pathans either deal in horses or run banks. His brother's a *shroff* in Delhi. For a generous commission he invests my money in ways no prying official will ever find out."

"I see." I felt exhausted, drained of all will. And yet

. . . "I'm sorry, Edward," I said, "truly sorry, but wherever it is you're going to run to, you'd better go."

He said softly, "And you? You'll come with me?"

I shook my head. "No. Never." How strange, I thought. There had been a time when I would have willingly died for this man. Suddenly I found myself laughing. "I don't wish to sound overdramatic, but I'd rather die."

"If you stay here till the Russians come," Edward said harshly, "you almost certainly will."

"I shan't stay here," I told him. "How can I? Adam . . . men may be dying while you waste time telling me about your greedy little schemes. Someone has got to tell the British authorities what is happening. So it had best be me."

"You'll never make the journey," Edward said.

"Perhaps not. But I can try." I walked past him out into the sunlight and shut the door behind me. I half expected him to try to stop me, but he did not follow. I glanced through the window into the room I had just left and saw that Edward was standing as if in thought. Then, with sudden decision, he picked up the bronze head and looked about him as though wondering what to take next. He had quite forgotten my existence. He was simply starting to pack.

14

Mercifully, there are times when one's memory behaves in a less serviceable manner than usual, so that one is left with a series of impressions rather than an ordered catalogue of events. And thus it was that much of what passed between the time I left Edward's house and my arrival in Calcutta remains to this day little more than a blur. I remember riding interminably, for what seemed day after day, even though I have no idea where I spent the nights, and I remember also the bewildered faces of such natives on the border as stared at the wild-eyed, dust-coated woman who, with glazed eyes, looked down from a weary horse and demanded the whereabouts of British soldiers.

I remember, and indeed it is the most vivid of all the pictures imprinted forever on my mind, the scarlet tunics of the troops when at last I found them. Resting briefly from the military exercise upon which they were engaged, the men were sprawled in the undergrowth beside the dusty track up which I rode, and their white, surprised faces stared up at me as I came up to them. I know that I reined in my horse and tried to ask for their commanding officer, failing at first to speak at all because of the dust that was clogging my throat. Then there was the blessed sensation of water from a canteen being dashed into my face, of guiding hands and rough, yet curiously tender speech. Within minutes I had blurted out my story to a small, black-bearded officer.

Russians . . . the pass . . . Adam McKenzie and his men riding against an army . . . gold . . .

I am not sure whether I fainted then or simply dropped my head upon my horse's neck and fell asleep, but either could only have been for a short time, for I was aroused by bugles, shouted orders, and the metallic bustle of armed men. Then someone was saying in my ear, "Am I correct, ma'am, in thinking you may be a Mrs. Hunt?"

It seemed so strange that at such a moment anyone should be worrying about the fact that we had not been introduced. "Of course," I told him, "that is my name."

The black-bearded face had stared into mine with what I suppose was compassion, although I did not understand that at the time. "My regrets, ma'am, but I have orders that should I meet you, I am to have you escorted to Calcutta without delay."

It had taken some little time for me to understand his meaning, and when it became clear, I believe that I cried out that I could not go, that at all costs I must ride back to discover the fate of the khan. If they listened at all, they took no heed but sent for their surgeon major, who, I suspect, gave me some kind of sleeping draft to drink and stayed with me till I slept.

I do not cry easily, so I imagine it was weakness that made me weep so readily in the days that followed as an officer and ten men escorted me down from the high hills. I know that at first I had fought against their restraining hands and cried that it was impossible that I leave without learning Adam's fate. But soon I had realized that there was to be no reprieve, my fate was sealed, and whatever my pleas, I should be taken to Calcutta. And so I left Adam and the hills behind me and headed, only half conscious of what I did, for the great city of the Hooghly and a government department that was waiting patiently to put me on trial for murder. . . .

I do not know how Mr. Whittle knew of my arrival at the great, rambling building that housed the government offices at Ballygunge, five miles distant from the sounds and smells of the teeming city. Perhaps as the proprietor of an influential newspaper he made it his business to know everything that happened in Bengal, but whatever alchemy he employed, it proved effective, for I had not been there an hour before his small, portly figure came bustling into the empty office in which I had been confined and he greeted me with a warmth that to one as friendless as I was touching in its obvious sincerity. I think that my appearance must have shocked him no little, for I was still wearing the jacket and breeches in which I had commenced my journey, and although they had been washed and pressed, I have no doubt that they were in no way what he considered to be acceptable ladies' dress.

"It grieves me to see you in this condition," he said once we had exchanged greetings, and his strangely froglike features became almost ludicrous as they strove to express their owners' concern. "Come at once, I have a phaeton waiting. My house is yours to use as you will until we clear up this sorry matter once and for all."

I protested that I had little option but to wait on the pleasure of whichever official was preparing himself to question me, but with his chin thrust high over his old-fashioned stock, Mr. Whittle dismissed the idea with impatience.

"Nonsense, m'dear. I've seen the legal member and the fool's running around in circles like a hen wondering what's to be done with you while they try to make some sort of case. Jumped at the chance when I told him it would cause a great deal less scandal if he released you into my care."

I found it hard to believe that even one of Mr. Whittle's influence would have been able to make such an arrangement as informally as he led me to believe, and I said as much.

Mr. Whittle shrugged his shoulders. "I am well able to meet the bond. Think no more of it and come home."

I did as I was told, although I must confess that it was not until I had walked unchecked past the uniformed lancers at the gates and settled myself in my benefactor's carriage that I breathed freely. I think that at any other time I would have thought with little enthusiasm of exchanging the clean, fresh air of Ballygunge with the traditional stench of Calcutta's notorious drains. But on this occasion, as we drew up at Mr. Whittle's tall, narrow-fronted house in Park Street, close by Chowringhee, I felt that, whatever the future might hold, my present was secure.

Mr. Whittle, with his prim, Old World manners that were so strangely at odds with his profession, had begged the assistance of a venerable widow by the name of Mrs. Clunes, who had installed herself as a kind of honorary housekeeper, to the outrage of an almost equally aged native butler. However, the arrangement eased Mr. Whittle's fears of what Calcutta society might have to say were I to reside at Park Street unchaperoned, and I in my turn was more than grateful for the presence of a woman who looked after me as though I were her own daughter.

I spent a curious two days accustoming myself to life in the house in Park Street, which was so typically British in its appointments. Yet it was pleasant to visit the premises of Kellner's and Hall and Anderson's and to be able to purchase more suitable clothing for myself, to such effect that I saw approval in my host's eyes when I appeared at dinner attired in a gown of pale yellow silk that fell in smooth folds to the floor, my hair gathered up and held by a jeweled tortoiseshell comb.

"That is very becoming, my dear. I confess I find it a great improvement on your—more practical attire."

"Thank you. Frankly, so do I." We sat at the old, dark mahogany table that reflected the warm glow of the candles in their silver holders. With the portraits looking down from the paneled walls and the Adams fireplace that must have been imported from England at enormous cost, it was indeed only the white-coated and turbaned abdar pouring the wine that reminded me that this was Park Street, Calcutta, and not some elegant apartment in Boston or London. And I was grateful that one, at least, of my worries had been lifted from me by the arrival of a letter from Rupert, from which it was clear that he was well and happy at his English school and in which he asked eagerly for my address. I had gone through much, I thought, to just this end, and whatever the future might hold for me, I had at least the satisfaction of knowing that none of it had been in vain.

"I have been thinking, ma'am—" Mr. Whittle broke in on my thoughts, but I stopped him before he could go further.

"Please," I said, "need there be this formality between us? I have had so much kindness at your hands, and it would make me happy if you called me by my given name."

My host's protuberant eyes met mine with what was obvious pleasure. "My dear lady—Harriet—I am deeply honoured. . . ."

"And I am deeply grateful. Only . . ."

"Yes?"

"I am a little mystified why you have done so much. Were you and my father such very close friends?"

Mr. Whittle shook his head and then hesitated in some embarrassment. "To tell the truth, no. Your father was a good man and one whom I greatly admired. Yet if I have been more than ordinarily concerned about your welfare, I suspect it is due more to the memory of your mother. I had the rare privilege of her friendship before she and your father ever met, and I had high hopes that friendship might become something more."

So that was why he had been so good to me. Because if things had been different, I might well have been his daughter. "I didn't know," I said, feeling a sudden ache of compassion for him. "And Mother married my father instead?"

"I have no doubt she chose the better man."

"And afterward . . . did you never marry?"

"No." Mr. Whittle shook his head. "No, I suppose it was man's age-old reluctance to accept second best. And anyone else *would* have been no more than that."

Abruptly he changed the subject. "To more pressing matters. As you can probably imagine, your case is causing a good deal of head scratching in high places. It is a poor enough reflection on the raj when some drunken fool of a planter kills the *bibi* he's living with, but for a white woman to be charged with murdering her husband would be a tasty tidbit for the native press indeed. On the other hand, we have given good law and honest courts to this country for the first time, and it may well be that in the years to come this may well be judged Britain's greatest gift to India. That being so, the matter can hardly be overlooked, particularly as the case hangs on the evidence of someone who has native blood in his veins."

I said levelly, "I am not asking for the case to be overlooked. I simply want de Souza's evidence discounted on the grounds that it is not true."

"Quite so, but you will appreciate that *proving* your point may well be another matter. On the other hand, there is another alternative."

Something in Mr. Whittle's voice made me look at him sharply. "And what is that?"

"I spent an hour with Mr. Ledbetter, the United States consul, this morning. Or had you forgotten that you are an American citizen?"

I shook my head. Indeed I had not forgotten, but it was true that I had overlooked the implications of the fact, whereas it was apparent that Mr. Whittle had not.

He went on. "It is a consul's duty to ensure that, in the event of their breaking the law, his countrymen get a fair trial in a foreign land. It is *not* his duty to help wrongdoers escape the consequences of their crimes."

I said hotly, "I am not a wrongdoer and I am not trying to avoid anything!"

"Please hear me out." Mr. Whittle raised a small, well-kept hand. "As I have said, your case is something of an embarrassment to Government House. Suppose—just suppose—that you are found guilty of murdering the late Mr. Hunt. It is inconceivable that they would hang you, equally unthinkable that you would serve years of imprisonment as the only white woman convict on the Andaman Islands. Were you a British subject, it would be a simple matter for you to serve your sentence in England. But you are not a British subject, you are American."

In spite of myself I felt my curiosity aroused. "So what does Mr. Ledbetter propose?"

"He does not propose anything. He merely made the observation that should the British authorities decide to serve you with an order of deportation, he would not oppose it. And a suggestion in the right quarter . . ."

"No!" The word was spoken before I even realized it, so instantaneous was my reaction. "Not on any account!"

Mr. Whittle sighed. "I suppose it is natural that you should feel this way, but consider, Harriet, I beg of you. In your case deportation means no more than returning to your native land. The matter could be arranged discreetly, with none of the publicity of a trial. . . ."

"It is unthinkable," I told him. And yet, oddly enough, I was by no means sure why it should be so. What was there left in this alien country for me now? Why, for that matter, should I not start my life again in New England, where Rupert could join me? But once again some instinct that was stronger than logic held me back. I shook my head fiercely. "Please thank Mr. Ledbetter for his concern. Tell him I realize that if the authorities decide for themselves that I must be deported, there is nothing I can do about it. But that it is the very last thing that I would wish."

Mr. Whittle shrugged his shoulders in a gesture of helplessness. "Naturally I shall tell him, since you feel so strongly about it. And in view of the universal admiration felt for your father, I doubt very much if anyone would banish you against your will. Although what the alternative will be I cannot at this moment imagine."

I managed to smile at him with a gaiety I certainly did not feel. "Well, all we can do," I said, "is wait and see." Then, "There is still no news from Khudistan?"

"None," Mr. Whittle told me. "But it may well take some time for word to get back from such a remote

236

area. Quite apart from the fact that this is hardly a military operation that should become public knowledge." He smiled faintly. "God knows we have quailed at the menace of the Bear for so long that one scarcely cares to imagine the panic that would ensue in the drawing rooms of Calcutta if it were known that there were real Russian soldiers operating upon Indian soil."

"Of course," I agreed. "I'm sure you are right." But at the back of my mind a voice said insistently, *Adam could be dead by now and you would never know it.*

First the days and then the weeks dragged by on leaden feet while the city suffocated in a haze of sweltering humidity. I, who had previously visited Calcutta only in winter, was able to verify through personal experience a world where mold grew on one's shoes overnight and even clothes hung in closets would be taken out each morning wringing wet. At night countless millions of insects clustered in great, droning clouds about the city's lamentably few streetlights, and through it all one suffered the sharp, needlelike stabs of pain about one's body, while the skin grew red and raw almost at a touch in the miseries of prickly heat.

It was on just such a day that I made my way back to Park Street at dusk after spending an hour walking in a desultory fashion through the teeming stalls of the Hog Market. A *palki* had passed me on the almost deserted road, and as I came to Mr. Whittle's house I saw that the same boxlike carriage was parked outside. For some reason I took it for granted that although he owned his own carriage, my host had hired it to bring him from his office near Writers' Buildings, and when Yakub, the butler, opened the door to me, I sought little more than confirmation.

"Sahib agir?"

"Ji-han. Barra kamera men hai."

I took off my bonnet and went into the big drawing room, with its Georgian elegance always at odds with the soft *shuff-shuff* of the swinging punkah, and then stopped dead, barely able to believe my eyes. Mr. Whittle was indeed there, but at his side were two familiar figures I had barely expected ever to see again.

237

"Oh, Harriet, it is so good to see you!" Sabina ran forward and threw her arms about me impulsively, and over her shoulder I could see Ram Gupta standing in the background, smiling broadly as he joined his fingertips in ritual greeting.

I felt my throat constrict and my eyes sting with sudden tears at the genuine pleasure in their eyes. I held Sabina at arm's length and studied her in admiration. She was dressed in purely European clothes, and her gown of heavy cream silk trimmed with matching bands of velvet was in vivid contrast to the warm gold of her skin. Her beautiful raven hair was twisted into a chignon under a shady straw hat. She looked a picture. Ram Gupta was immaculately dressed in white drill, and not for the first time I thought what a handsome pair they made.

"And it's wonderful to see you, too," I said, and meant it sincerely. I sat down in the nearest chair, feeling suddenly weak with excitement at the meeting. "When did you arrive? How did you know I was here . . . ?" I broke off abruptly, suddenly aware that these were not the questions I really wanted to ask.

"Yesterday. And one of the British officers who came to the palace said that you had been sent to Calcutta, so we asked about you at Government House." Sabina looked over her shoulder at Ram Gupta and then back at me, smiling, proud. "Harriet, won't you congratulate us? I mean, we are married."

I should have realized, I thought, that there was something special about the two of them. A kind of secret glow of happiness that I should have noticed from the start. I opened my mouth to speak but Sabina went on breathlessly. "Oh, it's quite all right! Adam gave us his permission. He even attended the wedding. . . ."

I felt the blood drain from my face and indeed it must have gone noticeably pale, for the girl gave me a look of concern.

"Harriet! Are you all right?"

"Yes," I told her. "Quite all right." My voice sounded a long way away, almost as though it belonged to another person. "I hadn't heard that Adam was safe. That he was—alive."

"Apparently McKenzie was quite unharmed." Mr. Whittle was addressing himself to me, his eyes bright with intelligence and understanding. "Strictly within these four walls, the situation in Khudistan now seems a good deal clearer. I was called to Government House today to discuss the formal announcement that will eventually appear in the press. But the main points are abundantly clear. Adam McKenzie and his men succeeded in driving the Russian advance party back through the pass, and by the time they could bring up reinforcements a sizable force of British and Indian troops had moved into the area. Our unwelcome visitors decided that having failed to attain their objective by stealth, any further action would result in a major action and they promptly withdrew. McKenzie then formally invited the government of India to assume control of Khudistan, and units of the Indian army will garrison the entrance to the pass. It is all highly satisfactory."

Which meant, I thought, that the independence that Adam and his father had clung to for so long had vanished overnight. I said in a low voice, "And Adam?"

"Nobody knows." It was Sabina who answered, and an expression of worry came over a face that had been bright with happiness. "He stayed long enough to hand over his responsibilities to the British general, then vanished one night without a word. He took his horse and a few necessities and no one has seen him since."

I thought of Edward packing his treasures swiftly in his deserted bungalow. So now there were two men fleeing from Khudistan, I thought. One with his honor and one without. I looked at the young couple in front of me and envied them their happiness as I asked, "And what do you plan to do now?"

"We laid our hopes before the khan sahib," Ram Gupta said quietly. "Happily, he agreed and has promised the necessary financial arrangements to make them possible." He looked toward Sabina with a smile. "We shall go to Europe almost immediately, where my wife will study painting, for which, as you know, she has a great talent. As for myself, I shall do my best to qualify as a doctor in order that I may better serve my fellow countrymen when we eventually return to India."

I felt a surge of happiness for them. "I hope that you do come back," I told him. "The country needs doctors. There will be a lot of work for you here."

"And you, Mrs. Hunt. What are you planning to do?"

I smiled wryly. "I am hardly my own mistress at the moment."

A look of surprise crossed Sabina's face. "Harriet! You mean you haven't heard about de Souza?"

"I've heard nothing." I shook my head.

"He was brought to me for treatment, suffering from cholera," Ram Gupta explained. "In his delirium he said things that caused me to question him later. Believing that he was dying, he confessed that your sister-in-law, Mrs. Scott-Barnard, had offered him a large sum of money if you could be brought back within reach of the British law. It seems that he lacked the courage to enter Khudistan himself, so he sent another with a false message while he himself waited close to the border. As you know, the messenger was discovered by the khan and de Souza himself fell ill. His companions abandoned him, and had he not been found by some hillmen, who brought him to me, he would most certainly have died."

I should have felt bitterness toward Ursula, I thought, but instead there was only a feeling that was very like pity for anyone for whom money meant so much. I asked, "And did de Souza eventually recover?"

Sabina laughed gaily. "Oh, yes. But not before Ram had made him sign a full confession, admitting that Mr. Hunt's death was an accident and that all the accusations against you were lies."

"You mean," I said incredulously, "that he actually made such a confession of his own free will?"

Ram Gupta smiled slightly. "It is possible that he was a little influenced by the fact that he thought I

240

would let him die if he did *not* sign it. But I assure you it is properly witnessed and quite legal, and it has already been handed into the proper authorities."

"And they will have no alternative but to decide that you have no case to answer," Mr. Whittle broke in. "In fact, my dear, I have already heard unofficially that you are free to go wherever you wish."

For a long minute I sat very still, trying to accustom myself to the idea that the long nightmare was really over. My nightmare, at least. Someone else's was just beginning. I said slowly, "And Adam?" Oh, God, I thought, how did one begin to find one man in a place the size of India?

Mr. Whittle said heavily, "The young fool appears to have vanished off the face of the earth and His Excellency is getting impatient."

I looked at him in surprise. "Impatient? Why?"

"Because he has to appoint a governor of Khudistan and McKenzie is the obvious man. The people trust him and in his own way he ruled the place remarkably well, and what with the strategic importance of the pass and the potential revenue from gold, Khudistan seems hardly the place to give to the charge of a stranger. But of course if he doesn't turn up soon . . ." Mr. Whittle left the sentence unfinished.

"Perhaps . . ." I began.

"Yes?"

I shook my head. "Nothing. It was just that there is something that Adam said to me once that I feel I should remember, but it's gone."

But it was not entirely gone, for it came back to me just before dawn as I lay sleepless in the sweltering heat. After that it seemed an age to wait before I could with decency present myself at the office of the consul for the United States. Mr. Ledbetter was a tall, cadaverous New Englander, and although my name could not so soon have escaped his memory, he listened to my query without comment.

"You say, ma'am, that this man's name is McKenzie and that he's been wanting to take passage to the United States?"

241

"That is his name, and I know only that he might be *thinking* of going. And as he's British, he may have decided to check if he'd be allowed to enter. If he did have any questions, you'd be the obvious person to ask."

The consul studied me for a long moment in silence, and it suddenly occurred to me that even if Adam had visited him, such a visit might be considered confidential. I said desperately, "I'm a friend. I mean him no harm. I just want to discover where he is."

Abruptly Mr. Ledbetter made up his mind. "Strictly speaking, ma'am, his whereabouts are his affair, but, yes, someone called McKenzie called on me yesterday, asking about settling in the United States. I told him that provided he could pass the medical authorities, there is at present nothing to prevent a British national either from visiting or settling."

I drew a deep breath. "Thank you very much. And do you know where he is now?"

"If he's set on going in a hurry, there's only one place he can be." Mr. Ledbetter permitted himself a wintry smile. "The *Chesapeake* is the only passenger-carrying vessel in port at the moment. As far as I know, she sails on the afternoon tide for San Francisco."

I gasped out my thanks and fled from the room. But lost amid the forest of masts that seemed to cover the waterfront, the *Chesapeake* took longer to discover than I had expected. Finally I discovered her moored at Garden Reach, a great four-masted iron ship with a tall funnel, from which issued thick clouds of black smoke.

My *tonga* driver, who had shared my search, stared up at the vessel incuriously. *"Yih hai?"*

"Yes," I said, "this is it." I paid him with a liberality that made him blink and made my way up the heavy teak gangway to the deck. Once there I did not have far to look. Despite the unfamiliar gray silk suit of a civilian and the fact that he had his back to me, there was no mistaking the lonely figure near the bow, leaning on the ship's rail and staring out across the slowly moving river.

"Adam."

He turned with the same swift, catlike movement I knew of old, and his blue eyes opened a little at the sight of me. Just for a fleeting moment the lean face, even more drawn now with strain, lit up and his hands reached out and gripped mine, holding me to him.

"Harriet!" Then, abruptly, the look vanished, to be replaced with the familiar mask. Almost harshly he said, "How the devil did you know I was here?"

"Don't you remember?" I reminded him. "You told me once that if you ever had to leave Khudistan, you'd leave India as well and start again in what you called 'my country.' "

He smiled fleetingly but without amusement. "I gather you visited the excellent Mr. Ledbetter."

"Yes." Then, as he said nothing, "Adam—Why are you doing this?"

Slowly he let go of my hands. "I should have thought that was obvious."

"The last time we saw each other you said that you should have loved me while you had the chance." It was strange, I thought, but it really made no difference that men were making the ship ready all around us. It was almost as though Adam and I were invisible, in our own private world. I said steadily, "You have the chance now. Because, Adam, I love you, too."

"It was all different then," Adam said slowly. "I had something to offer you—something I could have offered you long before if I hadn't been a fool. Now I have nothing—do you know that? I made over enough money to provide for Sabina and her husband and then presented the rest to the state. And frankly, my dear, you deserve better than a penniless leftover from a bygone age."

I said quietly, "You can hardly call yourself that, since half Government House is looking for you. Apparently they want you to go back to Khudistan as governor."

Adam gave me a quick, piercing look, as though for

a moment he thought that I was mocking him. Then he gave a small sigh. "It's no good, my dearest Harriet. You'd best forget me."

I said in bewilderment, "But Adam, why? I'll go back to Khudistan with you. What difference does it make whether you're khan or governor? You'll be ruler, just as you were before!"

Slowly Adam shook his head. "Harriet, can't you understand? It's past. All of it. Oh, I could have gone on being my father's son for the rest of my life if nothing had happened, but something *did* happen. And I stopped and looked at it all. Once you do that it's like trying to recapture ancient history. There's no going back."

I said desperately, "But they *need* you!"

"No, they don't. There are half a dozen perfectly sound men who can do that job. Not only do it but believe in what they're doing."

With rising anger, I said, "So you're going to run off to America. To do what?"

"I'm not sure. Farm, perhaps. Build something. Whatever it is, it'll be something new and mine!"

He was right, I thought. Of course he was right. I said, "Adam, do you want me?"

"Want you?" His hands gripped my shoulders, pulling me toward him. "Good God, Harriet, of course I want you! But I've nothing! Don't you realize I had just enough money to pay my fare?"

"I've money enough of my own," I reminded him. "And even if I hadn't, the begum gave me a diamond as a gift that must be worth a fortune. How much more do you need to make a new start?"

From the surprise in his eyes I think he had truly forgotten. Then he made a quick gesture of dismissal. "But that's impossible. I can't take your money. You know that."

"All I know," I said, "is that when you step off this ship at San Francisco, you won't be a khan anymore. You'll be just one more immigrant trying to make a fresh start. And if you're going to be too damn proud

244

to touch your own wife's money, that country's going to be a lot too big for you."

A sailor paused beside me and said approvingly, "That's telling him, lady!"

Adam looked at the man and then suddenly laughed. "And she's right." Oblivious of his audience, he pulled me toward him and his mouth came down on mine in a long, unhurried kiss, and though at first I tried to draw back, it was not long before I was clinging to him with a passion that matched his own. When at last he let me go, he said, "We'll give a note to a tonga driver. He'll get your baggage. Only say that you'll come with me."

Could this really be happening? I thought wonderingly. Could it really be as simple as this? I found myself remembering some of the events of the past few months and already they seemed hazy and far away, like incidents recalled from a dream. Only Adam, strong and alive in front of me, with all his promise of the future, was real.

As if from a long way off, I heard his voice, with something of its old rasp in it, asking, "Well, what's it to be, my dear? Yes or no?"

Huskily I said, "Of course I'll come with you. To San Francisco or anywhere else."

He gripped my hand silently and we turned and leaned against the rail. I looked out across the oily water for a last glimpse of Calcutta, but the mist had come up and the long, ragged skyline had vanished in the haze.

Adam pointed downriver. "Look that way," he said.

So I looked that way. And out toward the sea the sky was bright.

About the Author

Catherine Dillon has worked for many British magazines, as well as film and television companies. After spending some years in the United States she now divides her time between Norfolk and Buckinghamshire. Her main interests are antiques, modern jewelry, and travel. She has been all over the world and enjoys finding new and exotic settings for her novels. She is the author of *Constantine Cay* and *White Fires Burning*, available in Signet editions.

Big Bestsellers from SIGNET

☐ **CARIBEE by Christopher Nicole.** (#J7945—$1.95)

☐ **THE DEVIL'S OWN by Christopher Nicole.**
(#J7256—$1.95)

☐ **SOHO SQUARE by Clare Rayner.** (#J7783—$1.95)

☐ **CALDO LARGO by Earl Thompson.** (#E7737—$2.25)

☐ **A GARDEN OF SAND by Earl Thompson.**
(#E8039—$2.50)

☐ **TATTOO by Earl Thompson.** (#E8038—$2.50)

☐ **DESIRES OF THY HEART by Joan Carroll Cruz.**
(#J7738—$1.95)

☐ **RUNNING AWAY by Charlotte Vale Allen.**
(#E7740—$1.75)

☐ **THE ACCURSED by Paul Boorstin.** (#E7745—$1.75)

☐ **THE RICH ARE WITH YOU ALWAYS by Malcolm Mac-
donald.** (#E7682—$2.25)

☐ **THE WORLD FROM ROUGH STONES by Malcolm Mac-
donald.** (#J6891—$1.95)

☐ **THE FRENCH BRIDE by Evelyn Anthony.**
(#J7683—$1.95)

☐ **TELL ME EVERYTHING by Marie Brenner.**
(#J7685—$1.95)

☐ **ALYX by Lolah Burford.** (#J7640—$1.95)

☐ **MACLYON by Lolah Burford.** (#J7773—$1.95)

☐ **THE SHINING by Stephen King.** (#E7872—$2.50)

☐ **CARRIE by Stephen King.** (#J7280—$1.95)

☐ **'SALEM'S LOT by Stephen King.** (#E8000—$2.25)

☐ **COMA by Robin Cook.** (#E8202—$2.50)

☐ **THE YEAR OF THE INTERN by Robin Cook.**
(#E7674—$1.75)

More Big Bestsellers from SIGNET

☐ **FIRST, YOU CRY** by Betty Rollin. (#J7641—$1.95)

☐ **THE BRACKENROYD INHERITANCE** by Erica Lindley.
  (#W6795—$1.50)

☐ **THE DEVIL IN CRYSTAL** by Erica Lindley.
  (#E7643—$1.75)

☐ **LYNDON JOHNSON AND THE AMERICAN DREAM** by
  Doris Kearns. (#E7609—$2.50)

☐ **THIS IS THE HOUSE** by Deborah Hill. (#J7610—$1.95)

☐ **THE DEMON** by Hubert Selby, Jr. (#J7611—$1.95)

☐ **LORD RIVINGTON'S LADY** by Eileen Jackson.
  (#W7612—$1.50)

☐ **THE SURVIVOR** by James Herbert. (#E7393—$1.75)

☐ **RIVER RISING** by Jessica North. (#E7391—$1.75)

☐ **KINFLICKS** by Lisa Alther. (#E7390—$2.25)

☐ **LOVER: CONFESSIONS OF A ONE NIGHT STAND** by
  Lawrence Edwards. (#J7392—$1.95)

☐ **THE KILLING GIFT** by Bari Wood. (#J7350—$1.95)

☐ **CONSTANTINE CAY** by Catherine Dillon.
  (#E7583—$1.75)

☐ **WHITE FIRES BURNING** by Catherine Dillon.
  (#E7351—$1.75)

☐ **FOREVER AMBER** by Kathleen Winsor.
  (#E7675—$2.25)